The Life and Death
of Mr Badman

The Life and Death of Mr Badman

John Bunyan

ET REMOTISSIMA PROPE

Hesperus Classics

Hesperus Classics
Published by Hesperus Press Limited
4 Rickett Street, London sw6 1ru
www.hesperuspress.com

First published in 1680
First published by Hesperus Press Limited, 2007

Foreword © James Fenton, 2007

Designed and typeset by Fraser Muggeridge studio
Printed in Jordan by Jordan National Press

isbn: 1-84391-153-1
isbn13: 978-1-84391-153-1

CONTENTS

Are we really to read Bunyan's *Mr Badman* as a novel, or as one of the sources of the novel? We will be disappointed either way, unless we bear in mind that the source of a river does not resemble the river itself. *Pilgrim's Progress*, often filed as a novel, is an allegory. Isaac D'Israeli, in a nice phrase, called Bunyan 'the Spenser of the people', and Macaulay wrote that he

> is indeed as decidedly the first of the allegorists as Demosthenes is the first of the orators, or Shakespeare the first of dramatists. Other allegorists have shown equal ingenuity; but no other allegorist has ever been able to touch the heart, and to make abstractions objects of terror, pity, and of love.

Grace Abounding, Bunyan's next most famous work, is linked with the numerous spiritual autobiographies of its day, although it predates the term 'autobiography' by well over a century. It is Robert Southey, Bunyan's editor and champion in the Romantic age, who is credited with the first published use of the word, in an article in the *Quarterly Review* in 1809. It is interesting to read Southey's 1830 biographical essay on Bunyan (along with Macaulay's appreciation of it) because it seems to have been around the Romantic period that readers began generally to appreciate Bunyan *as literature*.

Macaulay says that *Pilgrim's Progress* had been

> during more than a century, the delight of pious cottagers and artisans before it took its proper place, as a classical work, in libraries. At length critics condescended to enquire where the secret of so wide and durable a popularity lay. They were compelled to own that the ignorant multitude had judged more correctly than the learned, and that the despised little book was really a masterpiece.

This implies that they were able to be somewhat detached about him as a religious instructor – to read him, as it were, without necessarily sharing his terrors.

It was Southey, so Macaulay tells us, who first realised or argued in print that the sins of Bunyan's youth, the accusations he hurls against himself in *Grace Abounding*, have to be interpreted in terms of the language of his milieu. To call Bunyan 'the wicked Tinker of Elstow' and to refer to him as depraved, as an early historian of the English Baptists did, was to take his self-reproaches too literally. Really, on the evidence of *Grace Abounding*, there is not much sign of gross debauchery in the young Bunyan (swearing and recreational bell-ringing aside), but there is very good evidence, indeed there is a brilliant, classic description, of religious mania and depression.

Bunyan believed, exactly as his eighteenth-century admirer William Cowper believed, that he had inadvertently committed the sin without a name, the sin against the Holy Ghost for which there is no forgiveness. Bunyan's admirers in the Romantic period were of course likely to be Christians (although my impression is that Macaulay had managed to push the Christianity of his childhood away from him), but they were Christians of a different stamp.

Coleridge, for instance, found Bunyan 'superstitious'. He comments, 'What genuine superstition is exemplified in that bandying of texts and half texts, and demi-semi-texts, just as memory happened to suggest them, or chance brought them before Bunyan's mind!' This is indeed what happens in *Grace Abounding*: a sentence forms in Bunyan's mind, and he searches for its origin, or its meaning, much like someone who has pointed at random to a line of text in a book. It is a superstitious method of divination.

Of *Pilgrim's Progress* Coleridge remarks that it is

one of those few books which may be read repeatedly over at different time, and each time with a different pleasure. I read it once as a theologian – once as a devotional book – another time as a poet &c. I could not have believed beforehand that Calvinism could be painted in such exquisitely delightful colours…

And Coleridge is struck, as Macaulay and Southey are struck, by the beauty of Bunyan's plain style. Coleridge remarks that

Pilgrim's Progress is composed in the lowest style of English, without slang or false grammar. If you were to polish it, you would at once destroy the reality of the vision. For works of imagination should be written in very plain language; the more purely imaginative they are the more necessary it is to be plain.

Southey himself reveals a sensitivity to the question of Bunyan's diction, even if his solutions to editorial problems are not those of a modern editor. He would have certainly liked to restore to his text of *Pilgrim's Progress* 'good old vernacular English which had been injudiciously altered, or carelessly corrupted'. He worried over restoring a certain 'vulgarism of diction', the contraction of 'have' to 'a', as in 'might *a* made me take heed' and 'like to *a* been smothered', but decided against. Nevertheless he valued Bunyan's 'homespun style':

If it is not a well of English undefiled to which the poet as well as the philologist must repair, if they would drink of the living waters, it is a clear stream of current English, – the vernacular speech of his age, sometimes indeed in its rusticity and coarseness, but always in its plainness and its strength. To this natural style Bunyan is in some degree beholden for his popularity…

Still, however admirable this plain style is, there is no disguising the fact that if we read Bunyan, of all people, for his style, we are almost owning up to not taking him seriously. We read *Grace Abounding* for the incomparable insights it gives us into the psychology of conversion. *The Life and Death of Mr Badman* is not a comparable description of the interior life. Bunyan knew very well what it was to believe yourself a sinner, but, as Southey and Macaulay were sharp to notice, he was quick to defend himself against accusations of the grosser sins that Mr Badman goes in for.

This is a systematic portrait of a type, not an individual. The world in which this type of sinful man lives, however, is not allegorised: it is the commercial world of Bedford or anywhere in Britain, in which the religious try to live their lives untroubled by informers and by persecution, and in which commercial principles have to be guided by religious precepts. Blasphemy, drunkenness, petty theft, false bankruptcy – all these have to be encountered. A woman has to choose between her duty to her husband and her duty to her soul. A midwife encounters an infanticide. God punishes the wicked. This is a book about the hazards and iniquities of daily life.

Sometimes when perusing this book I have fancied myself to be the only reader, specialists aside, who has ever taken it down off the shelf. Then, with a start, I came to the words 'he sleeps on the top of a Mast', and realised that it could have been here that Elizabeth Bishop found the inspiration for her poem 'The Unbeliever'. (I say 'could have' because the words occur in slightly different form in two passages of *The Pilgrim's Progress*.)

Here is the passage from *Mr Badman*, as Bishop would have read it:

Tell me, when did you see an old drunkard converted? No, no, such an one will sleep till he dies, though he sleeps on the top of a Mast, let his dangers be never so great, and Death and damnation never so near, he will not be awakened out of his sleep.

If Bishop, who had a drink problem, had been so struck by this passage as to make a poem out of it, she might also have cared to look at the passage in the Book of Proverbs to which Bunyan alludes:

Look not thou upon the wine when it is red, when it giveth his colour in the cup, when it moveth itself aright.
At the last it biteth like a serpent, and stingeth like an adder.
Thine eyes shall behold strange women, and thine heart shall utter perverse things.
Yea, thou shalt be as he that lieth down in the midst of the sea, or as he that lieth upon the top of a mast.

Bishop takes the image of the unbeliever as the sleeper at the top of the mast, but does not tell us that it is his drinking that puts him beyond the power of conversion. But perhaps alcoholism is that poem's secret subject.

But he sleeps at the top of his mast
with his eyes closed tight.
The gull inquired into his dream,
which was, 'I must not fall.
The spangled sea below wants me to fall.
It is as hard as diamonds; it wants to destroy us all.'

The unbeliever, fearing to be wakened from his precarious sleep, is Bunyan's gift to Bishop, with Marianne Moore, who knew *Mr Badman*, and who revered Bunyan, as a likely intermediary.

– James Fenton, 2007

The Life and Death
of Mr Badman

Courteous Reader,

I was considering with myself what I had written concerning the progress of the pilgrim from this world to glory, and how it had been acceptable to many in this nation. It came again into my mind to write as then of him who was going to heaven, so now of the life and death of the ungodly, and of their travel from this world to hell. The which in this I have done and have put it, as you see, under the name and title of Mr Badman, a name very proper for such a subject. I have also put it into the form of a dialogue, that I might with more ease to myself and pleasure to the reader perform the work.

And although, as I said, I have put it forth in this method, yet have I as little as may be, gone out of the road of mine own observation of things. Yea, I think I may truly say that to the best of my remembrance, all the things that here I discourse of, I mean as to matter of fact, have been acted upon the stage of this world, even many times before my eyes.

Here therefore, courteous reader, I present you with The Life and Death of Mr Badman indeed. Yea, I do trace him in his life, from his childhood to his death, that you may, as in a glass, behold with your own eyes, the steps that take hold of hell, and also discern, while you are reading of Mr Badman's death, whether you yourself are treading in his path thereto.

And let me entreat you to forbear quirking and mocking, for that I say Mr Badman is dead, but rather gravely enquire concerning yourself by the word, whether you are one of his lineage or no, for Mr Badman has left many of his relations behind him. Yea, the very world is overspread with his kindred. True, some of his relations, as he, are gone to their place and long home, but thousands of thousands are left behind as brothers, sisters, cousins, nephews, besides innumerable of his friends and associates.

I may say, and yet speak nothing but too much truth in so saying, that there is scarce a fellowship, a community, or fraternity of men in the world, but some of Mr Badman's relations are there. Yea, rarely can we find a family or household in a town where he has not left behind him either brother, nephew or friend.

The butt therefore that at this time I shoot at is wide, and 'twill be as impossible for this book to go into several families and not to arrest some as for the King's Messenger to rush into a house full of traitors and find none but honest men there.

I cannot but think that this shot will light upon many, since our fields are so full of this game. But how many it will kill to Mr Badman's course, and make alive to the Pilgrim's Progress, that is not in me to determine. This secret is with the Lord our God only, and He alone knows to whom He will bless it to so good and so blessed an end. However, I have put fire to the pan and doubt not but the report will quickly be heard.

I told you before, that Mr Badman had left many of his friends and relations behind him, but if I survive them (as that's a great question to me) I may also write of their lives. However, whether my life be longer or shorter, this is my prayer at present: that God will stir up witnesses against them that may either convert or confound them, for wherever they live and roll in their wickedness, they are the pest and plague of that country.

England shakes and totters already, by reason of the burden that Mr Badman and his friends have wickedly laid upon it. Yea, our earth reels and staggers to and fro like a drunkard, the transgression thereof is heavy upon it.

Courteous Reader, I will treat you now, even at the door and threshold of this house, but only with this intelligence that Mr Badman lies dead within. Be pleased therefore (if your leisure will serve you) to enter in, and behold the state in which he is laid, betwixt his deathbed and the grave. He is not buried as yet nor does he stink as is designed he shall before he lies down in oblivion.

Now as others have had their funerals solemnised according to their greatness and grandeur in the world, so likewise Mr Badman (forasmuch as he deserves not to go down to his grave with silence) has his funeral state according to his deserts.

Four things are usual at great men's funerals, which we will take leave, and I hope without offence to allude to in the funeral of Mr Badman.

First, they are sometimes, when dead, presented to their friends by their completely wrought images as lively as by cunning men's hands they can be, that the remembrance of them may be renewed to their survivors, the remembrance of them, and their deeds. And this I have endeavoured to answer in my discourse of Mr Badman, and therefore I have drawn him forth in his features and actions from his childhood to his grey hairs. Here therefore thou hast him lively set forth as in cuts:[i] both as to the minority, flower and seniority of his age, together with those actions of his life that he was most capable of doing, in and under those present circumstances of time, place, strength, and the opportunities that did attend him in these.

Secondly, there is also usual at great men's funerals those badges and escutcheons of their honour that they have received from their ancestors, or have been thought worthy of for the deeds and exploits they have done in their life. And here Mr Badman has his but such as vary from all men of worth, but so much the more agreeing with the merit of his doings. They all have descended in state, he only as an abominable branch. His deserts are the deserts of sin, and therefore the escutcheons of honour that he has are only that he died without honour, and at his end became a fool. You shall not be joined with them in burial – the seed of evil doers shall never be renowned.

The funeral pomp therefore of Mr Badman is to wear upon his hearse the badges of a dishonourable and wicked life. Since 'his bones are full of the sins of his youth, which shall lie down', as Job says, 'in the dust with him', (Job 20:11) nor is it fit that any should be his attendants now at his death. But such as with him conspired against their own souls in their life, persons whose transgressions have made them infamous to all who have or shall know what they have done.

Some notice therefore I have also here in this little discourse given the reader, of them who were his confederates in his life and attendants at his death, with a hint either of some high villainy committed by them, as also of those judgements that have overtaken and fallen upon them from the just and revenging hand of God. All which are things either fully known by me, as being eye- and ear-witness thereto, or that I have received from such hands whose relation as to this I am bound to believe. And that the reader may know them from other things and passages herein contained, I have pointed at them in the margin, as with a finger thus. ☞

5

Thirdly, the funerals of persons of quality have been solemnised with some suitable sermon at the time and place of their burial. But that I am not come to as yet, having got no further than to Mr Badman's death, but for as much as he must be buried, after he has stunk out his time before his beholders, I doubt not but some such that we read are appointed to be at the burial of Gog will do this work in my stead. Such as shall leave him neither skin nor bone above ground, but 'shall set a sign by it, till the buriers have buried it in the Valley of Hamon-gog' (Ezekiel 39:15).

Fourthly, at funerals there does use to be mourning and lamentation, but here also Mr Badman differs from others. His familiars cannot lament his departure, for they have not sense of his damnable state. They rather ring him and sing him to Hell in the sleep of death, in which he goes there. Good men count him no loss to the world, his place can well be without him, his loss is only his own, and 'tis too late for him to recover that damage or loss by a sea of bloody tears, could he shed them. Yea, God has said, He will laugh at his destruction who then shall lament for him, saying, 'Ah, my brother! He was but a stinking weed in his life, nor was he better at all in his death.' Such may well be thrown over the wall without sorrow, when once God has plucked them up by the roots in his wrath.

Reader, if you are of the race, lineage, stock or fraternity of Mr Badman, I tell you before you read this book, you will neither brook the author nor it, because he has written of Mr Badman as he has. For he who condemns the wicked that die so, passes also the sentence upon the wicked who live. I therefore expect neither credit of, nor countenance from you, for this narration of your kinsman's life.

For your old love to your friend, his ways, doings, etc. will stir up in you enmity rather in your very heart against me. I shall therefore incline to think of you that you will rent, burn, or throw it away in contempt, yea and wish also, that for writing so notorious a truth, some mischief may befall me. I look also to be loaded by you with disdain, scorn and contempt, yea, that you should railingly and vilifyingly say I lie and am a bespatterer of honest men's lives and deaths. For Mr Badman, when himself was alive, could not abide to be counted a knave (though his actions told all who went by that indeed he was such a one). How then should his brethren who survive him and who tread in his very steps, approve of the sentence that by this book is pronounced against him? Will they not rather imitate Corah, Dathan and Abiram's friends, even rail at me for condemning him, as they did at Moses for doing execution?[ii]

I know 'tis ill puddling in the cockatrice's den, and that they run hazards who hunt the wild boar. The man also who writes Mr Badman's life had need to be fenced with a coat of mail, and with the staff of a spear for that his surviving friends will know what he does. But I have adventured to do it, and to play, at this time, at the hole of these asps. If they bite, they bite. If they sting, they sting. Christ sends his lambs in the midst of wolves not to do like them but to suffer by them for bearing plain testimony against their bad deeds. But had one not need to walk with a guard and to have a sentinel stand at one's door for this? Verily, the flesh would be glad of such help. Yea, a spiritual man could he tell how to get it, Acts 23. But I am stripped naked of these, and yet am commanded to be faithful in my service for Christ. Well then, I have spoken what I have spoken, and now come on me what will, Job 13:13. True, the text says, rebuke a scorner and he will hate you, and that he who reproves a wicked man gets himself a blot and shame (Proverbs 9), but what then? Open rebuke is better than secret love, and he who receives it shall find it so afterwards.

So then whether Mr Badman's friends shall rage or laugh at what I have written, I know that the better end of the staff is mine. My endeavour is to stop a hellish course of life, and to 'save a soul from death' (James 5:20). And if for so doing, I meet with envy from them from whom in reason I should have thanks, I must remember the man in the dream who cut his way through his armed enemies and so got into the beauteous palace. I must, I say, remember him and do myself likewise.

Yet four things I will propound to the consideration of Mr Badman's friends before I turn my back upon them.

1. Suppose that there be a hell in very deed. Not that I do question it any more than I do whether there be a sun to shine, but I suppose it for argument sake with Mr Badman's friends. I say suppose there be a hell, and that too such a one as the scripture speaks of, one at the remotest distance from God and life eternal, one where the worm of

7

a guilty conscience never dies and where the fire of the wrath of God is not quenched.

Suppose, I say, that there is such a hell prepared of God (as there is indeed) for the body and soul of the ungodly world after this life to be tormented in. I say, do but with yourself suppose it and then tell me, is it not prepared for you, you being a wicked man? Let your conscience speak, I say, is it not prepared for you, you being an ungodly man? And do you think, were you there now, that you are able to wrestle with the judgement of God? Why then do the fallen angels tremble there? Your hands cannot be strong, nor can your heart endure, in that day when God shall deal with you (Ezekiel 22:14).

2. Suppose that someone who is now a soul in Hell for sin were permitted to come here again to dwell, and that they had a grant also, that upon amendment of life, next time they die, to change that place for Heaven and glory. What do you say, O wicked man? Would such a one (do you think) run again into the same course of life as before, and venture the damnation that for sin he had already been in? Would he choose again to lead that cursed life that afresh would kindle the flames of Hell upon him, and that would bind him up under the heavy wrath of God? O, he would not! He would not – the sixteenth of Luke insinuates it. Yea, reason itself awake would abhor it and tremble at such a thought.

3. Suppose again, that you who lives and rolls in your sin, and who as yet has known nothing but the pleasure thereof, should be by an angel conveyed to some place, where with convenience, from there you might have a view of Heaven and Hell, of the joys of the one and the torments of the other. I say, suppose that from there you might have such a view thereof as would convince your reason, that both Heaven and Hell are such realities as by the Word they are declared to be. Would you (do you think), when brought to your home again, choose to yourself your former life, to wit, to return to your folly again? No, if belief of what you saw remained with you, you would eat fire and brimstone first.

4. I will propound again. Suppose that there were amongst us such a law (and such a magistrate to inflict the penalty), that for every open wickedness committed by you, so much of your flesh should with

burning pincers be plucked from your bones. Would you then go on in your open way of lying, swearing, drinking and whoring, as you with delight do now? Surely, surely, no. The fear of the punishment would make you forbear, yea, would make you tremble, even then when your lusts were powerful, to think what a punishment you were sure to sustain so soon as the pleasure was over. But O, the folly, the madness, the desperate madness that is in the hearts of Mr Badman's friends, who in despite of the threatenings of a holy and sin revenging God, and of the outcries and warnings of all good men, yea, who will in despite of the groans and torments of those who are now in Hell for sin, (Luke 16:24–28) go on in a sinful course of life, yea, though every sin is also a step of descent down to that infernal cave. O how true is that saying of Solomon, 'the heart of the sons of men is full of evil, and madness is in their heart while they live, and after that they go to the dead,' Ecclesiastes 9:3. To the dead! That is, to the dead in Hell, to the damned dead. The place to which those who have died bad men are gone, and that those who live bad men are like to go to, when a little more sin, like stolen waters, has been imbibed by their sinful souls.

That which has made me publish this book is,

1. For that wickedness like a flood is like to drown our English world. It begins already to be above the tops of mountains. It has almost swallowed up all – our youth, our middle age, old age – and all are almost carried away of this flood. O, debauchery, debauchery, what have you done in England! You have corrupted our young men, and have made our old men beasts. You have deflowered our virgins, and have made matrons bawds. You have made our earth to reel to and fro like a drunkard. 'Tis in danger to be removed like a cottage, yea, it is, because transgression is so heavy upon it, like to fall and rise no more (Isaiah 24:20).

O, that I could mourn for England and for the sins that are committed therein, even while I see that without repentance, the men of God's wrath are about to deal with us, each having his slaughtering weapon in his hand (Ezekiel 9:1). Well, I have written, and by God's assistance shall pray, that this flood may abate in England, and could I but see the tops of the mountains above it, I should think that these waters were abating.

2. It is the duty of those who can to cry out against this deadly plague, yea, to lift up their voice as with a trumpet against it, that men may he awakened about it, fly from it, as from that which is the greatest of evils. Sin pulled angels out of Heaven, pulls men down to Hell, and overthrows kingdoms. Who, who sees a house on fire, will not give the alarm to them who dwell therein? Who, who sees the land invaded, will not set the beacons on a flame? Who, who sees the devils, as roaring lions, continually devouring souls, will not make an outcry? But above all, when we see sin, sinful sin, a swallowing up a nation, sinking of a nation, and bringing its inhabitants to temporal, spiritual and eternal ruin, shall we not cry out, and cry, 'They are drunk, but not with wine. They stagger, but not with strong drink. They are intoxicated with the deadly poison of sin, which will if its malignity be not by wholesome means allayed, bring soul and body, and estate and country, and all, to ruin and destruction?'

3. In and by this, my outcry, I shall deliver myself from the ruins of them who perish. For a man can do no more in this matter, I mean a man in my capacity, than to detect and condemn the wickedness, warn the evildoer of the judgement, and fly therefrom myself. But O, that I might not only deliver myself! O, that many would hear, and turn at this my cry, from sin, that they may be secured from the death and judgement that attend it!

Why I have handled the matter in this method is best known to myself, and why I have concealed most of the names of the persons whose sins or punishments I here and there in this book make relation of, is:

1. For that neither the sins nor judgements were all alike open. The sins of some were committed, and the judgements executed for them only in a corner. Not to say that I could not learn some of their names, for could I, I should not have made them public, for this reason.

2. Because I would not provoke those of their relations who survive them. I would not justly provoke them, and yet, as I think I should, should I have entailed their punishment to their sins, and both to their names, and so have turned them into the world.

3. Nor would I lay them under disgrace and contempt, which would, as I think, unavoidably have happened unto them had I withal inserted their names.

As for those whose names I mention, their crimes or judgements were manifest, public almost as anything of that nature that happens to mortal men. Such therefore have published their own shame by their sin, and God, his anger, by taking of open vengeance.

As Job says, God has struck them as wicked men in the open sight of others (Job 34:26). So that I cannot conceive, since their sin and judgement were so conspicuous, that my admonishing the world thereof should turn to their detriment. For the publishing of these things are, so far as relation is concerned, intended for remembrancers. That they may also bethink themselves, repent and turn to God, lest the judgements for their sins should prove hereditary. For the God of Heaven hath threatened to visit 'the iniquity of the fathers upon the children unto the third and fourth generation of them that hate me' (Exodus 20:5).

Nebuchadnezzar's punishment for his pride being open (for he was for his sin, driven from his kingly dignity, and from among men, too, to eat grass like an ox, and to company with the beasts), Daniel did not stick to tell Belshazzar his son to his face thereof, nor to publish it that it might be read and remembered by the generations to come. The same may be said of Judas and Ananias, etc., for their sin and punishment were known to all the dwellers at Jerusalem (Acts 5).

Nor is it a sign but of desperate impenitence and hardness of heart, when the offspring or relations of those who have fallen by open, fearful and prodigious judgements for their sin shall overlook, forget, pass by or take no notice of such high outgoings of God against them and their house. Thus Daniel aggravates Belshazzar's crime, for that he hardened his heart in pride, though he knew that for that very sin and transgression his father was brought down from his height and made to be a companion for asses. 'And thou his son, O Belshazzar,' says he, 'hast not humbled thine heart, though thou knewest all this' (Daniel 5:22). A home reproof indeed, but home is most fit for an open and continued-in transgression.

Let those then that are the offspring or relations of such, who by their own sin and the dreadful judgements of God, are made to become a sign (Deuteronomy 16:9–10) having been swept as dung from off the face of the earth, beware, lest when Judgement knocks at their door for their sins, as it did before at the door of their progenitors, it falls also with as heavy a stroke as on them that went before them. Lest, I say, they in that day, instead of finding mercy, find for their high, daring, and judgement-affronting sins, judgement without mercy.

To conclude, let those who would not die Mr Badman's death, take heed of Mr Badman's ways, for his ways bring to his end. Wickedness will not deliver him who is given to it, though they should cloak all with a profession of religion.

If it was a transgression of old for a man to wear a woman's apparel, surely it is a transgression now for a sinner to wear a Christian profession for a cloak. Wolves in sheep's clothing swarm in England this day – wolves both as to doctrine and as to practice, too. Some men make a profession, I doubt, on purpose that they may twist themselves into a trade, and then into an estate, yea, and if need be, into an estate knavishly by the ruins of their neighbour. Let such take heed for those who do such things have the greater damnation.

Christian, make your profession shine by a conversation according to the Gospel, or else you will damnify religion, bring scandal to your brethren and give offence to the enemies. And 'twould be better that a millstone were hung about your neck, and that you, as so adorned, were cast into the bottom of the sea, than so to do.

Christian, a profession according to the Gospel is, in these days, a rare thing. Seek then after it, put it on and keep it without spot, and, as becomes you, white and clean, and you shall be a rare Christian.

The prophecy of the last times is, that professing men (for so I understand the text) shall be many of them base (2 Timothy 3). But continue you in the things that you have learned, not of wanton men, not of licentious times, but of the Word and doctrine of God that is according to godliness, and you shall walk with Christ in white.

Now God Almighty gives his people grace, not to hate or malign sinners nor yet to choose any of their ways, but to keep themselves pure from the blood of all men, by speaking and doing according to that name and those rules that they profess to know, and love, for Jesus Christ's sake.

– John Bunyan.

THE LIFE AND DEATH OF MR BADMAN

Presented to the World in a Familiar DIALOGUE

Betwixt

Mr WISEMAN
&
Mr ATTENTIVE

WISEMAN: Good morrow my good neighbour, Mr Attentive. Where are you walking so early this morning? Methinks you look as if you were concerned about something more than ordinary. Have you lost any of your cattle, or what is the matter?

ATTENTIVE: Good sir, good morrow to you. I have not as yet lost ought, but yet you give a right guess of me, for I am, as you say, concerned in my heart, but 'tis because of the badness of the times. And sir you, as all our neighbours know, are a very observing man, pray therefore what do you think of them?

WISE: Why? I think, as you say, to wit, that they are bad times, and bad they will be until men are better, for they are bad men that make bad times. If men therefore would mend, so would the times. 'Tis a folly to look for good days so long as sin is so high, and those that study its nourishment so many. God bring it down, and those that nourish it to repentance, and then my good neighbour, you will be concerned, not as you are now: Now you are concerned because times are so bad; but then you will be so, 'cause times are so good: Now you are concerned so as to be perplexed, but then you will be concerned so as to lift up your voice with shouting; for I dare say, could you see such days they would make you shout.

ATTEN: Aye, so they would. Such times I have prayed for. Such times I have longed for. But I fear they'll be worse before they be better.

WISE: Make no conclusions, man. For He who has the hearts of men in His hand can change them from worse to better, and so bad times into good. God gives long life to them who are good, and especially to those of them who are capable of doing him service in the world. The ornament and beauty of this lower world, next to God and his wonders, are the men that spangle and shine in godliness.

Now as MR WISEMAN *said this, he gave a great sigh.*

ATTEN: Amen. Amen. But why, good sir, do you sigh so deeply? Is it for ought else than that for the which, as you have perceived, I myself am concerned?

WISE: I am concerned with you for the badness of the times, but that was not the cause of that sigh, of the which, as I see, you take notice. I sighed at the remembrance of the death of that man for whom the bell tolled at our town yesterday.

ATTEN: Why? I trow Mr Goodman your neighbour is not dead. Indeed I did hear that he had been sick.

WISE: No, no, it is not he. Had it been he, I could not but have been concerned, but yet not as I am concerned now. If he had died, I should only have been concerned for that the world had lost a light. But the man that I am concerned for now was one that never was good, therefore such a one who is not dead only, but damned. He died that he might die, he went from life to death, and then from death to death, from death natural to death eternal.

And as he spoke this, the water stood in his eyes.

ATTEN: Indeed, to go from a deathbed to Hell is a fearful thing to think on. But good neighbour Wiseman, be pleased to tell me who this man was, and why you conclude him so miserable in his death?

WISE: Well, if you can stay, I will tell you who he was, and why I conclude thus concerning him.

ATTEN: My leisure will admit me to stay, and I am willing to hear you out. And I pray God your discourse may take hold on my heart, that I may be bettered thereby.

So they agreed to sit down under a tree.
Then Mr Wiseman *proceeded as follows.*

Wise: The man that I mean is one Mr Badman. He has lived in our town a great while, and now, as I said, he is dead. But the reason of my being so concerned at his death is, not for that he was at all related to me, or for that any good conditions died with him, for he was far from them, but for that, as I greatly fear, he has, as was hinted before, died two deaths at once.

Atten: I perceive what you mean by two deaths at once. And to speak truth, 'tis a fearful thing thus to have ground to think of any. For although the death of the ungodly and sinners is laid to heart but of few, yet to die in such a state is more dreadful and fearful than any man can imagine. Indeed, if a man had no soul, if his state was not truly immortal, the matter would not be so much. But for a man to be so disposed of by his maker as to be appointed a sensible being for ever, and for him too to fall into the hands of revenging justice that will be always to the utmost extremity that his sin deserves, punishing of him in the dismal dungeon of Hell, this must needs be unutterably sad and lamentable.

Wise: There is no man, I think, that is sensible of the worth of one soul but must, when he hears of the death of unconverted men, be stricken with sorrow and grief. Because, as you said well, that man's state is such that he has a sensible being for ever. For 'tis sense that makes punishment heavy. But yet sense is not all that the damned have. They have sense and reason, too. So then, as sense receives punishment with sorrow because it feels and bleeds under the same, so by reason and the exercise thereof, in the midst of torment, all present affliction is aggravated, and that three manner of ways:

One – reason will consider thus with himself, 'for what am I thus tormented?' and will easily find 'tis for nothing but that base and filthy thing, sin. And now will vexation be mixed with punishment, and that will greatly heighten the affliction.

Two – reason will consider thus with himself: 'how long must this be my state?' and will soon return to himself this answer: 'this must be my state forever and ever.' Now this will greatly increase the torment.

Three – reason will consider thus with himself: 'what have I lost more than present ease and quiet by my sins that I have committed?' and will quickly return himself this answer: 'I have lost communion with God, Christ, saints and angels, and a share in Heaven and eternal life.' And this also must needs greaten the misery of poor damned souls. And this is the case of Mr Badman.

ATTEN: I feel my heart even shake at the thoughts of coming into such a state. Hell! Who knows that is yet alive what the torments of Hell are? This word Hell gives a very dreadful sound.

WISE: Aye, so it does in the ears of him that has a tender conscience. But if, as you say, and that truly the very name of Hell is so dreadful, what is the place itself, and what are the punishments that are there inflicted, and that without the least intermission upon the souls of damned men forever and ever.

ATTEN: Well, but passing this, my leisure will admit me to stay. And therefore pray tell me what it is that makes you think that Mr Badman has gone to Hell.

WISE: I will tell you. But first do you know which of the Badmans I mean?

ATTEN: Why was there more of them than one?

WISE: O yes. A great many, both brothers and sisters. And yet all of them the children of a godly parent, the more a great deal is the pity.

ATTEN: Which of them therefore was it who died?

WISE: The eldest. Old in years, and old in sin. But the sinner that dies a hundred years old shall be accursed.

ATTEN: Well, but what makes you think he has gone to Hell?

WISE: His wicked life and fearful death, especially since the manner of his death was so corresponding with his life.

ATTEN: Pray let me know the manner of his death, if yourself did perfectly know it.

WISE: I was there when he died. But I desire not to see another such man, while I live, die in such sort as he did.

ATTEN: Pray therefore let me hear it.

WISE: You say you have leisure and can stay. And therefore, if you please, we will discourse even orderly of him. First, we will begin with his life and then proceed to his death. Because a relation of the first may the more affect you when you shall hear of the second.

ATTEN: Did you then so well know his life?

WISE: I knew him of a child. I was a man when he was but a boy, and I made special observation of him from first to last.

ATTEN: Pray then let me hear from you an account of his life. But be as brief as you can, for I long to hear of the manner of his death.

WISE: I will endeavour to answer your desires. And first, I will tell you that from a child he was very bad. His very beginning was ominous and presaged that no good end was, in likelihood, to follow thereupon. There were several sins that he was given to when but a little one that manifested him to be notoriously infected with original corruption. For I dare say he learned none of them of his father or mother, nor was he admitted to go much abroad among other children that were vile to learn to sin of them. Nay, contrariwise, if at any time he did get abroad amongst others, he would be as the inventor of bad words and an example in bad actions. To them all he used to be, as we say, the ringleader and master sinner from a child.

ATTEN: This was a bad beginning indeed and did demonstrate that he was, as you say, polluted, very much polluted with original corruption. For to speak my mind freely, I do confess that it is my opinion that children come polluted with sin into the world, and that oft-times the sins of their youth, especially while they are very young, are rather by virtue of indwelling sin than by examples that are set before them by others. Not but that they learn to sin by example too, but example is not the root but rather the temptation unto wickedness. The root is sin within, for from within, out of the heart of man proceeds sin.[1,2]

WISE: I am glad to hear that you are of this opinion and to confirm what you have said by a few hints from the Word. Man in his birth is compared to an ass – an unclean beast – and to a wretched infant in its blood. Besides, all the firstborn of old that were offered unto the Lord were to be redeemed at the age of a month, and that was before

1. Original sin is the root of actual transgressions.
2. Mark 7.

they were sinners by imitation. The scripture also affirms,[3] that by the sin of one, judgement came upon all, and renders this reason, for that all have sinned: nor is that objection worth a rush, that Christ by his death has taken away Original Sin. First, because it is scriptureless. Secondly, because it makes them incapable of salvation by Christ, for none but those who in their own persons are sinners are to have salvation by him. Many other things might be added, but between persons so well agreed as you and I are, these may suffice at present. But when an antagonist comes to deal with us about this matter, then we have for him often other strong arguments, if he be an antagonist worth the taking notice of.[4]

ATTEN: But, as was hinted before, he used to be the ring leading sinner, or the master of mischief among other children. Yet these are but generals. Pray therefore tell me in particular which were the sins of his childhood.

WISE: I will so. When he was but a child, he was so addicted to lying,[5] that his parents scarce knew when to believe he spoke true. Yea, he would invent, tell, and stand to the lies that he invented and told, and that with such an audacious face, that one might even read in his very countenance the symptoms of a hard and desperate heart this way.

ATTEN: This was an ill beginning indeed, and argues that he began to harden himself in sin betimes. For a lie cannot be knowingly told and stood in – and I perceive that this was his manner of way in lying – but he must as it were force his own heart into it. Yea, he must make his heart hard[6], and bold to do it. Yea, he must be arrived to an exceeding pitch of wickedness thus to do, since all this he did against that good education, that before you seemed to hint, he had from his father and mother.

WISE: The want of good education, as you have intimated, is many times a cause why children do so easily, so soon, become bad, especially when there is not only a want of that but bad examples enough, as, the more is the pity, there is in many families. By virtue of which poor children are trained up in sin, and nursed therein for the Devil

3. Job 11:12. Ezekiel 16. Exodus 13:13, 34:20.
4. Romans 5.
5. Badman addicted to lying from a child.
6. A lie knowingly told demonstrates that the heart is desperately hard.

and Hell. But it was otherwise with Mr Badman, for to my knowledge, this his way of lying was a great grief to his parents, for their hearts were much dejected at this beginning of their son. Nor did there want counsel and correction from them to him, if that would have made him better. He wanted not to be told, in my hearing, and that over and over and over, that all liars should have their part in the lake that burns with fire and brimstone, and that whosoever loves and makes a lie should not have any part in the new and heavenly Jerusalem.[7] But all availed nothing with him. When a fit or an occasion to lie came upon him, he would invent, tell, and stand to his lie – as steadfastly as if it had been the biggest of truths – that he told, and that with that hardening of his heart and face, that it would be to those that stood by a wonder. Nay, and this he would do when under the rod of correction which is appointed by God for parents to use that thereby they might keep their children from Hell.[8]

ATTEN: Truly it was, as I said, a bad beginning. He served the Devil betimes. Yea he became a nurse to one of his brats,[9] for a spirit of lying is the Devil's brat,[10] for he is a liar and the father of it.

WISE: Right, he is the father of it indeed. A lie is begot by the Devil as the father and is brought forth by the wicked heart as the mother. Wherefore another scripture also says, 'why hath Satan filled thine heart to lie?'[11] etc. Yea, he calls the heart that is big with a lie, a heart that has conceived, that is, by the Devil. Why have you conceived this thing in your heart? You have not lied unto men but unto God. True, his lie was a lie of the highest nature, but every lie hath the same father and mother as had the lie last spoken of.[12] For he is a liar, and the father of it. A lie then is the brat of Hell, and it cannot be in the heart before the person has committed a kind of spiritual adultery with the Devil.[13] That soul therefore that tells a known lie,

7. The liar's portion. Revelation 21:8, 27, 22:15.

8. Proverbs 22:15, 23:13–14.

9. John 8:44.

10. The Devil's brat.

11. Acts 5:3–4.

12. The father and mother of a lie.

13. Mark.

has lain with and conceived it by lying with the Devil, the only father of lies. For a lie has only one father and mother: the Devil and the heart. No marvel therefore if the hearts that hatch and bring forth lies be so much of complexion with the Devil. Yea, no marvel though God and Christ have so bent their word against liars. A liar is wedded to the Devil himself.

ATTEN: It seems a marvellous thing in my eyes that since a lie is the offspring of the Devil, and since a lie brings the soul to the very den of devils, to wit, the dark dungeon of Hell, that men should be so desperately wicked as to accustom themselves to so horrible a thing.

WISE: It seems also marvellous to me, especially when I observe for how little a matter some men will study, contrive, make and tell a lie. You shall have some that will lie it over and over, and that for a penny profit.[14] Yea, lie and stand in it, although they know that they lie. Yea, you shall have some men that will not stick to tell lie after lie, though themselves get nothing thereby. They will tell lies in their ordinary discourse with their neighbours, also their news, their jests and their tales must needs be adorned with lies, or else they seem to bear no good sound to the ear, nor show much to the fancy of him to whom they are told. But alas, what will these liars do, when, for their lies they shall be tumbled down into Hell to that Devil that did beget those lies in their heart, and so be tormented by fire and brimstone, with him, and that forever and ever, for their lies?

ATTEN: Can you not give one some example of God's judgements upon liars, that one may tell them to liars when one hears them lie, if perhaps they may by the hearing thereof, be made afraid and ashamed to lie?

WISE: Examples! why, Sapphira and his wife are examples enough to put a stop, one would think, to a spirit addicted thereto, for they both were stricken down dead for telling a lie, and that by God himself, in the midst of a company of people.[15] But if God's threatening of liars with hellfire and with the loss of the kingdom of Heaven will not prevail with them to leave off to lie and make lies, it cannot be imagined that a relation of temporal judgements that

14. Some will tell a lie for a penny profit.
15. An example for liars: Acts 5.

have swept liars out of the world heretofore should do it. Now, as I said, this lying was one of the first sins that Mr Badman was addicted to, and he could make them and tell them fearfully.

ATTEN: I am sorry to hear this of him and so much the more because, as I fear, this sin did not reign in him alone.[16] For usually one who is accustomed to lying is also accustomed to other evils besides, and if it were not so also with Mr Badman, it would be indeed a wonder.

WISE: You say true. The liar is a captive slave of more than the spirit of lying, and therefore this Mr Badman, as he was a liar from a child, so he was also much given to pilfer and steal.[17] So that what he could, as we say, handsomely lay his hands on, that was counted his own, whether they were the things of his fellow children, or if he could lay hold of anything at a neighbour's house, he would take it away. You must understand me of trifles, for being let but a child he attempted no great matter, especially at first. But yet as he grew up in strength and ripeness of wit, so he attempted to pilfer and steal things still of more value than at first. He took at last great pleasure in robbing of gardens and orchards, and as he grew up, to steal pullen[iii] from the neighbourhood. Yea, what was his father's, could not escape his fingers.[18] All was fish that came to his net, so hardened, at last was he in this mischief also.

ATTEN: You make me wonder more and more. What, play the thief too! What, play the thief so soon! He could not but know, though he was but a child, that what he took from others was none of his own. Besides, if his father was a good man, as you say, it could not be but he must also hear from him that to steal was to transgress the law of God, and so to run the hazard of eternal damnation.

WISE: His father was not wanting to use the means to reclaim him, often urging, as I have been told, that saying in the law of Moses, 'Thou shalt not steal.'[19] And also that, 'This is the curse that goeth forth over the face of the whole earth: for every one that stealeth shall be cut off,' etc.[20] The light of nature also, though he was little, must

16. A spirit of lying accompanied with other sins.
17. Badman given to pilfer.
18. Badman would rob his father.
19. Exodus 20:15.
20. Zechariah 5:3.

needs show him that what he took from others was not his own, and that he would not willingly have been served so himself. But all was to no purpose, let father and conscience say what they would to him, he would go on, he was resolved to go on in his wickedness.

ATTEN: But his father would, as you intimate, sometimes rebuke him for his wickedness. Pray, how would he carry it then?

WISE: How! Why, like to a thief that is found. He would stand gloating and hanging down his head in a sullen, pouching manner[21] – a body might read, as we use to say, the picture of ill luck in his face. And when his father did demand his answer to such questions concerning his villainy, he would grumble and mutter at him, and that should be all he could get.

ATTEN: But you said that he would also rob his father. Methinks that was an unnatural thing.

WISE: Natural or unnatural, all is one to a thief. Beside, you must think that he had likewise companions to whom he was, for the wickedness that he saw in them, more firmly knit, than either to father or mother.[22] Yea, and what had he cared if father and mother had died for grief for him? Their death would have been, as he would have counted, great release and liberty to him. For the truth is, they and their counsel was his bondage. Yea, and if I forget not, I have heard some say that when he was at times among his companions, he would greatly rejoice to think that his parents were old and could not live long.[23] And then, quoth he, 'I shall be my own man to do what I list without their control.'

ATTEN: Then it seems he counted that robbing of his parents was no crime.

WISE: None at all, and therefore he fell directly under that sentence, 'Whoso robbeth his father or his mother, and saith, It is no transgression; the same is the companion of a destroyer.'[24] And for that he set so light by them as to their persons and counsels, 'twas a sign

21. Jeremiah 2:26. How Badman did use to carry it when his father used to chide him for his sins.
22. Badman more firmly knit to his companions than either to father or mother.
23. Badman would rejoice to think that his parents' deaths were at hand.
24. Proverbs 28:24.

that at present he was of a very abominable spirit, and that some judgement waited to take hold of him in time to come.[25]

ATTEN: But can you imagine what it was, I mean, in his conceit – for I speak not now of the suggestions of Satan, by which doubtless he was put on to do these things – I say, what it should be in his conceit that should make him think that this his manner of pilfering and stealing was no great matter?

WISE: It was for that the things that he stole were small, to rob orchards and gardens, and to steal pullen and the like. These he counted tricks of youth,[26] nor would he be beat out of it by all that his friends could say. They would tell him that he must not covet or desire – and yet to desire is less than to take – even anything. The least thing that was his neighbours', and that if he did, it would be a transgression of the law. But all was one to him. What through the wicked talk of his companions, and the delusion of his own corrupt heart, he would go on in his pilfering course, and where he thought himself secure, would talk of and laugh at it when he had done.

ATTEN: Well, ☞ I heard a man once, when he was upon the ladder with the rope about his neck, confess – when ready to be turned off by the hangman – that that which had brought him to that end was his accustoming of himself when young to pilfer and steal small things. To my best remembrance he told us that he began the trade of a thief by stealing pins and points, and therefore did forewarn all the youth that then were gathered together to see him die to take heed of beginning, though but with little sins, because by tampering at first with little ones, way is made for the commission of bigger.

WISE: Since you are entered upon stories, I also will tell you one. The which,[27] though I heard it not with my own ears, yet my author I dare believe.[28] It is concerning one old tod[iv] who was hanged about twenty years ago or more at Hartford for being a thief. The story is this:

At ☞ a summer assizes held at Hartford, while the judge was sitting upon the bench, came this old tod into the court, clothed in a green suit with his leather girdle in his hand, his bosom open and all

25. 1 Samuel 2:25.
26. Badman counted his thieving no great matter.
27. The Story of Old Tod.
28. Young thieves take notice.

on a dung sweat as if he had run for his life. And having come in, he spoke aloud as follows:

'My lord,' said he, 'here is the veriest rogue that breathes upon the face of the earth. I have been a thief from a child. When I was but a little one, I gave myself to rob orchards and to do other such like wicked things, and I have continued a thief ever since.[29] My lord, there has not been a robbery committed thus many years within so many miles of this place, but I have either been at it or privy to it.'

The judge thought the fellow was mad, but after some conference with some of the justices, they agreed to indict him. And so they did of several felonious actions, to all which he heartily confessed guilty, and so was hanged with his wife at the same time.

ATTEN: This is a remarkable story indeed, and you think it is a true one.

WISE: It is not only remarkable, but pat to our purpose. This thief, like Mr Badman, began his trade betimes. He began too where Mr Badman began, even at robbing of orchards and other such things, which brought him, as you may perceive, from sin to sin till at last it brought him to the public shame of sin, which is the gallows.

As for the truth of this story, the relator told me that he was at the same time himself in the court and stood within less than two yards of old Tod when he heard him aloud to utter the words.

ATTEN: These two sins of lying and stealing were a bad sign of an evil end.

WISE: So they were, and yet Mr Badman came not to his end like old Tod. Though I fear, to as bad, nay, worse than was that death of the gallows, though less discerned by spectators. But more of that by and by. But you talk of these two sins as if these were all that Mr Badman was addicted to in his youth. Alas, alas, he swarmed with sins, even as a beggar does with vermin, and that when he was but a boy.

ATTEN: Why, what other sins was he addicted to, I mean, while he was but a child?

WISE: You need not ask to what other sins was he, but to what other sins was he not addicted, that is, of such as suited with his age, for a man may safely say that nothing that was vile came amiss to him if he

29. Old Tod began his way to the gallows by robbing of orchards and the like.

was but capable to do it. Indeed, some sins there are that childhood knows not how to be tampering with. But I speak of sins that he was capable of committing, of which I will nominate two or three more. And:

First, he could not endure the Lord's Day,[30] because of the holiness that did attend it. The beginning of that day was to him as if he was going to prison, except he could get out from his father and mother and lurk in by-holes among his companions until holy duties were over. Reading the scriptures, hearing sermons, godly conference, repeating of sermons and prayer were things that he could not away with. And therefore if his father on such days – as often he did, though sometimes notwithstanding his diligence, he would be sure to give him the slip – did keep him strictly to the observation of the day, he would plainly show by all carriages that he was highly discontent therewith: he would sleep at duties, would talk vainly with his brothers, and as it were, think every godly opportunity seven times as long as it was, grudging till it was over.

ATTEN: This his abhorring of that day was not, I think, for the sake of the day itself. For as it is a day, it is nothing else but as other days of the week. But I suppose it were think every godly as it was, grudging till it that day, was not, I think, as it is a day, it is nothing of the week: But I suppose that the reason of his loathing of it was for that God has put sanctity and holiness upon it. Also because it is the day above all the days of the week that ought to be spent in holy devotion, in remembrance of our Lord's resurrection from the dead.[31]

WISE: Yes, 'twas therefore that he was such an enemy to it, even because more restraint was laid upon him on that day from his own ways than were possible should be laid upon him on all others.

ATTEN: Does not God, by instituting a day unto holy duties, make great proof how the hearts and inclinations of poor people do stand to holiness of heart, and a conversation in holy duties?

WISE: Yes doubtless.[32] And a man shall show his heart and his life what they are more by one Lord's Day than by all the days of the week

30. Badman could not abide the Lord's Day.

31. Why Badman could not abide the Lord's Day.

32. God proves the heart what it is by instituting the Lord's Day and setting it apart to His service.

besides. And the reason is because on the Lord's Day, there is a special restraint laid upon men as to thoughts and life, more than upon other days of the week besides. Also, men are enjoined on that day to a stricter performance of holy duties and restraint of worldly business than upon other days they are. Wherefore if their hearts incline not naturally to good, now they will show it, now they will appear what they are. The Lord's Day is a kind of an emblem of the heavenly Sabbath above, and it makes manifest how the heart stands to the perpetuity of holiness, more than to be found in a transient duty does.

On other days, a man may be in and out of holy duties, and all in a quarter of an hour. But now, the Lord's Day is, as it were, a day that enjoins to one perpetual duty of holiness. Remember that thou keep holy the Sabbath day[33] – which by Christ is not abrogated but changed into the first of the week – not as it was given in particular to the Jews but as it was sanctified by Him from the beginning of the world. And therefore is a greater proof of the frame and temper of a man's heart and does more make manifest to what he is inclined than doth his other performance of duties. Therefore God puts great difference between them that truly call and walk in this day as holy and count it honourable,[34] upon the account that now they have an opportunity to show how they delight to honour him[35] in that they have not only an hour but a whole day to show it in. I say, He puts great difference between these and that other sort who say, 'when will the Sabbath be gone, that we may be at our worldly business?'[36] The first He calls a blessed man but brands the other for an unsanctified worldling. And indeed, to delight ourselves in God's service upon his holy days gives a better proof of a sanctified nature, than to grudge at the coming and to be weary of the holy duties of such days, as Mr Badman did.

ATTEN: There may be something in what you say, for he who cannot abide to keep one day holy to God, to be sure he has given a

33. Genesis 2:2; Exodus 31:13–17; Mark 2:27–28, 16:1; Acts 20:7; 1 Corinthians 16:1–2; Revelation 1:10.
34. Isaiah 5:8, 13.
35. Isaiah 56:2.
36. Amos 8:5.

sufficient proof that he is an unsanctified man. And as such, what should he do in Heaven, that being the place where a perpetual Sabbath is to be kept to God,[37] I say, to be kept forever and ever? And for ought I know one reason why, one day in seven, has been by our Lord set apart unto holy duties for men may be to give them conviction that there is enmity in the hearts of sinners to the God of Heaven, for he who hates holiness hates God Himself. They pretend to love God, and yet love not a holy day, and yet love not to spend that day in one continued act of holiness to the Lord. They had as good say nothing as to call him Lord, Lord, and yet not do the things that he says. And this Mr Badman was such a one. He could not abide this day nor any of the duties of it. Indeed, when he could get from his friends and so spend it in all manner of idleness and profaneness,[38] then he would be pleased well enough. But what was this but a turning the day into night, or other than taking an opportunity at God's forbidding, to follow our callings to solace and satisfy our lusts and delights of the flesh. I take the liberty to speak thus of Mr Badman upon a confidence of what you sir have said of him is true.

WISE: You needed not to have made that apology for your censuring of Mr Badman, for all that knew him will confirm what you said of him to be true. He could not abide either that day or anything else that had the stamp or image of God upon it. Sin, sin, and to do the thing that was naught was that which he delighted in and that from a little child.

ATTEN: I must say again I am sorry to hear it, and that for his own sake and also for the sake of his relations who must needs be broken to pieces with such doings as these. For these things' sake comes 'the wrath of God upon the children of disobedience',[39] and doubtless he must have gone to Hell if he died without repentance. And to beget a child for Hell is sad for parents to think on.

WISE: Of his dying, as I told you, I will give you a relation anon, but now we are upon his life and upon the manner of his life in his

37. Hebrews 4:9.
38. How Badman used to spend the Lord's Day.
39. Ephesians 5:6.

childhood, even of the sins that attended him then, some of which I have mentioned already. And indeed I have mentioned but some, for yet there are more to follow, and those not at all inferior to what you have already heard.

ATTEN: Pray, what were they?

WISE: Why, he was greatly given, and that while a lad, to grievous swearing and cursing.[40] Yea, he then made no more of swearing and cursing than I do of telling my fingers. Yea, he would do it without provocation thereto. He counted it a glory to swear and curse, and it was as natural to him, as to eat and drink and sleep.

ATTEN: Oh! What a young villain was this! Here is, as the apostle says, a yielding of members as instruments of unrighteousness unto sin indeed![41] This is proceeding from evil to evil with a witness. This argues that he was a black-mouthed young wretch indeed.

WISE: He was so. And yet, as I told you, he counted above all this kind of sinning to be a badge of his honour.[42] He reckoned himself a man's fellow when he had learnt to swear and curse boldly.

ATTEN: I am persuaded that many do think, as you have said, that to swear is a thing that does bravely become them, and that it is the best way for a man when he would put authority or terror into his words to stuff them full of the sin of swearing.

WISE: You say right, else, as I am persuaded, men would not so usually belch out their blasphemous oaths as they do. They take a pride in it. They think that to swear is gentlemanlike, and having once accustomed themselves unto it, they hardly leave it all the days of their lives.

ATTEN: Well, but now we are upon it, pray show me[43] the difference between swearing and cursing, for there is a difference, is there not?

WISE: Yes. There is a difference between swearing and cursing. Swearing – vain swearing – such as young badman accustomed himself unto. Now vain and sinful swearing[44] is a light and wicked calling of God, etc., to witness to our vain and foolish attesting of things, and those things are of two sorts.

40. Badman given to swearing and cursing.
41. Romans 6:13.
42. Swearing and cursing a badge of Mr Badman's honour.
43. Difference between swearing and cursing.
44. What swearing is.

One – things that we swear are, or shall, be done.

Two – things so sworn to, true or false.

One – things that we swear are, or shall, be done. You swear you have done such a thing that such a thing is so or shall be so. For it is no matter which of these it is that men swear about, if it be done lightly and wickedly, and groundlessly, it is vain, because it is a sin against the Third Commandment, which says, 'Thou shalt not take the name of the Lord thy God in vain.'[45] For this is a vain using of that holy and sacred name, and so a sin for which, without sound repentance, there is not, nor can be rightly expected, forgiveness.

ATTEN: Then it seems – though as to the matter of fact – a man swears truly, yet if he swears lightly and groundlessly, his oath is evil, and he by it, under sin.

WISE: Yes. A man may say,[46] 'the Lord lives', and that is true, and yet in so saying, swear falsely, because he swears vainly, needlessly, and without a ground. To swear groundedly and necessarily – which then a man does, when he swears as being called thereto of God – that is tolerated of the Word. But this was none of Mr Badman's swearing, and therefore that which now we are not concerned about.

ATTEN: I perceive, by the prophet, that a man may sin in swearing to a truth. They therefore must needs most horribly sin that swear to confirm their jests and lies. And as they think, the better to beautify their foolish talking.

WISE: They sin with a high hand, for they presume to imagine that God is as wicked as themselves, to wit, that he is an avoucher of lies to be true.[47] For, as I said before, to swear is to call God to witness. And to swear to a lie is to call God Himself to witness that that lie is true. This therefore must needs offend, for it puts the highest affront upon the holiness and righteousness of God. Therefore his wrath must sweep them away. This kind of swearing is put in with lying, and killing, and stealing and committing adultery, and therefore must not go unpunished.[48] For if God will not hold him guiltless who takes his name in vain, which a man may do when he swears to a

45. Exodus 20:7.

46. A man may sin in swearing to a truth, Jeremiah 5:2.

47. He who swears to a lie concludes that God is as wicked as himself.

48. Zechariah 5:3; Jeremiah 7:9; Hosiah 4:2–3.

truth, as I have showed before, how can it be imagined that He should hold such guiltless, who by swearing will appeal to God, if lies be not true, or that swear out of their frantic and bedlam madness. It would grieve and provoke a sober man to wrath, if one should swear to a notorious lie, and avouch that that man would attest it for a truth. And yet thus do men deal with the holy God. They tell their jestings, tales and lies and then swear by God that they are true. Now this kind of swearing was as common with young Badman, as it was to eat when he was hungry or to go to bed when it was night.

ATTEN: I have often mused in my mind what it should be that should make men so common in the use of the sin of swearing, since those that be wise will believe them never the sooner for that.

WISE: It cannot be anything that is good, you may be sure, because the thing itself is abominable.[49] One – therefore it must be from the promptings of the spirit of the Devil within them. Two – also it flows sometimes from hellish rage, when the tongue has set on fire of Hell even the whole course of nature.[50] Three – but commonly swearing flows from that daring boldness that bids defiance to the law that forbids it. Four – swearers think also that by their belching of their blasphemous oaths out of their black and polluted mouths, they show themselves the more valiant men. Five – and imagine also, that by these outrageous kind of villainies, they shall conquer those that at such a time they have to do with, and make them believe their lies to be true. Six – they also swear frequently to get gain thereby, and when they meet with fools, they overcome them this way. But if I might give advice in this matter, no buyer should lay out one farthing with him that is a common swearer in his calling, especially with such an oath master who endeavours to swear away his commodity to another, and that would swear his chapman's money into his own pocket.

ATTEN: All these causes of swearing, so far as I can perceive, flow from the same root as do the oaths themselves, even from a hardened and desperate heart. But pray show me now how wicked cursing is to be distinguished from this kind of swearing.

49. Six causes of vain swearing.
50. James 3:6–9.

WISE: Swearing,[51] as I said, has immediately to do with the name of God, and it calls upon him to be witness to the truth of what is said. That is, if they who swear, swear by Him. Some indeed swear by idols, as by the Mass, by our Lady, by saints, beasts, birds, and other creatures. But the usual way of our profane ones in England, is to swear by God, Christ, faith and the like. But however, or by whatever they swear, cursing is distinguished from swearing thus.

To curse[52] – to curse profanely – it is to sentence another or oneself for or to evil, or to wish that some evil might happen to the person or thing under the curse unjustly.

It is to sentence for or to evil, that is, without a cause. Thus Shimei cursed David. He sentenced him for and to evil unjustly when he said to him, 'Come out, come out, thou bloody man, and thou man of Belial. The Lord hath returned upon thee all the blood of the house of Saul, in whose stead thou hast reigned; and the Lord hath delivered the kingdom into the hand of Absalom thy son: and behold thou art taken in thy mischief, because thou art a bloody man.'[53]

This David calls a grievous curse. And behold, said he to Solomon his son, 'thou hast with thee Shimei the son of Gera, a Benjamite of Bahurim, which cursed me with a grievous curse in the day when I went to Mahanaim.'[54]

But what was this curse? Why, first, it was a wrong sentence passed upon David. Shimei called him bloody man, man of Belial, when he was not. Secondly, he sentenced him to the evil that at present was upon him for a bloody man – that is, against the house of Saul – when that present evil overtook David for quite another thing.

And we may thus apply it to the profane ones of our times who, in their rage and envy, have little else in their mouths but a sentence against their neighbour for and to evil unjustly.[55] How common is it with many when they are but a little offended with one to cry, 'Hang him, damn him, rogue!' This is both a sentencing of him for and to evil, and is in itself a grievous curse.

51. How cursing is distinguished from swearing.
52. Of cursing, what it is.
53. 2 Samuel 16:6–8.
54. 1 Kings 2:8.
55. How the profane ones of our times curse.

Two – the other kind of cursing is to wish that some evil might happen to and overtake this or that person or thing. And this kind of cursing Job counted a grievous sin. I have not suffered, says he, my mouth to sin,[56] by wishing a curse to his soul or, consequently, to body or estate. This then is a wicked cursing to wish that evil might either befall another or ourselves, and this kind of cursing young Badman accustomed himself unto.

One – he would wish that evil might befall others.[57] He would wish their necks broken, or that their brains were out, or that the pox or plague was upon them, and the like. All which is a devilish kind of cursing and is become one of the common sins of our age.

Two – he would also as often wish a curse to himself, saying, 'Would I might be hanged, or burned, or that the Devil might fetch me, if it be not so,' or the like. We count the Damme Blades[58,v] to be great swearers, but when in their hellish fury they say, 'God damn me, God perish me,' or the like, they rather curse than swear. Yea, curse themselves, and that with a wish that damnation might light upon themselves, which wish and curse of theirs in a little time, they will see accomplished upon them, even in hellfire, if they repent not of their sins.

ATTEN: But did this young Badman accustom himself to such filthy kind of language?

WISE: I think I may say that nothing was more frequent in his mouth, and that upon the least provocation. Yea, he was so versed in such kind of language, that neither father,[59] nor mother, nor brother, nor sister, nor servant, no nor the very cattle that his father had, could escape these curses of his. I say that even the brute beasts when he drove them or rid upon them, if they pleased not his humour, they must be sure to partake of his curse.[60] He would wish their necks broken, their legs broken, their guts out, or that the Devil might fetch them, or the like. And no marvel, for he that is so hardy to wish

56. Job 30:31.
57. Badman's way of cursing.
58. The Damme Blade.
59. Badman would curse his father, etc.
60. Badman would curse his father's cattle.

damnation or other bad curses to himself or dearest relations, will not stick to wish evil to the silly beast in his madness.

ATTEN: Well, I see still that this Badman was a desperate villain. But pray, sir, since you have gone thus far, now show me where this evil of cursing arises, and also what dishonour it brings to God, for I easily discern that it does bring damnation to the soul.

WISE: This evil of cursing arises, in general, from the desperate wickedness of the heart, but particularly from:[61, 62] One – envy, which is as I apprehend, the leading sin to witchcraft. Two – it also arises from pride, which was the sin of the fallen angels. Three – it arises too from scorn and contempt of others. Four – but for a man to curse himself must needs arise from desperate madness.

The dishonour that it brings to God[63] is this. It takes away from him His authority, in whose power it is only, to bless and curse. Not to curse wickedly, as Mr Badman, but justly and righteously, giving by His curse to those who are wicked, the due reward of their deeds.

Besides, these wicked men, in their wicked cursing of their neighbour, etc., do even curse God Himself in His handy work. Man is God's image, and to curse wickedly the image of God is to curse God Himself.[64] Therefore as when men wickedly swear, they rend and tear God's name, and make him, as much as in them lies, the avoucher and approver of all their wickedness. So he who curses and condemns in this sort his neighbour, or who wishes him evil, curses, condemns and wishes evil to the image of God, and consequently judges and condemns God Himself.

Suppose that a man should say with his mouth, 'I wish that the King's picture was burned.' Would not this man's so saying render him as an enemy to the person of the King? Even so it is with them that, by cursing, wish evil to their neighbour, or to themselves, they condemn the image, even the image of God Himself.

ATTEN: But do you think that the men who do thus, do think that they do so vilely, so abominably?

61. Job 15; Ecclesiastes 7:22.
62. Four causes of cursing.
63. The dishonour it brings to God.
64. James 3:9.

WISE: The question is not what men do believe concerning their sin, but what God's Word says of it. If God's Word says that swearing and cursing are sins, though men should count them for virtues, their reward will be a reward for sin, to wit, the damnation of the soul.

To curse another[65] and to swear vainly and falsely are sins against the light of nature.

One – to curse is so, because whoso curses another knows that at the same time he would not be so served himself.

Two – to swear also is a sin against the same law, for nature will tell me, that I should not lie, and therefore much less swear to confirm it. Yea, the heathens have looked upon swearing to be a solemn ordinance of God, and therefore not to be lightly or vainly used by men, though to confirm a matter of truth.[66]

ATTEN: But I wonder, since cursing and swearing are such evils in the eyes of God, that He does not make some examples to others for their committing such wickedness.

WISE: Alas! So he has, a thousand times twice told as may be easily gathered by any observing people in every age and country. I could present you with several myself, but waving the abundance that might be mentioned, I will here present you with two:[67] one was that dreadful judgement of God upon one N P at Wimbleton in Surrey, who, after a horrible fit of swearing at and cursing of some persons who did not please him, suddenly fell sick and in little time died raving, cursing and swearing.

But above all, take that dreadful story of Dorothy Mately, an inhabitant of Ashover in the county of Derby.

This Dorothy Mately, ☞ said the relator, was noted by the people of the town to be a great swearer, and curser, and liar, and thief, just like Mr Badman. And the labour that she did usually follow was to wash the rubbish that came forth of the lead mines, and there to get sparks of lead ore. And her usual way of asserting of things, was with these kind of imprecations: 'I would I might sink into the earth if it be not so, or I would God would make the earth open and swallow

65. Swearing and cursing are sins against the light of nature.
66. Genesis 31.
67. Examples of God's anger against them that swear and curse.

34

me up.' Now upon the 23rd of March 1660, this Dorothy was washing of ore upon the top of a steep hill, about a quarter of a mile from Ashover, and was there taxed by a lad for taking of two single pence out of his pocket, for he had laid his breeches by and was at work in his drawers. But she violently denied it, wishing that the ground might swallow her up if she had them. She also used the same wicked words on several other occasions that day.

Now one George Hodgkinson of Ashover, a man of good report there, came accidentally by where this Dorothy was and stood still awhile to talk with her as she was washing her ore. There stood also a little child by her tub side, and another a distance from her, calling aloud to her to come away. Wherefore the said George took the girl by the hand to lead her away to her that called her. But behold, they had not gone above ten yards from Dorothy, but they heard her crying out for help. So looking back, he saw the woman, and her tub, and sieve, twirling round and sinking into the ground. Then said the man, 'Pray to God to pardon thy sin, for you are never like to be seen alive any longer.' So she and her tub twirled round and round, till they sunk about three yards into the earth, and then for a while stayed. Then she called for help again, thinking, as she said, that she should stay there. Now the man though greatly amazed, did begin to think which way to help her, but immediately a great stone that appeared in the earth fell upon her head and broke her skull, and then the earth fell in upon her and covered her. She was afterwards digged up and found about four yards within ground, with the boy's two single pence in her pocket, but her tub and sieve could not be found.

ATTEN: You bring to my mind a sad story, the which I will relate unto you. ☞ The thing is this: about a bow shoot from where I once dwelt, there was a blind alehouse, and the man who kept it had a son whose name was Edward. This Edward was, as it were, a half-fool, both in his words and manner of behaviour. To this blind alehouse, certain jovial companions would once or twice a week come, and this Ned – for so they called him – his father would entertain his guests withal, to wit, by calling for him to make them sport by his foolish words and gestures. So when these boon blades came to this man's house, the father would call for Ned. Ned therefore would come forth, and the villain was devilishly addicted to cursing. Yea, to cursing his father and mother, and anyone else who did cross him. And because, though he was a half-fool, he saw that his practice was pleasing, he would do it with the more audaciousness.

Well, when these brave fellows did come at their times to this tippling house, as they call it, to fuddle and make merry, then must Ned be called out. And because his father was best acquainted with Ned and best knew how to provoke him, therefore he would usually ask him such questions or command him such business as would be sure to provoke him indeed. Then would he, after his foolish manner, curse his father most bitterly, at which the old man would laugh. And so would the rest of the guests, as at that which pleased them best, still continuing to ask that Ned still might be provoked to curse that they might still be provoked to laugh. This was the mirth with which the old man did use to entertain his guests.

The curses wherewith this Ned did use to curse his father, and at which the old man would laugh, were these and such like: 'The Devil take you,' 'The Devil fetch you.' He would also wish him plagues and destructions many. Well, so it came to pass, through the righteous judgement of God, that Ned's wishes and curses were in a little time fuelled upon his father. For not many months passed between them after this manner, but the Devil did indeed take him, possess him, and also in few days carried him out of this world by death. I say, Satan did take him and possess him. I mean, so it was judged by those that knew him, and had to do with him in that his lamentable condition. He could feel him like a live thing goes up and down in his body. But when tormenting time was come, as he had often tormenting fits, then he would lie like a hard bump in the soft place of his chest – I mean, I saw it so – and so would rent and tear him, and make him roar till he died away.

I told you before, that I was an ear- and eyewitness of what I here say, and so I was. I have heard Ned in his roguery, cursing his father and his father laughing thereat most heartily, still provoking of Ned to curse that his mirth might be increased. I saw his father also, when he was possessed, I saw him in one of his fits and saw his flesh – as 'twas thought – by the Devil, gathered up on a heap, about the bigness of half an egg, to the unutterable torture and affliction of the old man. There was also one freeman – who was more than an ordinary doctor – sent for, to cast out this Devil, and I was there when he attempted to do it. The manner whereof was this: they had the possessed into an out-room, and laid him on his belly upon a form with his head hanging over the form's end. Then they bound him down thereto, which done, they set a pan of coals under his mouth and put something therein which made a great smoke. By this means – as 'twas said – to fetch out the Devil. There therefore they kept the man till he was almost smothered in the smoke, but no devil came out of him, at which the freeman was somewhat abashed, the man greatly afflicted, and I made to go away wondering and fearing. In a little time, therefore that which possessed the man carried him out of the world, according to the cursed wishes of his son. And this was the end of this hellish mirth.

WISE: These were all sad judgements.

ATTEN: These were dreadful judgements indeed.

WISE: Aye, and they look like the threatening of that text, though chiefly it concerned Judas, 'As he loved cursing, so let it come unto him: as he delighted not in blessing, so let it be far from him. As he clothed himself with cursing like as with his garment, so let it come into his bowels like water, and like oil into his bones.'[68]

ATTEN: It is a fearful thing for youth to be trained up in a way of cursing and swearing.

WISE: Trained up in them! That I cannot say Mr Badman was, for his father had ofttimes in my hearing bewailed the badness of his children and of this naughty boy in particular. I believe that the wickedness of his children made him, in the thoughts of it, go many a night with heavy heart to bed, and with as heavy a one to rise in the morning. But all was one to his graceless son. Neither wholesome counsel nor fatherly sorrow would make him mend his manners.

There[69] are some indeed who do train up their children to swear, curse, lie and steal, and great is the misery of such poor children

68. Psalm 109:17–18.
69. A grievous thing to bring up children wickedly.

whose hard hap it is to be ushered into the world by, and to be under the tuition too of such ungodly parents. It had been better for such parents had they not begat them, and better for such children had they not been born. O, methinks for a father or a mother to train up a child in that very way that leads to Hell and damnation, what thing so horrible! But Mr Badman was not by his parents so brought up.

ATTEN: But methinks, since this young Badman would not be ruled at home, his father should have tried what good could have been done of him abroad, by putting him out to some man of his acquaintance that he knew to be able to command him, and to keep him pretty hard to some employ. So should he, at least, have been prevented of time to do those wickednesses that could not be done without time to do them in.

WISE: Alas, his father did so.[70] He put him out betimes to one of his own acquaintance, and entreated him of all love that he would take care of son and keep him from extravagant ways. His trade also was honest and commodious. He had besides a full employ therein, so that this young Badman had no vacant seasons nor idle hours yielded him by his calling, therein to take opportunities to do badly. But all was one to him, as he had begun to be vile in his father's house, even so he continued to be when he was in the house of his master.

ATTEN: I have known some children who, though they have been very bad at home, yet have altered much when they have been put out abroad, especially when they have fallen into a family where the governors thereof have made conscience of maintaining of the worship and service of God therein. But perhaps that might be wanting in Mr Badman's master's house.

WISE: Indeed some children do greatly mend when put under other men's roofs. But, as I said, this naughty boy did not so, nor did his badness continue because he wanted a master that both could and did correct it. For his master was a very good man,[71] a very devout person. One who frequented the best soul means that set up the worship of God in his family, and also who walked himself thereafter. He was also a man very meek and merciful, one who did never

70. Badman put to be an apprentice.
71. Young Badman's master and his qualifications.

overdrive young Badman in business, nor who kept him at it at unseasonable hours.

ATTEN: Say you so! This is rare. I, for my part, can see but few who can parallel in these things with Mr Badman's master.

WISE: Nor I neither, yet Mr Badman had such a one, for, for the most past,[72] masters are nowadays such as mind nothing but their worldly concerns, and if apprentices do but answer their commands therein, soul and religion may go where they will. Yea, I much fear that there have been many towardly lads put out by their parents to such masters who have quite undone them as to the next world.

ATTEN: The more is the pity. But pray, now you have touched upon this subject, show me how many ways a master may be the ruin of his poor apprentice.

WISE: Nay, I cannot tell you of all the ways, yet some of them I will mention.

Suppose then that a towardly lad be put to be an apprentice with one who is reputed to be a godly man, yet that lad may be ruined many ways, that is, if his master be not circumspect in all things that respect both God and man, and that before his apprentice.

One – if[73] he be not moderate in the use of his apprentice, if he drives him beyond his strength, if he holds him to work at unseasonable hours, if he will not allow him convenient time to read the Word, to pray, etc. This is the way to destroy him, that is, in those tender beginnings of good thoughts, and good beginnings about spiritual things.

Two – if he suffers his house to be scattered with profane and wicked books, such as stir up to lust, to wantonness, such as teach idle, wanton, lascivious discourse and such as has a tendency to provoke to profane drollery and jesting. And lastly, such as tend to corrupt and pervert the doctrine of faith and holiness. All these things will eat as does a canker and will quickly spoil, in youth, etc., those good beginnings that may be putting forth themselves in them.

Three – if there be a mixture of servants. That is, if some very bad be in the same place, that's a way also to undo such tender lads. For

72. A bad master, a bad thing.

73. How many ways a master may be the ruin of an apprentice.

they who are bad and sordid servants will be often – and they have an opportunity too, to be – distilling and fomenting of their profane and wicked words and tricks before them. And these will easily stick in the flesh and minds of youth to the corrupting of them.

Four – if the master have one guise for abroad, and another for home. That is, if his religion hangs by in his house as his cloak does, and he be seldom in it, except he be abroad. This young beginners will take notice of and stumble at. We say, 'Hedges have eyes, and little pitchers have ears.'[74] And indeed, children make a greater inspection into the lives of fathers, masters, etc., than ofttimes they are aware of. And therefore should masters be careful, else they may soon destroy good beginnings in their servants.

Five – if the master be unconscionable in his dealing, and trades with lying words, or if bad commodities be avouched to be good, or if he seeks after unreasonable gain, or the like, his servant sees it, and it is enough to undo him. Eli's sons being bad before the congregation made men despise the sacrifices of the Lord.[75]

But these things, by the by, only they may serve for a hint to masters to take heed that they take not apprentices to destroy their souls. But young Badman had none of these hindrances.[76] His father took care and provided well for him, as to this: he had a good master, he wanted not good books, nor good instruction, nor good sermons, nor good examples, no nor good fellow servants neither. But all would not do.

ATTEN: 'Tis a wonder that in such a family, amidst so many spiritual helps, nothing should take hold of his heart! What? Not good books, nor good instruction, nor good sermons, nor good examples, nor good fellow servants, nor nothing do him good!

WISE: You talk, he minded none of these things. Nay, all these were abominable to him.[77]

One – for good books, they might lie in his master's house till they rotted for him, he would not regard to look into them, but contrariwise would get all the bad and abominable books that he could,

74. Children are great observers of what older folks do.
75. 1 Samuel 2.
76. Badman had all advantages to be good, but continued Badman still.
77. All good things abominable to Badman.

as beastly romances and books full of ribaldry, even such as immediately tended to set all fleshly lusts on fire. True, he dared not be known to have any of these to his master, therefore would he never let them be seen by him, but would keep them in close places and peruse them at such times as yielded him fit opportunities thereto.

Two – for good instruction, he liked that much as he liked good books. His care was to hear but little thereof and to forget what he heard as soon as 'twas spoken. Yea, I have heard some that knew him then say that one might evidently discern by the show of his countenance and gestures that good counsel was to him like little ease, even a continual torment to him. Nor did he ever count himself at liberty but when farthest off of wholesome words. He would hate them that rebuked him, and count them his deadly enemies.[78]

Three – for good example, which was frequently set him by his master, both in religious and civil matters, these young Badman would laugh at, and would also make a byword of them, when he came in place where he with safety could.

Four – his master indeed would make him go with him to sermons, and that where he thought the best preachers were, but this ungodly young man, what shall I say, was – I think – a master of art in all mischief. He had these wicked ways to hinder himself of hearing, let the preacher thunder never so loud.[79]

One – his way was, when come into the place of hearing, to sit down in some corner and then to fall fast asleep.

Two – or else to fix his adulterous eyes upon some beautiful object that was in the place, and so all sermon while therewith be feeding of his fleshly lusts.

Three – or, if he could get near to some that he had observed would fit his humour, he would be whispering, giggling and playing with them till such time as sermon was done.

ATTEN: Why, he was grown to a prodigious height of wickedness!

WISE: He was so, and that which aggravates all was this was his practice as soon as he was come to his master. He was as ready at all

78. Good counsel to Badman like little ease, Proverbs 9:8, 15:12.

79. How Badman used to behave himself at sermons.

these things as if he had, before he came to his master, served an apprenticeship to learn them.

ATTEN: There could not but be added, as you relate them, rebellion to his sin. Methinks it is as if he had said, 'I will not hear, I will not regard, I will not mind good, I will not mend, I will not turn, I will not be converted.'

WISE: You say true, ☞ and I know not to whom more fitly to compare him[80] than to that man, who when I myself rebuked him for his wickedness, in this great huff replied, 'what would the Devil do for company, if it was not for such as I?'

ATTEN: Why, did you ever hear any man say so?

WISE: Yes, that I did. And this young Badman was as like him, as an egg is like an egg. Alas! The scripture makes mention of many who by their actions speak the same. They say unto God, 'Depart from us, for we desire not the knowledge of your ways.' Again, they refuse to harken, and pull away their shoulder, and stop their ears. Yea, they make their hearts hard as an adamant stone, lest they should hear the law and the words that the Lord of hosts has sent.[81] What are all these but such as Badman, and such as the young man but now mentioned? That young man was my playfellow when I was solacing myself in my sins. I may make mention of him to my shame, but he has a great many fellows.

ATTEN: Young Badman was like him indeed, and he trod his steps as if his wickedness had been his very copy. I mean, as to his desperateness, for had he not been a desperate one, he would never have made you such a reply, when you were rebuking of him for his sin. But when did you give him such a rebuke?

WISE: Awhile after God had parted him and I, by calling of me as I hope by his grace, still leaving him in his sins. And so far as I could ever gather, as he lived, so he died, even as Mr Badman did. But we will leave him and return again to our discourse.

ATTEN: Ha, poor obstinate sinners! Do they think that God cannot be even with them?

80. The desperate words of one HS who once was my companion. He was one brother to Ned, of whom you read before.
81. Job 21:14; Zechariah 1:11–13.

42

WISE: I do not know what they think, but I know that God hath said, 'That as He cried, and they would not hear; so they cried, and I would not hear, saith the Lord.'[82] Doubtless there is a time a coming when Mr Badman will cry for this.

ATTEN: But I wonder that he should be so expert in wickedness so soon! Alas, he was but a stripling, I suppose, he was as yet not twenty.

WISE: No, nor eighteen neither. But, as with Ishmael and with the children who mocked the prophet, the seeds of sin did put forth themselves betimes in him.[83]

ATTEN: Well, he was as wicked a young man as commonly one shall hear of.

WISE: You will say so, when you know all.

ATTEN: All, I think here is a great all, but if there is more behind, pray let us hear it.

WISE: Why, then I will tell you that he had not been with his master much above a year and a half, but he came acquainted with three young villains[84] – who here shall be nameless – who taught him to add to his sin much of like kind, and he as aptly received their instructions. One of them was chiefly given to uncleanness, another to drunkenness, and the third to purloining, or stealing from his master.

ATTEN: Alas, poor wretch, he was bad enough before, but these, I suppose, made him much worse.

WISE: That they made him worse you may be sure of, for they taught him to be an arch, a chief one in all their ways.

ATTEN: It was an ill hap that he ever came acquainted with them.

WISE: You must rather word it thus. It was the judgement of God that he did.[85] That is, he came acquainted with them through the anger of God. He had a good master, and before him a good father. By these he had good counsel given him for months and years together, but his heart was set upon mischief. He loved wickedness more than to do good, even until his iniquity came to be hateful. Therefore, from

82. Zechariah 7:13.
83. Genesis 21:9–10; 2 Kings 2:23–24.
84. Badman's acquaintances.
85. A sign of God's anger.

the anger of God it was, that these companions of his and he did at last so acquaint together. Says Paul, 'they did not like to retain God in their knowledge',[86] and what follows? Wherefore God gave them over or up to their own hearts' lusts. And again, 'as for such as turn aside unto their own crooked ways, the Lord shall lead them forth with the workers of iniquity.'[87] This therefore was God's hand upon him, that he might be destroyed, be damned, because he received not the love of the truth that he might be saved. He chose his delusions and deluders for him, even the company of base men, of fools, that he might be destroyed.[88, 89]

ATTEN: I cannot but think indeed that it is a great judgement of God for a man to be given up to the company of vile men. For what are such but the Devil's decoys,[90] even those by whom he draws the simple into the net? A whoremaster, a drunkard, a thief: what are they but the Devil's baits by which he catches others?

WISE: You say right. But this young Badman was no simple one, if by simple, you mean one uninstructed, for he had often good counsel given him. But if by simple you mean he who is a fool as to the true knowledge of and faith in Christ, then he was a simple one indeed, for he chose death rather than life, and to live in continual opposition to God rather than to be reconciled unto Him. According to that saying of the wise man, the fools 'hated knowledge, and did not choose the Fear of the Lord'.[91] And what judgement more dreadful can a fool be given up to than to be delivered into the hands of such men who have skill to do nothing but to ripen sin and hasten its finishing unto damnation? And therefore men should be afraid of offending God because He can in this manner punish them for their sins. I ☞ knew a man that once was, as I thought, hopefully awakened about his condition. Yea, I knew two who were so awakened, but in time they began to draw back, and to incline again to their lusts, wherefore God gave them up to the company of three

86. Romans 1:28.
87. Psalm 125:5.
88. 2 Thessalonians 2:10–12.
89. Proverbs 12:20.
90. The Devil's decoys.
91. Proverbs 1:29.

or four men who, in less than three years' time, brought them roundly to the gallows where they were hanged like dogs because they refused to live like honest men.[92]

ATTEN: But such men do not believe that thus to be given up of God is in judgement and anger. They rather take it to be their liberty and do count it their happiness. They are glad that their cord is loosened and that the reins are in their neck. They are glad that they may sin without control, and that they may choose such company as can make them more expert in an evil way.

WISE: Their judgement is therefore so much the greater, because thereto is added blindness of mind and hardness of heart in a wicked way. They are turned up to the way of death but must not see to what place they are going. They must go 'as an ox goeth to the slaughter, or as a fool to the correction of the stocks, till a dart strike through his liver',[93] not knowing that it is for their life. This, I say, makes their judgement double. They are given up of God for a while to sport themselves with that which will assuredly make them mourn at last, when their flesh and their body is consumed.[94] These are those of whom Peter speaks, who shall utterly perish in their own corruptions. These, I say, who count it pleasure to riot in the daytime, and who sport themselves with their own deceivings are as natural brute beasts, made to be taken and destroyed.[95]

ATTEN: Well, but I pray now concerning these three villains that were young Badman's companions. Tell me more particularly how he carried it then.

WISE: How he carried it! Why, he did as they. I intimated so much before when I said they made him an arch, a chief one in their ways.

First, he became a frequenter of[96] taverns and tippling-houses and would stay there until he was even as drunk as a beast. And if it was so that he could not get out by day, he would, be sure, get out by night. Yea, he became so common a drunkard at last that he was taken notice of to be a drunkard even by all.

92. This was done at Bedford.
93. Proverbs 7:22–23.
94. Proverbs 5:11.
95. 2 Peter 2:12–13.
96. Badman becomes a frequenter of taverns.

ATTEN: This was swinish, for drunkenness is so beastly a sin. A sin so much against nature that I wonder that any who have but the appearance of men can give up themselves to so beastly – yea, worse than beastly – a thing.

WISE: It is a swinish vanity indeed. I will tell you another story. ☞ 97 There was a gentleman who had a drunkard to be his groom, and coming home one night very much abused with beer, his master saw it. 'Well,' quoth his master within himself, 'I will let you alone tonight, but tomorrow morning I will convince you that you are worse than a beast by the behaviour of my horse.' So when morning had come, he bade his man go and water his horse, and so he did. But coming up to his master, he commands him to water him again. So the fellow rid into the water the second time, but his master's horse would now drink no more, so the fellow came up and told his master. Then said his master, 'You drunken sot! You are far worse than my horse. He will drink but to satisfy nature, but you will drink to the abuse of nature. He will drink but to refresh himself, but you to your hurt and damage. He will drink that he may be more serviceable to his master, but you till you are uncapable of serving either God or man. O you beast, how much are you worse than the horse that you ride on!'

ATTEN: Truly I think that his master served him right, for in doing as he did, he showed him plainly, as he said, that he had not so much government of himself as his horse had of himself. And consequently that his beast did live more according to the law of his nature by far than did his man. But pray go on with what you have further to say.

WISE: Why, I say that there are[98] four things that if they were well considered would make drunkenness to be abhorred in the thoughts of the children of men.

One – it greatly tends to impoverish and beggar a man. 'The drunkard,' says Solomon, 'shall come to poverty.'[99] Many who have begun the world with plenty have gone out of it in rags through drunkenness. Yea, many children who have been born to good estates have yet been brought to a flail and a rake through this beastly sin of their parents.

97. A story for a drunkard.
98. Four evils attend drunkenness.
99. Proverbs 23:20–21.

Two – this sin of drunkenness, it brings upon the body many, great and incurable diseases by which men do in little time come to their end, and none can help them. So because they are overmuch wicked, therefore they die before their time.[100]

Three – drunkenness is a sin that is often times attended with abundance of other evils. 'Who hath woe? who hath sorrow? who hath contentions? who hath babbling? who hath wounds without cause? who hath redness of eyes? They that tarry long at the wine; they that go to seek mixed wine.'[101] That is the drunkard.

Four – by drunkenness, men do often times shorten their days, go out of the alehouse drunk, and break their necks before they come home. Instances not a few might be given of this, but this is so manifest, a man need say nothing.

ATTEN: But[102, 103] that which is worse than all is it also prepares men for everlasting burnings.

WISE: Yea, and it so stupefies and besots the soul that a man who is far gone in drunkenness is hardly ever recovered to God. Tell me, when did you see an old drunkard converted? No, no such a one will sleep till he dies. Though he sleeps on the top of a mast, [104] let his dangers be never so great, and death and damnation never so near, he will not be awaked out of his sleep. So that if a man have any respect either to credit, health, life or salvation, he will not be a drunken man. But the truth is, where this sin gets the upper hand, men are, as I said before, so intoxicated and bewitched with the seeming pleasures and sweetness thereof that they have neither heart nor mind to think of that which is better in itself, and would, if embraced, do them good.

ATTEN: You said that drunkenness tends to poverty, yet some make themselves rich by drunken bargains.

WISE: I[105] said so, because the Word says so. And as to some men's getting thereby, that is indeed but rare and base, and base will be the end of such gettings. The Word of God is against such ways, and the

100. Ecclesiastes 7:17.
101. Proverbs 23:29–30.
102. 1 Corinthians 6:10.
103. The fifth evil, the worst.
104. Proverbs 23:34–35.
105. An objection answered.

curse of God will be the end of such doings. An inheritance may sometimes thus be hastily gotten at the beginning, but the end thereof shall not be blessed. Hark what the prophet saith, 'Woe to him that coveteth an evil covetousness to his house, that he may set his nest on high.'[106] Whether he makes drunkenness or ought else the engine and decoy to get it, for that man does but consult the shame of his own house, the spoiling of his family, and the damnation of his soul, for that which he gets by working of iniquity is but a getting by the devices of Hell. Therefore he can be no gainer neither for himself nor family that gains by an evil course. But this was one of the sins that Mr Badman was addicted to after he came acquainted with these three fellows, nor could all that his master could do break him of this beastly sin.

ATTEN: But where, since he was but an apprentice, could he get money to follow this practice, for drunkenness, as you have intimated, is a very costly sin.

WISE: His master[107] paid for all. For, as I told you before, as he learned of these three villains to be a beastly drunkard, so he learned of them to pilfer and steal from his master. Sometimes he would sell off his master's goods, but keep the money – that is, when he could. Also sometimes he would beguile his master by taking out of his cashbox. And when he could do neither of these, he would convey away of his master's wares, what he thought would be least missed, and send or carry them to such and such houses where he knew they would be laid up to his use, and then appoint set times there to meet and make merry with these fellows.

ATTEN: This was as bad, nay I think, worse than the former. For by thus doing, he did not only run himself under the wrath of God but endangered the undoing of his master and his family.

WISE: Sins go not alone but follow one the other as do the links of a chain. He who will be a drunkard must have money either of his own or of some other man's – either of his fathers, mother's, master's, or at the highway, or some way.

ATTEN: I fear that many an honest man is undone by such kind of servants.

106. Habakkuk 2:5, 9–12, 15.

107. Badman's master's purse paid for his drunkenness.

WISE: I am of the same mind with you, but[108] this should make the dealer the more wary what kind of servants he keeps and what kind of apprentices he takes. It should also teach him to look well to his shop himself, also to take strict account of all things that are bought and sold by his servants. The master's neglect herein may embolden his servant to be bad and may bring him too in short time to rags and a morsel of bread.

ATTEN: I am afraid that there is much of this kind of pilfering among servants in these bad days of ours.

WISE: Now, while it is in my mind, I will tell you a story. ☞ When I was in prison, there came a woman to me who was under a great deal of trouble. So I asked her – she being a stranger to me – what she had to say to me. She said she was afraid she should be damned. I asked her the cause of those fears. She told me that she had sometime since lived with a shopkeeper at Wellingborough and had robbed his box in the shop several times of money to the value of more than now I will say. And 'pray,' says she, 'tell me what I shall do.' I told her I would have her go to her master and make him satisfaction. She said she was afraid. I asked her why. She said she doubted he would hang her. I told her that I would intercede for her life and would make use of other friends too to do the like. But she told me she dared not venture that. 'Well,' said I, 'shall I send to your master while you abide out of sight, and make your peace with him before he sees you?' And with that, I asked her her master's name. But all that she said in answer to this was, 'Pray let it alone till I come to you again.' So away she went and neither told me her master's name nor her own. This is about ten or twelve years since, and I never saw her again. I tell you this story for this cause to confirm your fears that such kind of servants too many there be, and that God makes them sometimes like old Tod, of whom mention was made before, through the terrors that he lays upon them, to betray themselves.

I could tell you of another ☞ who came to me with a like relation concerning herself, and the robbing of her mistress, but at this time let this suffice.

108. A caution for masters.

ATTEN: But what was that other villain addicted to? I mean young Badman's third companion.

WISE: Uncleanness.[109] I told you before, but it seems you forgot.

ATTEN: Right, it was uncleanness. Uncleanness is also a filthy sin.

WISE: It is so. And yet it is one of the most reigning sins in our day.

ATTEN: So they say, and that too among those whom one would think had more wit, even among the great ones.

WISE: The more is the pity, for usually examples that are set by them who are great and chief[110] spread sooner and more universally than do the sins of other men. Yea, and when such men are at the head in transgressing, sin walks with a bold face through the land. As Jeremiah said of the prophets, so may it be said of such, from them 'is profaneness gone forth into all the land',[111] that is, with bold and audacious face.

ATTEN: But pray let us return again to Mr Badman and his companions. You say one of them was very vile in the commission of uncleanness.

WISE: Yes, so I say. Not but that he was a drunkard and also thievish, but he was most arch in this sin of uncleanness. This roguery was his masterpiece, for he was a ringleader to them all in the beastly sin of whoredom. He was also best acquainted with such houses where they were, and so could readily lead the rest of his gang unto them. The strumpets also, because they knew this young villain, would at first discover themselves in all their whorish pranks to those that he brought with him.

ATTEN: That is a deadly thing. I mean it is a deadly thing to young men when such beastly queens shall, with words and carriages that are openly tempting, discover themselves unto them. It is hard for such to escape their snare.

WISE: That is true. Therefore the wise man's counsel is the best: 'Come not nigh the door of her house,'[112] for they are, as you say, very tempting, as is seen by her in the Proverbs. 'I looked,' says the wise man, 'through my casement, and beheld among the simple

109. Badman's third companion addicted to uncleanness.
110. Sins of great men dangerous.
111. Jeremiah 23:15.
112. Proverbs 5:8.

ones, I discerned among the youths, a young man void of under-standing, passing through the street near her corner; and he went the way to her house, in the twilight, in the evening, in the black and dark night. And, behold, there met him a woman with the attire of an harlot, and subtle of heart. (She is loud and stubborn; her feet abide not in her house. Now is she without, now in the streets, and lieth in wait at every corner.)[113] So she caught him, and kissed him, and with an impudent face said unto him, I have peace offerings with me. This day have I paid my vows. Therefore came I forth to meet thee, diligently to seek thy face, and I have found thee. I have decked my bed with coverings of tapestry, with carved works, with fine linen of Egypt. I have perfumed my bed with myrrh, aloes and cinnamon. Come, let us take our fill of love until the morning. Let us solace ourselves with loves.'[114] Here was a bold beast. And indeed, the very eyes, hands, words and ways of such are all snares and bands to youthful, lustful fellows, and with these was young Badman greatly snared.

ATTEN: This sin of uncleanness[115] is mightily cried out against by Moses, the prophets, Christ and His apostles. And yet, as we see, for all that, how men run headlong to it!

WISE: You have said the truth. And I will add that God, to hold men back from so filthy a sin, has set such a stamp of his indignation upon it, and commanded such evil effects to follow it, that were not they who use it bereft of all fear of God and love to their own health, they could not but stop and be afraid to commit it. For, besides the eternal damnation that does attend such in the next world, for these have no inheritance in the kingdom of Christ and of God,[116] the evil effects thereof in this world are dreadful.

ATTEN: Pray show me some of them, that as occasion offers itself, I may show them to others for their good.

WISE: So I will.[117] One – it brings a man, as was said of the sin before, to want and poverty, for by means of a whorish woman, a man is

113. Signs of a whore.
114. Proverbs 7: 6–18.
115. The sin of uncleanness cried out against.
116. Ephesians 5.
117. What evils attend this sin. Proverbs 6:26.

brought to a piece of bread. The reason is for that a whore will not yield without hire, and men when the Devil and lust is in them, and God and his fear far away from them, will not stick so they may accomplish their desire to lay their signet, their bracelets, and their staff to pledge[118] rather than miss of the fulfilling of their lusts. Two – again, by this sin men diminish their strength and bring upon themselves, even upon the body, a multitude of diseases. This King Lemuel's mother warned him of. 'What, my son?' said she, 'and what, the son of my womb? and what, the son of my vows? Give not thy strength unto women, nor thy ways to that which destroyeth kings.'[119] This sin is destructive to the body. Give me leave to tell you another story. ☞ [120] I have heard of a great man who was a very unclean person, and he had lived so long in that sin that he had almost lost his sight. So his physicians were sent for to whom he told his to disease, but they told him that they could do him no good unless he would forbear his women. 'Nay then,' said he, 'farewell sweet sight!' Whence observe that this sin, as I said, is destructive to the body, and also that some men be so in love therewith that they will have it though it destroy their bodies.

ATTEN: Paul says also that he who sins this sin, sins against his own body. But what of that? He who will run the hazard of eternal damnation of his soul, but he will commit this sin, will for it run the hazard of destroying his body. If young Badman feared not the damnation of his soul, do you think that the consideration of impairing of his body would have deterred him therefrom?

WISE: You say true. But yet, methinks there are still such bad effects follow often upon the commission of it, that if men would consider them, it would put at least a stop to their career therein.

ATTEN: What other evil effects attend this sin?

WISE: Outward shame and disgrace, and that in these particulars:[121]

First, there often follows this foul sin the foul disease, now called by us the pox. A disease so nauseous and stinking, so infectious to the whole body – and so entailed to this sin – that hardly are any

118. Genesis 38:18.
119. Proverbs 31:1–2.
120. A story for unclean persons to take notice of.
121. More evils attend this sin.

common with unclean women but they have more or less a touch of it to their shame.

ATTEN: That is a foul disease indeed. I knew ☞ a man once that rotted away with it, and another who had his nose eaten off, and his mouth almost quite sewed up thereby.

WISE: It is a disease that, where it is, it commonly declares that the cause thereof is uncleanness. It declares to all who behold such a man that he is an odious, a beastly, unclean person. This is that strange punishment that Job speaks of that is appointed to seize on these workers of iniquity.[122]

ATTEN: Then it seems you think that the strange punishment that Job there speaks of should be the foul disease.

WISE: I have thought so indeed, and that for this reason: we see that this disease is entailed, as I may say, to this most beastly sin. Nor is there any disease so entailed to any other sin, as this to this. That this is the sin to which the strange punishment is entailed, you will easily perceive when you read the text. 'I made a covenant with mine eyes,' said Job, 'why then should I think upon a Maid? For what portion of God is there [for that sin] from above? and what inheritance of the Almighty from on high?' And then he answers himself, 'Is not destruction to the wicked? And a strange punishment to the workers of iniquity?'[123] This strange punishment is the pox.

Also I think that this foul disease is that which Solomon intends when he says, speaking of this unclean and beastly creature, 'A wound and dishonour shall he get; and his reproach shall not be wiped away.'[124] A punishment Job calls it. A wound and dishonour, Solomon calls it. And they both do set it as a remark upon this sin: Job calling it a strange punishment, and Solomon a reproach that shall not be turned away from them who are common in it.

ATTEN: What other things follow upon the commission of this beastly sin?

WISE: Why, oftentimes it is attended with murder – with the murder of the babe begotten on the defiled bed. How common it is for the

122. Job 31.
123. Job 31:1–3.
124. Proverbs 6:33.

bastard-getter and bastard-bearer to consent together to murder their children will be better known at the day of Judgement, yet something is manifest now.

I will tell you another story. ☞ An ancient man – one of my acquaintance, a man of good credit in our country – had a mother who was a midwife who was mostly employed in laying great persons. To this woman's house, upon a time, came a brave young gallant on horseback to fetch her to lay a young lady. So she addressed herself to go with him, wherefore he took her up behind him and away they rode in the night. Now they had not ridden far, but the gentleman lit off his horse and, taking the old midwife in his arms from the horse, turned round with her several times and then set her up again. Then he got up, and away they went till they came at a stately house into which he had her, and so into a chamber where the young lady was in her pains. He then bade the midwife do her office. And she demanded help, but he drew out his sword and told her if she did not make speed to do her office without, she must look for nothing but death. Well, to be short, this old midwife laid the young lady, and a fine, sweet babe she had. Now there was made in a room hard by a very great fire. So the gentleman took up the babe, went and drew the coals from the stock, cast the child in and covered it up, and there was an end of that. So when the midwife had done her work, he paid her well for her pains but shut her up in a dark room all day, and when night came, took her up behind him again and carried her away, till she came almost at home. Then he turned her round and round, as he did before, and had her to her house, set her down, bid her farewell and away he went. And she could never tell who it was.

This story the midwife's son, who was a minister, told me, and also protested that his mother told it him for a truth.

ATTEN: Murder doth often follow indeed, as that which is the fruit of this sin. But sometimes God brings even these adulterers and adulteresses to shameful ends. I heard ☞ of one – I think a doctor of physic – and his whore who had had three or four bastards betwixt them and had murdered them all, but at last themselves were hanged for it in or near to Colchester. It came out after this manner: the whore was so afflicted in her conscience about it that she could not be quiet until she had made it known. Thus God many times makes the actors of wickedness their own accusers and brings them by their own tongues to condign punishment for their own sins.

WISE: There have been many such instances, but we will let that pass. I was once in the presence of a woman, a married woman, who lay sick of the sickness whereof she died. And being smitten in her conscience for the sin of uncleanness, which she had often committed with other men, I heard ☞ her, as she lay upon her bed, cry out thus, 'I am a whore, and all my children are bastards! And I must go to Hell for my sin. And look! There stands the Devil at my bed's feet to receive my soul when I die.'

ATTEN: These are sad stories. Tell no more of them now, but if you please, show me yet some other of the evil effects of this beastly sin.

WISE: This sin is such a snare to the soul that unless a miracle of grace prevents, it unavoidably perishes in the enchanting and bewitching pleasures of it. This is manifest by these and such like texts.

'The Adulteress will hunt for the precious life. Whoso committeth adultery with a woman lacketh understanding: he that doeth it destroyeth his own soul.'[125] 'A whore is a deep ditch; and a strange woman is a narrow pit.'[126] 'Her house inclineth unto death, and her paths unto the dead. None that go unto her return again, neither take they hold of the paths of life.'[127] 'She hath cast down many wounded: yea, many strong men have been slain by her. Her house is the way to hell, going down to the chambers of death.'[128]

ATTEN: These are dreadful sayings, and do show the dreadful state of those who are guilty of this sin.

WISE: Verily so they do. But yet that which makes the whole more dreadful is that men are given up to this sin, because they are abhorred of God, and because abhorred, therefore they shall fall into the commission of it and shall live there. 'The mouth,' that is, the flattering lips, 'of a strange woman is a deep pit: he that is

125. Proverbs 6:26, 32.
126. Proverbs 23:27.
127. Proverbs 2:18–19.
128. Proverbs 7:25–27.

abhorred of the Lord shall fall therein.'[129] Therefore it says again of such, that they have no inheritance in the kingdom of Christ and of God.[130]

ATTEN: Put all together, and it is a dreadful thing to live and die in this transgression.

WISE: True. But suppose, that instead of all these judgements, this sin had attending of it all the felicities of this life, and no bitterness, shame or disgrace mixed with it, yet one hour in Hell will spoil all. Oh, this Hell, hellfire, damnation in Hell! It is such an inconceivable punishment, that were it but thoroughly believed, it would nip this sin with others in the head. But here is the mischief: those who give up themselves to these things do so harden themselves in unbelief and atheism about the things, the punishments that God has threatened to inflict upon the committers of them, that at last they arrive to almost an absolute and firm belief that there is no judgement to come hereafter. Else they would not – they could not, no, not – attempt to commit this sin, by such abominable language as some do.

I heard ☞ of one that should say to his miss, when he tempted her to the committing of this sin, 'If you will venture your body, I will venture my soul.'[131] And I myself heard another say, when he was tempting of a maid to commit uncleanness with him – it was in Oliver's days – that if she did prove with child, he would tell her how she might escape punishment, and that was then somewhat severe. 'Say,' said he, 'when you come before the judge, that you are with child by the Holy Ghost.' I heard ☞ him say thus, and it greatly afflicted me. I had a mind to have accused him for it before some magistrate. But he was a great man, and I was poor and young. So I let it alone, but it troubled me very much.

ATTEN: 'Twas the most horrible thing that ever I heard in my life. But how far off are these men from that spirit and grace that dwelt in Joseph!

WISE: Right. When Joseph's mistress tempted him – yea, tempted him daily[132] – yea, she laid hold on him, and said with her whore's

129. Proverbs 22:14.
130. Ephesians 5:5.
131. Desperate words.
132. Genesis 39:10.

56

forehead, 'Come lie with me,' but he refused. He hearkened not to lie with her, or to be with her. Mr Badman would have taken the opportunity.

And a little to comment upon this of Joseph.[133]

One – Here is a miss, a great miss, the wife of the Captain of the Guard, some beautiful dame, I'll warrant you.

Two – Here is a miss won, and in her whorish affections comes over to Joseph, without his speaking of a word.

Three – Here is her unclean desire made known: 'Come lie with me,' said she.

Four – Here was a fit opportunity. There was none of the men of the house there within.

Five – Joseph was a young man, full of strength, and therefore the more in danger to be taken.

Six – This was to him a temptation from her that lasted days.

Seven – And yet Joseph refused, one – her daily temptation; two – her daily solicitation; three – her daily provocation heartily, violently and constantly. For when she caught him by the garment, saying, 'Lie with me,' he left his garment in her hand and got himself out. Aye, and although contempt, treachery, slander, accusation, imprisonment and danger of death followed – for a whore cares not what mischief she does when she cannot have her end – yet Joseph will not defile himself, sin against God and hazard his own eternal salvation.

ATTEN: Blessed Joseph! I would you had more fellows!

WISE: Mr Badman has more fellows than Joseph, else there would not be so many whores as there are. For though I doubt not but that that sex is bad enough this way, yet I verily believe that many of them are made whores at first by the flatteries of Badman's fellows. Alas, there is many a woman plunged into this sin at first even by promises of marriage.[134] I say, by these promises they are flattered, yea, forced into consenting to these villainies, and so being in and growing hardened in their hearts, they at last give themselves up, even as wicked men do, to act this kind of wickedness with greediness. But Joseph, you see, was of another mind for the fear of God was in him.

133. Of chaste Joseph.
134. Many are made whores by promises of marriage, etc.

I will, before I leave this, tell you here two notable stories, and I wish Mr Badman's companions may hear of them. They are found in *Clark's Looking-glass for Sinners* and are these.

Mr Cleaver, says Mr Clark, reports of one whom he knew who had committed the act of uncleanness, whereupon he fell into such horror of conscience that he hanged himself, leaving it thus written in a paper. 'Indeed,' said he, 'I acknowledge it to be utterly unlawful for a man to kill himself, but I am bound to act the magistrate's part because the punishment of this sin is death.'

Clark does also in the same page make mention of two more, who as they were committing adultery in London, were immediately struck dead with fire from Heaven in the very act. Their bodies were so found, half burnt up, and sending out a most loathsome savour.

ATTEN: These are notable stories indeed.

WISE: So they are, and I suppose they are as true as notable.

ATTEN: Well, but I wonder if young Badman's master knew him to be such a wretch that he would suffer him in his house.

WISE: They liked one another even as[135] fire and water do. Young Badman's ways were odious to his master, and his master's ways were such as young Badman could not endure. Thus in these two was fulfilled that saying of the Holy Ghost: 'An unjust man is an abomination to the just: and he that is upright in the way is abomination to the wicked.'[136]

The good man's ways Mr Badman could not abide, nor could the good man abide the bad ways of his base apprentice. Yet would his master, if he could have, kept him and also have taught him his trade.

ATTEN: If he could! Why he might, if he would, might he not?

WISE: Alas, Badman ran away[137] from him once and twice and would not at all be ruled. So the next time he did run away from him, he did let him go indeed. For he gave him no occasion to run away, except it was by holding of him as much as he could – and that he could do but little – to good and honest rules of life. And had it been one's own case, one should have let him go. For what should a man do,

135. *Clark's Looking-glass for Sinners*, Chapter 2, Page 12. Badman and his Master abhor one another.
136. Proverbs 29:27.
137. Young Badman runs away from his master.

who had either regard to his own peace, his children's good or the preservation of the rest of his servants from evil, but let him go? Had he stayed, the house of correction had been most fit for him, but there his master was loath to send him because of the love that he bore to his father. A house of correction, I say, had been the fittest place for him, but his master let him go.

ATTEN: He ran away you say, but where did he run?

WISE: Why, to one of his own trade[138] and also like himself. Thus the wicked joined hand-in-hand, and there he served out his time.

ATTEN: Then, sure, he had his heart's desire, when he was with one so like himself.

WISE: Yes. So he had, but God gave it him in His anger.

ATTEN: How do you mean?

WISE: I mean as before, that for a wicked man to be, by the providence of God, turned out of a good man's doors, into a wicked man's house to dwell, is a sign of the anger of God.[139] For God by this and such judgements says thus to such a one: 'You wicked one, you don't love me, my ways or my people. You cast my law and good counsel behind your back. Come, I will dispose of you in my wrath. You shall be turned over to the ungodly. You shall be put to school to the Devil. I will leave you to sink and swim in sin, till I shall visit you with death and judgement.' This was therefore another judgement that did come upon this young Badman.

ATTEN: You have said the truth, for God by such a judgement as this in effect says so indeed. For He takes them out of the hand of the just and binds them up in the hand of the wicked, and where they then shall be carried, a man may easily imagine.

WISE: It is one of the saddest tokens of God's anger that happens to such kind of persons, and that for several reasons.[140]

One – such a one, by this judgement, is put out of the way and from under the means that ordinarily are made use of to do good to the soul. For a family where godliness is professed and practised, is God's ordinance, the place that he has appointed to teach young

138. He gets a new master like himself.
139. A sign of God's anger upon young Badman.
140. Demonstration of God's anger towards him.

ones the way and fear of God.[141] Now to be put out of such a family into a bad, a wicked one, as Mr Badman was, must needs be in judgement and a sign of the anger of God, for in ungodly families, men learn to forget God, to hate goodness and to estrange themselves from the ways of those who are good.

Two – in bad families, they have continually fresh examples, and also incitements to evil and fresh encouragements to it, too. Yea, moreover, in such places evil is commended, praised, well-spoken of, and they who do it are applauded. And this, to be sure, is a drowning judgement.

Three – such places are the very haunts and walks of the infernal spirits who are continually poisoning the cogitations and minds of one or another in such families, that they may be able to poison others. Therefore observe it, usually in wicked families, some one or two are more arch for wickedness than are any other who are there. Now such are Satan's conduit pipes, for by them he conveys of the spawn of Hell through their being crafty in wickedness into the ears and souls of their companions. Yea, and when they have once conceived wickedness, they travel with it, as does a woman with child, till they have brought it forth. 'Behold, he travaileth with iniquity, and hath conceived mischief, and brought forth falsehood.'[142] Some men, as here is intimated in the text and as was hinted also before, have a kind of mystical but hellish copulation with the Devil, who is the father, and their soul the mother of sin and wickedness. And they, so soon as they have conceived by him, finish by bringing forth sin: both it and their own damnation.[143]

ATTEN: How[144] much then does it concern those parents who love their children to see that if they go from them, they be put into such families as be good, that they may learn there betimes to eschew evil and to follow that which is good?

WISE: It does concern them indeed. And it does also concern them[145] who take children into their families to take heed which children

141. Genesis 18:18–19.

142. Psalm 7:14.

143. James 1:15.

144. It concerns parents to put their children into good families.

145. Masters should also beware of which servants they entertain.

they receive. For a man may soon by a bad boy be damaged both in his name, estate and family, and also hindered in his peace and peaceable pursuit after God and godliness, I say, by one such vermin as a wicked and filthy apprentice.

ATTEN: True, for one sinner destroys much good, and a poor man is better than a liar. But many times a man cannot help it, for such as at the beginning promise very fair are by a little time proved to be very rogues, like young Badman.

WISE: That is true also, but when a man has done the best he can to help it, he may with the more confidence expect the blessing of God to follow, or he shall have the more peace if things go contrary to his desire.

ATTEN: Well, but did Mr Badman and his master agree so well? I mean his last master, since they were birds of a feather, I mean, since they were so well met for wickedness.

WISE: This second master was, as before I told you, bad enough, but yet he would often fall out[146] with young Badman his servant, and chide, yea, and some times beat him, too, for his naughty doings.

ATTEN: What! for all he was so bad himself! This is like the proverb the Devil corrects vice.

WISE: I will assure you 'tis as I say. For you must know that Badman's ways suited not with his master's gains. Could he have done as the damsel who we read of Acts 16.[147] He did, to wit, fill his master's purse with his badness, he had certainly been his white-boy.[vi] But it was not so with young Badman, and therefore, though his master and he did suit well enough in the main, yet in this and that point they differed. Young Badman[148] was for neglecting of his master's business, for going to the whorehouse, for beguiling of his master, for attempting to debauch his daughters and the like. No marvel then if they disagreed in these points. Not so much for that his master had an antipathy against the fact itself, for he could do so when he was an apprentice, but for that his servant by his sin made spoil of his commodities, etc., and so damnified his master.

146. Young Badman and his second master cannot agree.
147. Acts 16:16.
148. Reasons of their disagreeing.

Had, as I said before, young Badman's wickedness had only a tendency to his master's advantage, as could he have sworn, lied, cozened, cheated and defrauded customers for his master – and indeed sometimes he did so – but had that been all that he had done. He had not had, no, not a wry word from his master. But this was not always Mr Badman's way.

ATTEN: That was well brought in, even the maid that we read of in the Acts, and the distinction was as clear between the wickedness and wickedness of servants.

WISE: Alas! Men who are wicked themselves yet greatly hate it in others, not simply because it is wickedness but because it opposes their interest. Do you think that that maid's master would have been troubled at the loss of her, if he had not lost with her his gain? No, I'll warrant you. She might have gone to the Devil for him. But when her master saw that the hope of his gain was gone then, then he fell to persecuting Paul.[149] But Mr Badman's master did sometimes lose by Mr Badman's sins, and then Badman and his master were at odds.

ATTEN: Alas poor Badman! Then it seems you could not at all times please your like.

WISE: No, he could not, and the reason I have told you.

ATTEN: But do not bad masters condemn themselves in condemning the badness of their servants?[150]

WISE: Yes,[151] in that they condemn that in another that they either have or do allow in themselves. And the time will come when that very sentence that has gone out of their own mouths against the sins of others, themselves living and taking pleasure in the same, shall return with violence upon their own pates. The Lord pronounced judgement against Baasha, as for all his evils in general, so for this in special because he was like the house of Jeroboam, and yet killed him.[152] This is Mr Badman's master's case. He is like his man, and yet he beats him. He is like his man, and yet he rails at him for being bad.

ATTEN: But why did not young Badman run away from this master as he ran away from the other?

149. Acts 16:17–20.
150. Romans 14:22.
151. Bad masters condemn themselves when they for badness beat their bad servants.
152. 1 Kings 16:7.

WISE: He did not. And if I am not mistaken, the reason[153] why was this: there was godliness in the house of the first, and that young Badman could not endure. For fare, for lodging, for work and time, he had better and more by this master's allowance than ever he had by his last, but all this would not content because godliness was promoted there. He could not abide this praying, this reading of scriptures and hearing and repeating of sermons. He could not abide to be told of his transgressions in a sober and godly manner.

ATTEN: There is a great deal in the manner of reproof. Wicked men both can and cannot abide to hear their transgressions spoken against.

WISE: There is a great deal of difference indeed. This last master of Mr Badman's would tell Mr Badman of his sins in Mr Badman's own dialect. He would swear and curse and damn when he told him of his sins, and this he could bear better[154] than to be told of them after a godly sort. Besides, that last master would, when his passions and rage was over, laugh at and make merry with the sins of his servant Badman, and that would please young Badman well. Nothing offended Badman but blows, and those he had but few of now because he was pretty well grown up. For the most part, when his master did rage and swear, he would give him oath for oath and curse for curse, at least secretly, let him go on as long as he would.

ATTEN: This was hellish living.

WISE: 'Twas hellish living indeed. And a man might say that with this master, young Badman completed himself[155] yet more and more in wickedness as well as in his trade. For by that he came out of his time – what with his own inclination to sin, what with his acquaintance with his three companions, and what with this last master and the wickedness he saw in him – he became a sinner in grain. I think he had a bastard laid to his charge before he came out of his time.

ATTEN: Well, but it seems he did live to come out of his time.[156] But what did he then?

153. Why young Badman did not run away from this master, though he did beat him.
154. Why Badman could bear his last master's reproof better than he could the first.
155. By what means Badman came to be completed in his wickedness.
156. Badman out of his time.

WISE: Why, he went home to his father, and he like a loving and tender-hearted father received him into his house.

ATTEN: And how did he carry it there?

WISE: Why, the reason why he went home[157] was for money to set up for himself. He stayed but a little at home, but that little while that he did stay, he refrained himself[158] as well he could and did not so much discover himself to be base, for fear his father should take distaste and so should refuse or, for a while, forbear to give him money.

Yet even then he would have his times and companions and the fill of his lusts with them, but he used to blind all with this. He was glad to see his old acquaintance, and they as glad to see him, and he could not in civility but accommodate them with a bottle or two of wine, or a dozen or two of drink.

ATTEN: And did the old man give him money to set up with?

WISE: Yes, above two hundred pounds.

ATTEN: Therein I think the old man was out. Had I been his father, I would have held him a little at stave's end, till I had had far better proof of his manners to be good, for I perceive that his father did know what a naughty boy he had been, both by what he used to do at home and because he changed a good master for a bad, etc. He should not therefore have given him money so soon. What if he had pinched a little and gone to journeywork for a time, that he might have known what a penny was by his earning of it? Then, in all probability, he had known better how to have spent it. Yea, and by that time perhaps have better considered with himself how to have lived in the world. Aye, and who knows but he might have come to himself with the prodigal and have asked God and his father forgiveness for the villainies that he had committed against them.[159]

WISE: If his father could also have blessed this manner of dealing to him and have made it effectual for the ends that you have propounded, then I should have thought as you. But alas! Alas, you talk as if you never knew or had at this present forgot what the bowels and compassions of a father are. Why did you not serve your own

157. He goes home to his father.
158. He refrains himself for money.
159. Severity what it inclines to.

64

son so? But 'tis evident enough that we are better at giving good counsel to others than we are at taking good counsel ourselves.[160] But my honest neighbour, suppose that Mr Badman's father had done as you say and by so doing had driven his son to ill courses, what had he bettered either himself or his son in so doing?

ATTEN: That's true, but it does not follow that if the father had done as I said, the son would have done as you suppose. But if he had done as you have supposed, what had he done worse than what he had done already?[161]

WISE: He had done bad enough, that's true. But suppose his father had given him no money, and suppose that young Badman had taken a pet thereat, and in an anger had gone beyond sea, and his father had neither seen him nor heard of him more. Or suppose that of a mad and headstrong stomach he had gone to the highway for money, and so had brought himself to the gallows, and his father and family to great contempt. Or if by so doing he had not brought himself to that end, yet he had added to all his wickedness, such and such evils besides. And what comfort could his father have had in this?

Besides, when his father had done for him what he could with desire to make him an honest man, he would then, whether his son had proved honest or no, have laid down his head with far more peace than if he had taken your counsel.

ATTEN: Nay, I think I should not have been forward to have given advice in the cause. But truly you have given me such an account of his villainies that the hearing thereof has made me angry with him.

WISE: In an angry mood we may soon outshoot ourselves, but poor wretch, as he is, he has gone to his place. But as I said, when a good father has done what he can for a bad child, and that child shall prove never the better, he will lie down with far more peace than if through severity he had driven him to inconveniencies.

I remember that I have heard of a good woman who had, as this old man, a bad and ungodly[162] son. And she prayed for him, counselled him and carried it motherly to him for several years together,

160. We are better at giving than taking good counsel.
161. This is to be considered.
162. A good woman and her bad son.

but still he remained bad. At last, upon a time, after she had been at prayer as she was wont for his conversion, she came to him and thus or to this effect began again to admonish him. 'Son,' said she, 'You have been and are a wicked child. You have cost me many a prayer and tear, and yet you remain wicked. Well, I have done my duty. I have done what I can to save you. Now I am satisfied that if I shall see you damned at the day of Judgement, I shall be so far off from being grieved for you that I shall rejoice to hear the sentence of your damnation at that day.' And it converted him.

I tell you that if parents carry it lovingly towards their children, mixing their mercies with loving rebukes and their loving rebukes with fatherly and motherly compassions, they are more likely to save their children than by being churlish and severe toward them. But if they do not save them, if their mercy does them no good, yet it will greatly ease them at the day of death to consider, 'I have done by love as much as I could to save and deliver my child from Hell.'

ATTEN: Well, I yield. But pray let us return again to Mr Badman. You say that his father gave him a piece of money that he might set up for himself.

WISE: Yes, his father did give him a piece of money, and he did set up [163] and almost as soon set down again. For he was not long set up, but by his ill-managing of his matters at home, together with his extravagant expenses abroad, he was got so far into debt and had so little in his shop to pay that he was hard put to it to keep himself out of prison. But when his creditors understood that he was about to marry and in a fair way to get a rich wife, they said among themselves, 'We will not be hasty with him. If he gets a rich wife, he will pay us all.'

ATTEN: But how could he so quickly run out, for I perceive 'twas in little time, by what you say?

WISE: 'Twas in little time indeed, I think he was not above two years and a half in doing of it. But the reason[164] is apparent, for he being a wild young man, and now having the bridle loose before him, and being wholly subjected to his lusts and vices, he gave himself up to

163. Mr Badman sets up for himself and quickly runs to the land's end.
164. The reason of his running out.

the way of his heart and to the sight of his eye, forgetting that for all these things God will bring him to judgement.[165] And he that doth thus, you may be sure, shall not be able long to stand on his legs.

Besides, he had now an addition of [166] new companions: companions you must think, most like himself in manners, and so such who cared not who sunk if they themselves might swim. These would often be haunting of him and of his shop, too, when he was absent. They would commonly egg him to the alehouse, but yet make him Jack-pay-for-all. They would be borrowing also money of him but take no care to pay again, except it was with more of their company, which also he liked very well. And so his poverty came like one who travels, and his want like an armed man.

But all the while they studied his temper.[167] He loved to be flattered, praised and commanded for wit, manhood and personage, and this was like stroking him over the face. Thus they collogued with him and got yet more and more into him, and so like horse-leaches, they drew away that little that his father had given him and brought him quickly down, almost to dwell next door to the beggar.

ATTEN: Then was the saying of the wise man fulfilled, 'He that keepeth company with harlots,' and 'a companion of fools, shall be destroyed'.[168]

WISE: Aye, and that too 'a companion of riotous persons shameth his father'.[169] For he, poor man, had both grief and shame to see how his son – now at his own hand – behaved himself in the enjoyment of those good things, in and under the lawful use of which he might have lived to God's glory, his own comfort and credit among his neighbours. But 'he that followeth vain persons shall have poverty enough'.[170] The way that he took led him directly into this condition, for who can expect other things of one who follows such courses? Besides, when he was in his shop, he could not abide to be doing. He was naturally given to idleness. He loved to live high,

165. Ecclesiastes 11:9.
166. New companions.
167. Mr Badman's temper.
168. Proverbs 29:3, 13:20.
169. Proverbs 28:7.
170. Proverbs 28:19.

but his hands refused to labour. And what else can the end of such a one be but that which the wise man says? 'The drunkard and the glutton shall come to poverty: and drowsiness shall clothe a man with rags.'[171]

ATTEN: But now, methinks, when he was brought thus low, he should have considered the hand of God that was gone out against him, and should have smote upon the breast and have returned.

WISE: Consideration – good consideration – was far from him. He was as stout and proud now as ever in all his life, and was as high too in the pursuit of his sin as when he was in the midst of his fullness. Only he went now[172] like a tired jade. The Devil had rid him almost off of his legs.

ATTEN: Well, but what did he do when all was almost gone?

WISE: Two things were now his play.[173] One – he bore all in hand by swearing and cracking and lying that he was as well to pass as he was the first day he set up for himself, yea, that he had rather got than lost. And he had at his beck some of his companions who would swear to confirm it as fast as he.

ATTEN: This was double wickedness. 'Twas a sin to say it and another to swear it.

WISE: That's true, but what evil is that that he will not do that is left of God, as I believe Mr Badman was?

ATTEN: And what was the other thing?

WISE: Why, that which I hinted before. He was for looking out for a rich wife.[174] And now I am come to some more of his invented, devised, designed and abominable roguery, such that will yet declare him to be a most desperate sinner.

The thing was this: a wife he wanted, or rather money, for as for a woman, he could have whores enow at his whistle. But as I said, he wanted money, and that must be got by a wife or no way. Nor could he so easily get a wife neither, except he became an artist at the way of dissembling. Nor would dissembling do among that people who could dissemble as well as he. But there dwelt a maid not far

171. Proverbs 23:21.
172. His behaviour under his decays.
173. How he covered his decays.
174. Badman is for a rich wife.

from him who was both godly[175] and one who had a good portion. But how to get her: there lay all the craft.[176] Well, he calls a council of some of his most trusty and cunning companions[177] and breaks his mind to them, to wit, that he had a mind to marry, and he also told them to whom. 'But,' said he, 'how shall I accomplish my end? She is religious, and I am not.' Then one of them made reply saying, 'Since she is religious, you must pretend to be so likewise, and that for some time before you go to her. Mark therefore where she goes daily to hear, and do you go there also. But there you must be sure to behave yourself soberly and make as if you liked the Word wonderful well. Stand also where she may see you, and when you come home, be sure that you walk the street very soberly and go within sight of her. This done for a while, then go to her. And first talk of how sorry you are for your sins and show great love to the religion that she is of, still speaking well of her preachers and of her godly acquaintance, bewailing your hard hap, that it was not your lot to be acquainted with her and her fellow professors sooner. And this is the way to get her. Also you must write down sermons, talk of scriptures and pro-test that you came a wooing to her only because she is godly and because you should count it your greatest happiness if you might but have such a one. As for her money: slight it. It will be never the further off. That's the way to come soonest at it, for she will be jealous at first that you come for her money. You know what she has, but make not a word about it. Do this, and you shall see if you do not entangle the lass.'

Thus was the snare laid for this poor honest maid, and she was quickly caught in his pit.

ATTEN: Why, did he take this counsel?

WISE: Did he! Yes! And after a while he went as boldly to her,[178] and that under a vizard of religion as if he had been, for honesty and godliness, one of the most sincere and upright-hearted in England. He observed all his points and followed the advice of his counsellors, and quickly obtained her, too. For natural parts, he had: he was tall

175. Badman has a godly maid in his eye.
176. He seeks to get her, why and how.
177. He calls his companions together, and they advise him how to get her.
178. Badman goes to the damsel as his counsel advised him.

and fair, and had plain but very good clothes on his back. And his religion was the more easily attained, for he had seen something in the house of his father and first master, and so could the more readily put himself into the form and show thereof.

So he appointed his day and went to her, as that he might easily do, for she had neither father nor mother to oppose. Well, when he had come and had given her a civil compliment[179] to let her understand why he had come, then he began and told her that he had found in his heart a great deal of love to her person, and that of all the damsels in the world, he had pitched upon her, if she thought fit to make her his beloved wife. The reasons, as he told her, why he had pitched upon her were her religious and personal excellences, and therefore entreated her to take his condition into her tender and loving consideration. 'As for the world,' quoth he, 'I have a very good trade and can maintain myself and family well while my wife sits still on her seat. I have got thus, and thus much already, and feel money come in every day. But that is not the thing that I aim at. 'Tis an honest and godly wife.' Then he would present her with a good book or two, pretending how much good he had got by them himself. He would also be often speaking well of godly ministers, especially of those that he perceived she liked and loved most. Besides, he would be often telling of her what a godly father he had, and what a new man he was also become himself. And thus did this treacherous dealer deal with this honest and good girl to her great grief and sorrow, as afterward you shall hear.

ATTEN: But had the maid no friend to look after her?

WISE: Her father and mother were dead, and that he knew well enough, and so she was the more easily overcome by his naughty, lying tongue. But if she had never so many friends, she might have been beguiled by him. It is too much the custom of young people now to think themselves wise enough to make their own choice, and that they need not ask counsel of those who are older and also wiser then they.[180] But this is a great fault in them, and many of them have paid dear for it. Well, to be short, in little time Mr Badman obtains

179. Badman's compliment, his lying compliment.
180. Neglect of counsel about marriage dangerous.

his desire,[181] gets this honest girl and her money, is married to her, brings her home, makes a feast, entertains her royally, but her portion must pay for all.

ATTEN: This was wonderful deceitful doings. A man shall seldom hear of the like.

WISE: By this his doing, he showed how little he feared God[182] and what little dread he had of His judgements. For all this carriage, and all these words were by him premeditated evil, he knew he lied, he knew he dissembled. Yea, he knew that he made use of the name of God, of religion, good men and good books, but as a stalking horse, thereby the better to catch his game. In all this his glorious pretence of religion, he was but a glorious painted hypocrite, and hypocrisy is the highest sin that a poor carnal wretch can attain unto. It is also a sin that most dares God and that also brings the greater damnation. Now was he a whited wall, now was he a painted sepulchre,[183] now was he a grave that appeared not. For this poor honest, godly damsel, little thought that both her peace, and comfort, and estate, and liberty, and person, and all, were going to her burial[184] when she was going to be married to Mr Badman. And yet so it was, she enjoyed herself but little afterwards. She was as if she was dead and buried to what she enjoyed before.

ATTEN: Certainly some wonderful judgement of God must attend and overtake such wicked men as these.

WISE: You may be sure that they shall have judgement to the full for all these things when the day of Judgement has come. But as for judgement upon them in this life, it does not always come – no, not upon those that are worthy thereof. 'They that work wickedness are set up; yea, they that tempt God are even delivered.'[185] But they are reserved to the day of wrath, and then for their wickedness, God will repay them to their faces.[186] 'The wicked is reserved to the day of destruction? They shall be brought forth to the day of wrath. Who shall

181. Badman obtains his desire, is married, etc.
182. His carriage judged ungodly and wicked.
183. Matthew 23.
184. The great alteration that quickly happened to Badman's wife.
185. Malachi 3:15.
186. Expectation of judgement is for such things.

declare his way to his face? And who shall repay him what he hath done? Yet shall he be brought to the grave, and shall remain in the tomb.'[187] That is, ordinarily they escape God's hand in this life, save only a few examples are made that others may be cautioned and take warning thereby. But at the day of Judgement, they must be rebuked for their evil with the lashes of devouring fire.

ATTEN: Can you give me no examples of God's wrath upon men who have acted this tragical wicked deed of Mr Badman?

WISE: Yes.[188] Hamor and Shechem, and all the men of their city, for attempting to make God and religion the stalking horse to get Jacob's daughters to wife, were together slain with the edge of the sword. A judgement of God upon them, no doubt, for their dissembling in that matter. All manner of lying and dissembling is dreadful, but to make God and religion a disguise, therewith to blind your dissimulation from others eyes, is highly provoking to the divine majesty.

I knew ☞ one that dwelt not far off from our town who got him a wife as Mr Badman got his, but he did not enjoy her long. For one night as he was riding home from his companions, where he had been at a neighbouring town, his horse threw him to the ground, where he was found dead at break of day, frightfully and lamentably mangled with his fall, and besmeared with his own blood.

ATTEN: Well, but pray return again to Mr Badman. How did he carry it to his wife after he was married to her?

WISE: Nay, let us take things along as we go. He had not been married but a little while but his creditors came upon him[189] for their money. He deferred them a little while, but at last things were come to that point that pay he must or must do worse. So he appointed them a time, and they came for their money, and he paid them down with her money before her eyes for those goods that he had profusely spent among his whores long before, besides the portion that his father gave him, to the value of two hundred pounds.

187. Job 21:30–32.
188. An example of God's anger on such as have heretofore committed this sin of Mr Badman. Genesis 34.
189. After Badman is married, his creditors come upon him, and his wife's portion pays for that which his whores were feasted with before he was married.

ATTEN: This beginning was bad, but what shall I say? 'Twas like Mr Badman himself. Poor woman. This was but a bad beginning for her. I fear it filled her with trouble enough, as I think such a beginning would have done one perhaps much stronger than she.

WISE: Trouble, aye, you may be sure of it, but now 'twas too late to repent.[190] She should have looked better to herself when being wary would have done her good. Her harms may be an advantage to others that will learn to take heed thereby, but for herself, she must take what follows even such a life now as Mr Badman her husband will lead her, and that will be bad enough.

ATTEN: This beginning was bad, and yet I fear it was but the beginning of bad.

WISE: You may be sure that it was but the beginning of badness, for other evils came on apace. As for instance, it was but a little while after he was married,[191] but he hangs his religion upon the hedge, or rather dealt with it as men deal with their old clothes, who cast them off or leave them to others to wear. For his part, he would be religious no longer.

Now therefore he had pulled off his vizard and began to show himself in his old shape: a base, wicked, debauched fellow. And now the poor woman saw that she was betrayed indeed. Now also his old companions began to flock about him and to haunt his house and shop as formerly. And who with them but Mr Badman? And who with him again but they?

Now those good people who used to company with his wife began to be amated[vii] and discouraged.[192] Also he would frown and gloat upon them, as if he abhorred the appearance of them, so that in little time he drove all good company from her and made her sit solitary by herself. He also began now to go out a nights to those drabs[193] who were his familiars before, with whom he would stay sometimes till midnight and sometimes till almost morning, and then would come home as drunk as a swine. And this was the course of Mr Badman.

190. Now she reaps the fruits of her unadvisedness.
191. Now Badman has got him a wife by religion, he hangs it by as a thing out of use and entertains his old companions.
192. He drives good company from his wife.
193. He goes to his whores.

Now when he came home in this case, if his wife did but speak a word to him about where he had been, and why he had so abused himself, though her words were spoken in never so much meekness and love, then she was whore,[194] and bitch, and jade, and 'twas well if she missed his fingers and heels. Sometimes also he would bring his punks home to his house, and woe be to his wife when they were gone, if she did not entertain them with all varieties possible, and also carry it lovingly to them.

Thus this good woman was made by Badman her husband to possess nothing but disappointments as to all that he had promised her, or that she hoped to have at his hands.

But that which added pressing weight to all her sorrow was that, as he had cast away all religion himself, so he attempted, if possible, to make her do so too.[195] He would not suffer her to go out to the preaching of the Word of Christ, nor to the rest of his appointments for the health and salvation of her soul. He would now taunt at and reflectingly speak of her preachers,[196] and would receive, yea, raise scandals of them to her very great grief and affliction.

Now she scarce dared go to an honest neighbour's house, or have a good book in her hand, especially when he had his companions in his house or had got a little drink in his head. He would also, when he perceived that she was dejected, speak tauntingly[197] and mockingly to her in the presence of his companions, calling of her his religious wife, his demure dame, and the like. Also he would make a sport of her among his wanton ones abroad.

If she did ask him, as sometimes she would, to let her go out to a sermon, he would in a currish manner reply, 'Keep at home, keep at home, and look to your business. We cannot live by hearing of sermons.'[198] If she still urged that he would let her go, then he would say to her, 'Go if you dare.' He would also charge her with giving of what he had to her ministers when, vile wretch, he had spent it on his vain companions before.

194. He rails at his wife.
195. He seeks to force his wife from her religion.
196. He mocks at her preachers.
197. He mocks his wife in her dejections.
198. He refuses to let her go out to good company.

This was the life that Mr Badman's good wife lived within few months after he had married her.

ATTEN: This was a disappointment indeed.

WISE: A disappointment indeed as ever, I think, poor woman had. One would think that the knave might a little let her have had her will, since it was nothing but to be honest, and since she brought him so sweet, so lumping a portion, for she brought hundreds into his house. I say, one would think he should have let her had her own will a little since she desired it only in the service and worship of God. But could she win him to grant her that? No, not a bit if it would have saved her life. True, sometimes she would steal out when he was from home on a journey, or among his drunken companions, but with all privacy imaginable.[199] And, poor woman, this advantage she had, she carried it so to all her neighbours that, though many of them were but carnal, yet they would not betray her or tell of her going out to the Word, if they saw it, but would rather endeavour to hide it from Mr Badman himself.

ATTEN: This carriage of his to her was enough to break her heart.

WISE: It was enough to do it indeed. Yea, it did effectually do it. It killed her in time, yea, it was all the time a killing of her. She would oftentimes, when she sat by herself, thus mournfully bewail her condition.[200] ' "Woe is me, that I sojourn in Mesech, that I dwell in the tents of Kedar! My soul hath long dwelt with him that hateth peace." Oh, "what shall be given unto thee, thou deceitful tongue? or what shall be done unto thee, thou false tongue?"[201] I am a woman grieved in spirit. My husband has bought me and sold me for his lusts. 'Twas not me but my money that he wanted. Oh that he had had it, so I had had my liberty!'

This she said, not of contempt of his person but of his conditions, and because she saw that by his hypocritical tongue, he had brought her not only almost to beggary but robbed her of the Word of God.

ATTEN: It is a deadly thing, I see, to be unequally yoked with unbelievers. If this woman had had a good husband, how happily might

199. She gets out sometimes by stealth.
200. Her repentance and complaint.
201. Psalm 120.

they have lived together! Such a one would have prayed for her, taught her and also would have encouraged her in the faith and ways of God. But now, poor creature, instead of this, there is nothing but the quite contrary.

WISE: It is a deadly thing indeed, and therefore, by the Word of God his people are forbidden to be joined in marriage with them.[202] 'Be ye not,' says it, 'unequally yoked together with unbelievers: for what fellowship hath righteousness with unrighteousness? And what communion hath light with darkness? And what concord hath Christ with Belial? Or what part hath he that believeth with an infidel? And what agreement hath the temple of God with idols?'[203] There can be no agreement where such matches are made. Even God himself hath declared the contrary from the beginning of the world. 'I,' says He, 'will put enmity between thee and the woman, between thy seed and her seed.'[204] Therefore He says in another place, they can mix no better than iron and clay.[205] I say, they cannot agree, they cannot be one, and therefore they should be aware at first and not lightly receive such into their affections. God has often made such matches bitter, especially to His own. Such matches are, as God said of Elie's sons that were spared, 'to consume the eyes, and to cause sorrow of heart'.[206] Oh the wailing and lamentation that they have made who have been thus yoked, especially if they were such as would be so yoked against their light and good counsel to the contrary.

ATTEN: Alas! He deluded her with his tongue and feigned reformation.

WISE: Well, well. She should have gone more warily to work.[207] What if she had acquainted some of her best, most knowing, and godly friends therewith? What if she had engaged a godly minister or two to have talked with Mr Badman? Also, what if she had laid wait round about him to espy if he was not otherwise behind her back than he was before her face? And besides, I verily think – since in the

202. The evil of being unequally yoked together.
203. 2 Corinthians 6:14–16.
204. Genesis 3:15.
205. Daniel 2:43.
206. Leviticus 26:16.
207. Good counsel to those godly maids who are to marry.

multitude of counsellors there is safety – that if she had acquainted the congregation with it and desired them to spend some time in prayer to God about it, and if she must have had him, to have received him as to his godliness upon the judgement of others rather than her own, she knowing them to be godly, and judicious, and unbiased men, she had had more peace all her life after than to trust to her own poor, raw, womanish judgement, as she did. Love is blind and will see nothing amiss, where others may see a hundred faults. Therefore I say she should not have trusted to her own thoughts in the matter of his goodness.

As to his person, there she was fittest to judge because she was to be the person pleased, but as to his godliness, there the Word was the fittest judge, and they who could best understand it, because God was therein to be pleased. I wish[208] that all young maidens will take heed of being beguiled with flattering words, with feigning and lying speeches, and take the best way to preserve themselves from being bought and sold by wicked men, as she was. Lest they repent with her, when as to this repentance will do them no good, but for their unadvisedness go sorrowing to their graves.

ATTEN: Well, things are past with this poor woman and cannot be called back. Let others[209] beware by her misfortunes, lest they also fall into her distress.

WISE: That is the thing that I say. Let them take heed, lest for their unadvisedness they smart, as this poor woman has done. And ah! Methinks that they who yet are single persons and who are tempted to marry to such as Mr Badman would to inform and warn themselves in this matter before they entangle themselves, but go to some who already are in the snare and ask them how it is with them, as to the suitable or unsuitableness of their marriage, and desire their advice. Surely they would ring such a peal in their ears about the unequality, unsuitableness, disadvantages and disquietments, and sins that attend such marriages that would make them beware as long as they live. But the bird in the air knows not the notes of the bird in the snare until she comes there herself. Besides, to make up such

208. A caution to young women.

209. Let Mr Badman's wife be your example.

marriages, Satan and carnal Reason and Lust, or at least Inconsiderateness, have the chiefest hand. And where these things bear sway, designs, though never so destructive, will go headlong on. And therefore I fear that but little warning will be taken by young girls, at Mr Badman's wife's affliction.

ATTEN: But are there no dissuasive arguments to lay before such to prevent their future misery.

WISE: Yes. There is the law of God that forbids marriage with unbelievers. These kind of marriages also are condemned even by irrational creatures. One – it is forbidden by the law of God both in the Old Testament and in the New. One – in the Old: 'Thou shalt not make marriages with them; thy daughter thou shalt not give unto his son, nor his daughter shalt thou take unto thy son.'[210] Two – in the New Testament it is forbidden. 'Be ye not unequally yoked together with unbelievers.' Let them marry to whom they will, only in the Lord.[211]

Here now is a prohibition,[212] plainly forbidding the believer to marry with the unbeliever, therefore they should not do it. Again, these unwarrantable marriages are, as I may so say, condemned by irrational creatures who will not couple but with their own sort. Will the sheep couple with a dog, the partridge with a crow, or the pheasant with an owl? No, they will strictly tie up themselves to those of their own sort only. Yea, it sets all the world a-wondering when they see or hear the contrary. Man only is most subject to wink at and allow of these unlawful mixtures of men and women, because man only is a sinful beast, a sinful bird. Therefore he, above all, will take upon him by rebellious actions to answer, or rather, to oppose and violate the law of his God and Creator. Nor shall these or other interrogatories – what fellowship? what concord? what agreement? what communion can there be in such marriages? – be counted of weight, or thought worth the answering by him.

But further: the dangers[213] that such do commonly run themselves into should be to others a dissuasive argument to stop them

210. Deuteronomy 7:3.
211. 1 Corinthians 7:39; 2 Corinthians 6:14–16.
212. Rules for those that are to marry.
213. If you love your soul, take heed.

from doing the like. For besides the distresses of Mr Badman's wife, many who have had very hopeful beginnings for Heaven have, by virtue of the mischiefs that have attended these unlawful marriages, miserably and fearfully miscarried. Soon after such marriages, conviction – the first step toward Heaven – has ceased. Prayer – the next step toward Heaven – has ceased. Hungerings and thirstings after salvation – another step towards the kingdom of Heaven – have ceased. In a word, such marriages have estranged them from the Word, from their godly and faithful friends, and have brought them again into carnal company, among carnal friends, and also into carnal delights, where and with whom they have in conclusion both sinfully abode, and miserably perished.

And this is one reason why God hath forbidden this kind of unequal marriages. 'For they,' says He, meaning the ungodly, 'will turn away thy son from following me, that they may serve other gods: so will the anger of the Lord be kindled against you, and destroy thee suddenly.'[214] Now mark, there were some in Israel who would, notwithstanding this prohibition, venture to marry to the heathens and unbelievers. But what followed? 'They served their idols. … They sacrificed their sons and their daughters unto devils. … Thus were they defiled with their own works, and went a-whoring with their own inventions. … Therefore was the wrath of the Lord kindled against his people, insomuch that he abhorred his own inheritance.'[215]

ATTEN: But let's return again to Mr Badman. Had he any children by his wife?

WISE: Yes, seven.

ATTEN: I doubt they were but badly brought up.

WISE: One of them loved its mother dearly and would constantly harken to her voice. Now that child[216] she had the opportunity to instruct in the principles of Christian religion, and it became a very gracious child. But that child Mr Badman could not abide. He would seldom afford it a pleasant word but would scowl and frown upon it, speak churlishly and doggedly to it, and though as to nature it was

214. Deuteronomy 7:4.
215. Psalm 106:35–40.
216. Badman's children that he had by this good woman.

the most feeble of the seven, yet it oftenest felt the weight of its father's fingers. Three of his children did directly follow his steps and began to be as vile as in his youth he was himself. The other that remained became a kind of mongrel professors, not so bad as their father, nor so good as their mother, but were between them both. They had their mother's notions and their father's actions, and were much like those that you read of in the Book of Nehemiah: 'And their children spake half in the speech of Ashdod, and could not speak in the Jews' language, but according to the language of each people.'[217]

ATTEN: What you say in this matter is observable, and if I take not my mark amiss, it often happens after this manner where such unlawful marriages are contracted.

WISE: It sometimes does so, and the reason, with respect to their parents, is this: where the one of the parents is godly, and the other ungodly and vile, though they can agree in begetting of children yet, they strive for their children when they are born.[218] The godly parent strives for the child, and by prayers, counsel and good examples, labours to make it holy in body and soul, and so fit for the kingdom of Heaven. But the ungodly would have it like himself: wicked and base and sinful. And so they both give instructions accordingly. Instructions, did I say? Yea, and examples, too, according to their minds. Thus the godly, as Hannah, is presenting her Samuel unto the Lord. But the ungodly, like them who went before them, are for offering their children to Moloch, to an idol, to sin, to the Devil and to Hell. Thus one harkens to the law of their mother, and is preserved from destruction. But as for the other, as their fathers did, so do they. Thus did Mr Badman and his wife part some of their children between them. But as for the other three that were as 'twere mongrels, between both, they were like unto those that you read of in Kings, 'They feared the Lord, and served their own gods.'[219] They had, as I say, their mother's notions and, I will add, profession, too, but their father's lusts and something of his life. Now their father did not like them, because they had their mother's

217. Nehemiah 13:24.
218. How the ungodly father and godly mother do strive for the children that God does give them.
219. 2 Kings 17:33.

tongue. And the mother did not like them because they had still their father's heart and life. Nor were they indeed fit company for good or bad. The good would not trust them because they were bad, the bad would not trust them because they were good, viz. The good would not trust them because they were bad in their lives, and the bad would not trust them because they were good in their words. So they were forced with Esau to join in affinity with Ishmael, to wit, to look out a people that were hypocrites like themselves, and with them they matched, and lived, and died.

ATTEN: Poor woman! She could not but have much perplexity.

WISE: Yea, and poor children that ever they were sent into the world as the fruit of the loins and under the government of such a father as Mr Badman.

ATTEN: You say right, for such children lie almost under all manner of disadvantages. But we must say nothing because this also is the sovereign will of God.

WISE: We may not by any means object against God. Yet we may talk of the advantages and disadvantages that children have by having for their parents such as are either godly or the contrary.

ATTEN: You say right. We may so, and pray now since we are about it, speak something in brief unto it that is unto this: what advantage those children have above others that have for their parents such as indeed are godly.

WISE: So I will, only I must first premise these two or three things.[220]

One – they have not the advantage of election for their father's sakes.

Two – they are born, as others, the children of wrath, though they come of godly parents.

Three – grace comes not unto them as an inheritance because they have godly parents. These things premised, I shall now proceed.

One – the children of godly parents are the children of many prayers. They are prayed for before and prayed for after they are born, and the prayer of a godly father and godly mother does much.

Two – they have the advantage of what restraint is possible from what evils their parents see them inclinable to, and that is a second mercy.

220. The advantages that children have whose parents are both godly.

Three – they have the advantage of godly instruction, and of being told which are and which are not the right ways of the Lord.

Four – they have also those ways commended unto them, and spoken well of in their hearing, that are good.

Five – such are also, what may be, kept out of evil company, from evil books and from being taught the way of swearing, lying and the like, as Sabbath-breaking and mocking at good men and good things, and this is a very great mercy.

Six – they have also the benefit of a godly life set before them doctrinally by their parents, and that doctrine backed with a godly and holy example. And all these are very great advantages.

Now all these advantages the children of ungodly parents want,[221] and so are more in danger of being carried away with the error of the wicked. For ungodly parents neither pray for their children, nor do, nor can they heartily instruct them. They do not after a godly manner restrain them from evil, nor do they keep them from evil company. They are not grieved at, nor yet do they forewarn their children to beware of such evil actions that are abomination to God and to all good men. They let their children break the Sabbath, swear, lie, be wicked and vain. They commend not to their children a holy life, nor set a good example before their eyes. No, they do in all things contrary, estranging of their children what they can from the love of God and all good men so soon as they are born. Therefore it is a very great judgement of God upon children to be the offspring of base and ungodly men.[222]

ATTEN: Well, but before we leave Mr Badman's wife and children, I have a mind, if you please, to enquire a little more after one thing, the which I am sure you can satisfy me in.

WISE: What is that?

ATTEN: You said a while ago that this Mr Badman would not suffer his wife to go out to hear such godly ministers as she liked, but said if she did, she had as good never come home any more. Did he often carry it thus to her?

221. The disadvantages that the children of ungodly parents have.
222. Job 30:8.

WISE: He did say so. He did often say so. This I told you then, and had also then told you more, but that other things put me out.

ATTEN: Well said, pray therefore now go on.

WISE: So I will. Upon a time, she was on a Lord's day for going to hear a sermon, and Mr Badman was unwilling[223] she should. But she at that time, as it seems, did put on more courage than she was wont, and therefore, after she had spent upon him a great many fair words and entreaties, if perhaps she might have prevailed by them, but all to no purpose at all. At last she said she would go and rendered this reason for it: 'I have a husband but also a God. My God has commanded me, and that upon pain of damnation, to be a continual worshipper of Him, and that in the way of His own appointments. I have a husband but also a soul, and my soul ought to be more unto me than all the world besides. This soul of mine I will look after, care for and, if I can provide it, a Heaven for its habitation. You are commanded to love me as you love your own body, and so do I love you.[224] But I tell you true, I prefer my soul before all the world, and its salvation I will seek.'

At this, first[225] he gave her an ugly wish and then fell into a fearful rage and swore moreover that if she did go, he would make both her and all her damnable brotherhood, for so he was pleased to call them, to repent their coming there.

ATTEN: But what should he mean by that?

WISE: You may easily guess what he meant. He meant he would turn informer, and so either weary out those that she loved from meeting together to worship God, or make them pay dearly for their so doing, the which if he did, he knew it would vex every vein of her tender heart.

ATTEN: But do you think Mr Badman would have been so base?

WISE: Truly he had malice and enmity enough in his heart to do it, only he was a tradesman. Also he knew that he must live by his neighbours, and so he had that little wit in his anger that he refrained himself and did it not. But, as I said, he had malice and

223. A contest between Mr Badman and his wife.
224. Ephesians 5:28.
225. With which weapons Badman did deal with his wife.

83

envy enough in his heart[226] to have made him to do it, only he thought it would worst him in his trade. Yet these three things he would be doing.

One – he would be putting of others on to molest and abuse her friends.

Two – he would be glad when he heard that any mischief befell them.

Three – and would laugh at her when he saw her troubled for them. And now I have told you Mr Badman's way as to this.

ATTEN: But was he not afraid of the judgements of God that did fly about at that time?

WISE: He regarded not the judgement nor mercy of God, for had he at all done that, he could not have done as he did. But what judgements do you mean?

ATTEN: Such judgements that if Mr Badman himself had taken but sober notice of, they might have made him a-hung down his ears.

WISE: Why, have you heard of any such persons that the judgements of God have overtaken?

ATTEN: Yes, and so I believe have you, too, though you make so strange about it.

WISE: I have so indeed to my astonishment and wonder.

ATTEN: Pray therefore, if you please, tell me what it is as to this, that you know, and then, perhaps I may also say something to you of the same.

WISE: In[227] our town ☞ there was one WS – a man of a very wicked life. And he, when there seemed to be countenance given to it, would needs turn informer. Well, so he did and was as diligent in his business as most of them could be. He would watch a-nights, climb trees and range the woods a-days if possible to find out the meeters, for then they were forced to meet in the fields. Yea, he would curse them bitterly and swear most fearfully what he would do to them when he found them. Well, after he had gone on like a Bedlam in his course a while, and had done some mischiefs to the people, he was stricken by the hand of God and that in this manner.

226. Mr Badman's heart discovered as to its enmity against the friends of his wife.
227. Mark.

One – although he had his tongue naturally at will, now he was taken with a faltering in his speech and could not for weeks together speak otherwise than just like a man who was drunk.

Two – then he was taken with a drawling or slobbering at his mouth, which slobber sometimes would hang at his mouth well nigh halfway down to the ground.

Three – then he had such a weakness in the back sinews of his neck that ofttimes he could not look up before him unless he clapped his hand hard upon his forehead and held up his head that way by strength of hand.

Four – after this his speech went quite away, and he could speak no more than a swine or a bear. Therefore like one of them, he would gruntle and make an ugly noise, according as he was offended, or pleased, or would have anything done, etc.

In this posture he continued for the space of half a year or there-abouts, all the while otherwise well and could go about his business, save once that he had a fall from the bell as it hangs in our steeple, which 'twas a wonder it did not kill him. But after that he also walked about till God had made him a sufficient spectacle of his judgement for his sin, and then on a sudden he was stricken and died miserably. And so there was an end of him and his doings.

I will tell you ☞ of another. About four miles from St Neots, there was a gentleman had a man, and he would needs be an in-former, and a lusty young man he was. Well, an informer he was and did much distress some people, and had perfected his informations so effectually against some that there was nothing further to do but for the constables to make distress on the people that he might have the money or goods. And as I heard, he hastened them much to do it. Now while he was in the heat of his work, as he stood one day by the fireside, he had – it should seem – a mind to a sop in the pan, for the spit was then at the fire, so he went to make him one. But behold a dog – so say his own dog – took distaste at something and bit his master by the leg, the which bite notwithstanding all the means that was used to cure him, turned as was said to a gangrene. However, that wound was his death, and that a dreadful one, too, for my relator said that he lay in such a condition by this bite, as the beginning till his flesh rotted from off him before he went out of the world. But what need I instance in particular persons, when the judgement of God against this kind of people was made manifest, I think I may say, if not in all, yet in most of the counties in England where such poor creatures were? But I would, if it had been the will of God that neither I nor anybody else could tell you more of these stories, true stories that are neither lie nor romance.

ATTEN: Well, I also heard of both these myself, and of more too as remarkable in their kind as these, if I had any list to tell them. But let us leave those that are behind to others, or to the coming of Christ, who then will justify or condemn them as the merit of their work shall require. Or if they repented and found mercy, I shall be glad when I know it, for I wish not a curse to the soul of my enemy.

WISE: There can be no pleasure in the telling of such stories, though to hear of them may do us a pleasure. They may put us in mind that there is a God who judges in the earth and who does not always forget nor defer to hear the cry of the destitute. They also carry along with them both caution and counsel to those who are the survivors of such. Let us tremble at the judgements of God, and be afraid of sinning against him, and it shall be our protection. It shall go well with them who fear God, who fear before Him.

ATTEN: Well, sir, as you have intimated, so I think we have in this place spoken enough about these kind of men. If you please, let us return again to Mr Badman himself if you have any more to say of him.

WISE: More! We have yet scarce thoroughly begun with anything that we have said! All the particulars are in themselves so full of badness that we have rather only looked in them than indeed said anything to them. But we will pass them and proceed. You have heard of the sins of his youth, of his apprenticeship, and how he set up and married, and what a life he had led his wife. And now I will tell you some more[228] of his pranks. He had the very knack of knavery. Had he, as I said before, been bound to serve an apprenticeship to all these things, he could not have been more cunning, he could not have been more artificial at it.

228. New discourse of Mr Badman.

ATTEN: Nor perhaps so artificially neither. For as none can teach goodness like to God himself, so concerning sin and knavery, none can teach a man it like the Devil to whom, as I perceive, Mr Badman went to school from his childhood to the end of his life. But pray, sir, make a beginning.

WISE: Well, so I will. You may remember that I told you what a condition he was in for money before he did marry, and how he got a rich wife, with whose money he paid his debts. Now when he had paid his debts, he having some money left, he sets up again[229] as briskly as ever, keeps a great shop, drives a great trade and runs again a great way into debt. But now not into the debt of one or two, but into the debt of many, so that at last he came to owe some thousands, and thus he went on a good while. And to pursue his ends the better, he began now to study to please all men and to suit himself to any company. He could now be as they, say as they, that is, if he listed. And then he would list when he perceived that by so doing he might either make them his customers or creditors for his commodities. If he dealt with honest men, as with some honest men he did, then he would be as they: talk as they, seem to be sober as they, talk of justice and religion as they, and against debauchery as they, yea, and would too seem to show a dislike of them that said, did or were otherwise than honest.

Again, when he did light among those who were bad, then he would be as they, but yet more close and cautiously, except he were sure of his company. Then he would carry it openly, be as they, say, 'Damn'em' and 'Sink'em' as they. If they railed on good men, so could he.[230] If they railed on religion, so could he. If they talked beastly, vainly, idly, so would he. If they were for drinking, swearing, whoring or any the like villainies, so was he. This was now the path he trod in and could do all artificially as any man alive. And now he thought himself a perfect man. He thought he was always a boy till now. What think you now of Mr Badman?

ATTEN: Think? Why, I think he was an atheist, for no man but an atheist can do this. I say it cannot be, but that the man that is such as this

229. Mr Badman plays a new prank.
230. Mr Badman's perfection.

Mr Badman must be a rank and stinking atheist, for he that believes that there is either God or Devil, Heaven or Hell, or death and judgement after, cannot do as Mr Badman did. I mean, if he could do these things without reluctancy and check of conscience, yea, if he had not sorrow and remorse for such abominable sins as these.

WISE: Nay, he was so far off from reluctancies and remorse of conscience for these things that he counted them the excellency of his attainments, the quintessence of his wit, his rare and singular virtues, such as but few besides himself could be the masters of. Therefore, as for those who made boggle and stop at things, and who could not in conscience and for fear of death and judgement, do such things as he, he would call them fools and noddies, and charge them for being frighted with the talk of unseen bugbears, and would encourage them, if they would be men indeed, to labour after the attainment of this his excellent art. He would oftentimes please himself[231] with the thoughts of what he could do in this matter, saying within himself, 'I can be religious and irreligious. I can be anything or nothing. I can swear and speak against swearing. I can lie and speak against lying. I can drink, wench, be unclean and defraud, and not be troubled for it. Now I enjoy myself and am master of my own ways, and not they of me. This I have attained with much study, great care and more pains.' But this his talk should be only with himself, to his wife, who he knew dared not divulge it, or among his intimates, to whom he knew he might say anything.

ATTEN: Did I call him before an atheist? I may call him now a devil, or a man possessed with one, if not with many. I think that there cannot be found in every corner such a one as this. True, it is said of King Ahaz, that he sinned more and more, and of Ahab, that he sold himself to work wickedness, and of the men of Sodom, that they were sinners exceedingly before the Lord.[232]

WISE: An atheist he was no doubt, if there be such a thing as an atheist in the world, but for all his brags of perfection and security in his wickedness, I believe that at times God did let down fire from Heaven into his conscience. True, I believe he would quickly put it

231. How Mr Badman came to enjoy himself.
232. 2 Chronicles 28:22; 1 Kings 21:25; Genesis 13:13.

out again and grow more desperate and wicked afterward, but this also turned to his destruction, as afterward you may hear.[233]

But I am not of your mind to think that there are but few such in the world, except you mean as to the degree of wickedness unto which he had attained. For otherwise, no doubt[234] there is abundance of such as he: men of the same mind, of the same principles, and of the same conscience, too, to put them into practice. Yea, I believe that there are many who are endeavouring to attain to the same pitch of wickedness, and all them are such as he, in the judgement of the law, nor will their want of hellish wit to attain thereto, excuse them at the day of Judgement. You know that in all science, some are more arch than some, and so it is in the art as well as in the practice of wickedness. Some are two-fold and some seven-fold more the children of Hell than others, and yet all the children of Hell, else they would all be masters and none scholars in the school of wickedness. But there must be masters, and there must be learners. Mr Badman was a master in this art, and therefore it follows that he must be an arch and chief one in that mystery.

ATTEN: You are in the right, for I perceive that some men, though they desire it, cannot be so arch in the practice thereof as others, but are, as I suppose they call them, fools and dunces to the rest. Their heads and capacities will not serve them to act and do so wickedly. But Mr Badman wanted not a wicked head to contrive, as well as a wicked heart to do his wickedness.

WISE: True, but yet I say, such men shall at the day of Judgement be judged not only for what they are but also for what they would be. For if the thought of foolishness is sin,[235] doubtless the desire of foolishness is more sin. And if the desire be more, the endeavour after it must needs be more and more.[236] He then that is not an artificial atheist and transgressor, yet if he desires to be so, if he endeavours to be so, he shall be judged and condemned to Hell for such a one. For the law judges men, as I said, according to what they would be. He who looks upon a woman to lust after her has

233. Job 21:17.
234. There are abundance like Mr Badman.
235. Proverbs 24:9.
236. He that would be bad is bad.

committed adultery with her already in his heart.[237] By the same rule, he who would steal does steal. He who would cheat does cheat. He who would swear does swear. And he who would commit adultery does do so. For God judges men according to the working of their minds and says, 'As he thinks, so is he.' That is, so is he in his heart, in his intentions, in his desires, in his endeavours. And God's law, I say, lays hold of the desires, intentions and endeavours, even as it lays hold of the act of wickedness itself.[238] A man then who desires to be as bad as Mr Badman, and desires to be so wicked have many in their hearts, though he never attains to that proficiency in wickedness as he, shall yet be judged for as bad a man as he, because 'twas in his desires to be such a wicked one.

ATTEN: But this height of wickedness in Mr Badman will not yet out of my mind. This hard, desperate, or what shall I call it, diabolical frame of heart was in him a foundation, a groundwork, to all acts and deeds that were evil.

WISE: The heart and the desperate wickedness of it is the foundation and groundwork of all. Atheism, professed and practical, spring both out of the heart, yea, and all manner of evils besides,[239] for they are not bad deeds that make a bad man, but he is already a bad man that does bad deeds. A man must be wicked before he can do wickedness. 'Wickedness proceedeth from the wicked.'[240] 'Tis an evil tree that bears evil fruit. Men gather no grapes of thorns. The heart therefore must be evil before the man can do evil, and good before the man does good.[241]

ATTEN: Now I see the reason why Mr Badman was so base as to get a wife by dissimulation and to abuse her so like a villain when he had got her. It was because he was before by a wicked heart prepared to act wickedness.

WISE: You may be sure of it. 'For from within, out of the heart of men, proceed evil thoughts, adulteries, fornications, murders, thefts, covetousness, wickedness, deceit, lasciviousness, an evil eye,

237. Matthew 5:28.
238. Proverbs 23:7; Matthew 5; Romans 7:7.
239. A bad heart makes a bad man.
240. 1 Samuel 24:13.
241. Matthew 7:16–18.

blasphemy, pride, foolishness: all these evil things come from within, and defile the man.'[242] And a man, as his naughty mind inclines him, makes use of these, or any of these, to gratify his lust, to promote his designs, to revenge his malice, to enrich, or to wallow himself in the foolish pleasures and pastimes of this life. And all these did Mr Badman do, even to the utmost, if either opportunity, or purse, or perfidiousness, would help him to the obtaining of his purpose.

ATTEN: Purse! Why he could not but have purse to do almost what he would, having married a wife with so much money.

WISE: Hold you there. Some of Mr Badman's sins were costly, as his drinking and whoring, and keeping other bad company, though he was a man who had ways too many to get money, as well as ways too many to spend it.

ATTEN: Had he then such a good trade, for all he was such a bad man? Or was his calling so gainful to him as always to keep his purse's belly full, though he was himself a great spender?

WISE: No. It was not his trade that did it, though he had a pretty trade, too. He had another way to get money, and that by hatfuls and pocketfuls at a time.

ATTEN: Why I trust he was no highwayman, was he?

WISE: I will be sparing in my speech as to that, though some have muttered as if he could ride out now and then, about nobody but himself knew what, overnight, and come home all dirty and weary next morning. But that is not the thing I aim at.

ATTEN: Pray let me know it, if you think it convenient that I should.

WISE: I will tell you. It was this: he had an art to break[243] and get hatfuls of money by breaking.

ATTEN: But what do you mean by Mr Badman's breaking? You speak mystically, do you not?

WISE: No, no, I speak plainly. Or, if you will have it in plainer language, 'tis this: when Mr Badman had swaggered and whored away most of his wife's portion, he began to feel that he could not much longer stand upon his legs in this course of life, and keep up his trade and repute, such as he had, in the world, but by the new engine of

242. Mark 7:20–23.

243. Mr Badman had an art to break and to get money that way.

breaking. Wherefore upon a time, he gives a great and sudden[244] rush into several men's debts to the value of about four or five thousand pound, driving at the same time a very great trade by selling many things for less than they cost him to get him custom, therewith to blind his creditors' eyes. His creditors therefore feeling that he had a great employ, and dreaming that it must needs at length turn to a very good account to them, trusted him freely without mistrust, and so did others too, to the value of what was mentioned before. Well, when Mr Badman had well feathered his nest with other men's goods and money, after a little time[245] he breaks. And by and by it is noised abroad that Mr Badman had shut up shop, was gone and could trade no longer. Now, by that time his breaking was come to his creditors' ears, he had by craft and knavery made so sure of what he had that his creditors could not touch a penny. Well, when he had done, he sends his mournful, sugared letters to his creditors to let them understand what had happened unto him, and desired them not to be severe with him,[246] for he bore towards all men an honest mind and would pay so far as he was able. Now he sends his letters by a man[247] confederate with him, who could make both the worst and best of Mr Badman's case, the best for Mr Badman and the worst for his creditors. So when he comes to them, he both bemoans them and condoles Mr Badman's condition, telling of them that without a speedy bringing of things to a conclusion, Mr Badman would be able to make them no satisfaction, but at present he both could, and would, and that to the utmost of his power. And to that end, he desired that they would come over to him. Well, his creditors appoint him a time and come over, and he, meanwhile, authorises another to treat with them but will not be seen himself, unless it was on a Sunday, lest they should snap him with a writ. So his deputed friend treats with them about their concern with Mr Badman, first telling them of the great care that Mr Badman took to satisfy them and all men for whatsoever he ought, as far as in him lay, and how little he thought a while since to be in this low condition. He pleaded also the greatness of his charge, the greatness of taxes, the

244. How he managed things in order to his breaking.
245. He breaks.
246. Mr Badman's sugar words to his creditors.
247. Badman's friend.

badness of the times and the great losses that he had by many of his customers, some of which died in his debt, others were run away, and for many that were alive, he never expected a farthing from them. Yet nevertheless, he would show himself an honest man and would pay as far as he was able, and if they were willing to come to terms, he would make a composition with them, for he was not able to pay them all. The creditors asked what he would give.[248] 'Twas replied, 'Half a crown in the pound.' At this they began to huff, and he to renew his complaint and entreaty. But the creditors would not hear, and so for that time their meeting without success broke up. But after his creditors were in cool blood and admitting of second thoughts, and fearing lest delays should make them lose all, they admit of a second debate, come together again and, by many words, and great ado, they obtained five shillings i'th' pound.[249] So the money was produced, releases and discharges drawn, signed, and sealed, books crossed and all things confirmed. And then Mr Badman can put his head out of doors again and be a better man than when he shut up shop by several thousands of pounds.

ATTEN: And did he do thus indeed?

WISE: Yes, once and again. I think he broke twice or thrice.

ATTEN: And did he do it before he had need to do it?

WISE: Need! What do you mean by need? There is no need at any time for a man to play the knave.[250] He did it of a wicked mind to defraud and beguile his creditors. He had wherewithal of his father, and also by his wife, to have lived upon with lawful labour like an honest man. He had also, when he made this wicked break, though he had been a profuse and prodigal spender, to have paid his creditors their own to a farthing. But had he done so, he had not done like himself, like Mr Badman. Had he, I say, dealt like an honest man, he had then gone out of Mr Badman's road. He did it therefore of a dishonest mind and to a wicked end, to wit, that he might have wherewithal, howsoever unlawfully gotten, to follow his cups and queens, and to live in the full swinge of his lusts, even as he did before.

248. What Mr Badman propounds to his creditors.
249. They at last agree, and Mr Badman gains by breaking.
250. There is no plea for his dishonesty.

ATTEN: Why, this was a mere cheat.

WISE: It was a cheat indeed. This way of breaking – it is else but a more neat way of thieving, of picking of pockets, of breaking open of shops and of taking from men what one has nothing to do with. But though it seem easy, it is hard to learn. No man who has conscience to God or man can ever be his craftsmaster in this hellish art.

ATTEN: Oh! Sirs! What a wicked man was this?

WISE: A wicked man indeed. By this art he could tell how to make men send their goods to his shop, and then be glad to take a penny for that for which he had promised, before it came there, to give them a groat. I say, he could make them glad to take a crown for a pound's worth, and a thousand for that for which he had promised before to give them four thousand pounds.

ATTEN: This argues that Mr Badman had but little conscience.

WISE: This argues that Mr Badman had no conscience at all, for conscience, the least spark of a good conscience, cannot endure this.

ATTEN: Before we go any further in Mr Badman's matters, let me desire you, if you please, to give me an answer to these two questions.[251]

One – what do you find in the Word of God against such a practice, as this of Mr Badman's is?[252]

Two – what would you have a man do who is in his creditor's debt, and can neither pay him what he owes him, nor go on in a trade any longer?

WISE: I will answer you as well as I can. And first to the first of your questions, to wit, what I find in the Word of God against such a practice, as this of Mr Badman's is.

Answer: the Word of God does forbid this wickedness, and to make it the more odious in our eyes, it joins it with theft and robbery: 'Thou shalt not,' says God, 'defraud thy neighbour, nor rob him.'[253] Thou shalt not defraud, that is, deceive or beguile. Now thus to break is to defraud, deceive and beguile, which is, as you see, forbidden by the God of Heaven: 'Thou shalt not defraud thy neighbour, nor rob him.' It is a kind of theft and robbery thus to defraud and beguile.[254]

251. An answer to two questions.
252. First question.
253. Leviticus 19:13.
254. The heinousness of this sin.

It is a wilily robbing of his shop and picking of his pocket: a thing odious to reason and conscience, and contrary to the law of nature. It is a designed piece of wickedness and therefore a double sin. A man cannot do this great wickedness on a sudden, and through a violent assault of Satan. He who will commit this sin must have time to deliberate, that by invention, he may make it formidable, and that with lies and high dissimulations. He who commits this wickedness must first hatch it upon his bed, beat his head about it and lay his plot strong, so that to the completing of such a wickedness, there must be adjoined many sins, and they too, must go hand in hand until it be completed. But what said the scripture? 'That no man go beyond and defraud his brother in any matter: because that the Lord is the avenger of all such.' [255, 256] But this kind of breaking is a-going beyond my brother. This is a compassing of him about that I may catch him in my net, and as I said, an art to rob my brother, and to pick his pocket, and that with his consent, which does not therefore mitigate, but so much the more greaten and make odious the offence. For men who are thus wilily abused cannot help themselves. They are taken in a deceitful net. But God will here concern himself. He will be the avenger. He will be the avenger of all such either here or in another world.

And this, the Apostle testifies again, where he says, 'But he that doeth wrong shall receive for the wrong which he hath done: and there is no respect of persons.'[257, 258] That is, there is no man, be he what he will, if he will be guilty of this sin of going beyond, of beguiling of and doing wrong to his brother, but God will call him to an account for it, and will pay him with vengeance for it, too, for there is no respect of persons.

I might add that this sin of wronging, of going beyond and defrauding of my neighbour: it is like that first prank that the Devil played with our first parents,[259] as the altar that Uriah built for Ahaz was taken from the fashion of that that stood at Damascus, to be the

255. 1 Thessolonians 4:6.
256. Fair warning.
257. Colossians 3:25.
258. Fair warning again.
259. He that designedly commits this sin is like the Devil.

very pattern of it. 'The serpent beguiled me,' says Eve. Mr Badman beguiles his creditors. The serpent beguiled Eve with lying promises of gain. And so did Mr Badman beguile his creditors. The serpent said one thing and meant another when he beguiled Eve, and so did Mr Badman when he beguiled his creditors.

That man therefore who does thus deceive and beguile his neighbour, imitates the Devil. He takes his examples from him, and not from God, the Word or good men. And this did Mr Badman.

And now to your second question: to wit, what I would have a man do, who is in his creditors' debt, and who can neither pay him nor go on in a trade any longer?[260]

Answer: first of all, if this is his case, and he knows it, let him not run one penny further in his creditors' debt, for that cannot be done with good conscience. He who knows he cannot pay and yet will run into debt, does knowingly wrong and defraud his neighbour, and falls under that sentence of the Word of God, 'The wicked borroweth, and payeth not again.'[261] Yea worse, he borrows though at the very same time he knows that he cannot pay again. He does also craftily take away what is his neighbours'. That is therefore the first thing that I would propound to such: let him not run any further into his creditors' debt.[262]

Secondly, after this, let him consider[263] how and by what means he was brought into such a condition that he could not pay his just debts. To wit, whether it was by his own remissness in his calling, by living too high in diet or apparel, by lending too ravishingly that which was none of his own, to his loss, or whether by the immediate hand and judgement of God.

If by searching he finds that this has come upon him through remissness in his calling, extravagancies in his family or the like, let him labour for a sense of his sin and wickedness[264] for he has sinned against the Lord. First in his being slothful in business and in not providing, to wit, of is own by the sweat of his brows, or other

260. Second question.
261. Psalm 37:21.
262. How those who are bankrupt should deal with their consciences.
263. Good advice.
264. Romans 12:11.

honest ways, for those of his own house,[265] and secondly in being lavishing in diet and apparel in the family, or in lending to others that which was none of his own. This cannot be done with good conscience. It is both against reason and nature, and therefore must be a sin against God. I say therefore, if thus this debtor has done, if ever he would live quietly in conscience and comfortably in his condition for the future, let him humble himself before God and repent of this his wickedness. For 'he also that is slothful in his work is brother to him that is a great waster'.[266] To be slothful and a waster, too, is to be, as it were, a double sinner.

But again, as this man should enquire into these things, so he should also into this: 'How came I into this way of dealing in which I have now miscarried? Is it a way that my parents brought me up in, put me apprentice to, or that by providence I was first thrust into? Or is it a way into which I have twisted myself, as not being contented with my first lot, that by God and my parents I was cast into?' This ought duly to be considered.[267] And if upon search,[268] a man shall find that he is out of the place and calling into which he was put by his parents, or the providence of God, and has miscarried in a new way that, through pride and dislike of his first state, he has chosen rather to embrace. His miscarriage is his sin, the fruit of his pride and a token of the judgement of God upon him for his leaving of his first state. And for this he ought, as for the former, to be humble and penitent before the Lord.

But if by search, he finds that his poverty came by none of these – if by honest search, he finds it so – and can say with good conscience, 'I went not out of my place and state in which God by his providence had put me, but have abode with God in the calling wherein I was called, and have wrought hard and fared meanly, been civilly apparelled and have not directly nor indirectly made away with my creditors' goods,' then has his fall come upon him by the immediate hand of God, whether by visible or invisible ways. For sometimes it comes by visible ways: to wit, by fire, by thieves, by loss

265. 1 Timothy 5:8.
266. Proverbs 18:9.
267. Good counsel again.
268. How to find that your decay came by the judgement of God, or by your miscarriage.

of cattle or the wickedness of sinful dealers, etc. And sometimes by means invisible, and then no man knows how. We only see things are going, but cannot see by what way they go. Well, now suppose that a man by an immediate hand of God is brought to a morsel of bread, what must he do now?[269] I answer: his surest way is still to think that this is the fruit of some sin, though possibly not sin in the management of his calling, yet of some other sin. God 'casteth away the substance of the wicked'.[270] Therefore let him still humble himself before his God,[271] because His hand is upon him, and say, 'What sin is this for which this hand of God is upon me?' And let him be diligent to find it out, for some sin is the cause of this judgement, for God 'doth not afflict willingly nor grieve the children of men'.[272] Either the heart is too much set upon the world, or religion is too much neglected in your family or something. There is a snake in the grass, a worm in the gourd, some sin in your bosom for the sake of which God does thus deal with you.

Thirdly, this thus done, let that man again consider thus with himself, 'perhaps God is now changing of my condition and state in the world. He has let me live in fashion, in fullness and abundance of worldly glory, and I did not to His glory improve, as I should, that his good dispensation to me.[273] But when I lived in full and fat pasture, I did there lift up the heel. Therefore He will now turn me into hard commons that with leanness, and hunger, and meanness, and want, I may spend the rest of my days.' But let him do this without murmuring and repining. Let him do it in a godly manner, submitting himself to the judgement of God. Let the rich rejoice in that 'he is made low'.[274]

This is duty, and it may be privilege to those that are under this hand of God. And for your encouragement to this hard work – for this is a hard work – consider of these four things.[275]

269. Another question.
270. Proverbs 10:3.
271. 1 Peter 5:6.
272. Lamentations 3:33.
273. Good advice again. Deuteronomy 32:15.
274. James 1:9–10.
275. Consider four things.

One – this is right lying down under God's hand, and the way to be exalted in God's time. When God would have Job embrace the dunghill, he embraces it, and says, 'The Lord giveth, and the Lord taketh away; blessed be the name of the Lord.'[276]

Two – consider that there are blessings also that attend a low condition more than all the world are aware of. A poor condition has preventing mercy attending of it. The poor, because they are poor, are not capable of sinning against God as the rich man does.

Three – the poor can more clearly see himself preserved by the providence of God than the rich, for he trusts in the abundance of his riches.[277]

Four – it may be God has made you poor, because he would make you rich. 'Hearken, my beloved brethren, hath not God chosen the poor of this world rich in faith, and heirs of the kingdom which he hath promised to them that love him?'[278]

I am persuaded if men upon whom this hand of God is would thus quietly lie down, and humble themselves under it, they would find more peace, yea, more blessing of God attending them in it than the most of men are aware of. But this is a hard chapter, and therefore I do not expect that many should either read it with pleasure, or desire to take my counsel.

Having thus spoken to the broken man with reference to his own self, I will now speak to him as he stands related to his creditors.

In the next place, therefore let him fall upon the most[279] honest way of dealing with his creditors, and that I think must be this.

First, let him timely make them acquainted with his condition, and also do to them these three things.

One – let him heartily and unfeignedly ask them forgiveness for the wrong that he has done them.

Two – let him proffer them all, and the whole all that ever he has in the world. Let him hide nothing. Let him strip himself to his raiment for them. Let him not keep a ring, a spoon or anything from them.

276. Job 1:21, 2:8.
277. Psalm 49:6.
278. James 2:5.
279. Honest dealing with creditors.

Three – if none of these two will satisfy them, let him proffer them his body to be at their disposal, to wit, either to abide imprisonment their pleasure, or to be at their service till by labour and travel he has made them such amends as they in reason think fit, only reserving something for the succour of his poor and distressed family out of his labour, which in reason, and conscience, and nature, he is bound also to take care of. Thus shall he make them what amends he is able for the wrong that he has done them in wasting and spending of their estates.

By thus doing, he submits himself to God's rod, commits himself to the dispose of his providence. Yea, by thus doing, he casts the lot of his present and future condition into the lap of his creditors, and leaves the whole disposing thereof to the Lord,[280] even as he shall order and incline their hearts to do with him. And let that be either to forgive him, or to take that which he has for satisfaction, or to lay his body under affliction, this way or that, according to law. Can he, I say, thus leave the whole dispose to God, let the issue be what it will, that man shall have peace in his mind afterward. And the comforts of that state, which will be comforts that attend equity, justice and duty, will be more unto him, because more is accorded to godliness than can be the comforts that are the fruits of injustice, fraudulency and deceit. Besides, this is the way to engage God to favour him by the sentence of his creditors, for He can entreat them to use him kindly, and He will do it when His ways are pleasing in His sight. 'When a man's ways please the Lord, he maketh even his enemies to be at peace with him.'[281] And surely, for a man to seek to make restitution for wrongs done to the utmost of his power by what he is, has and enjoys in this world, is the best way, in that capacity and with reference to that thing, that a man can at this time be found active in.

But he that does otherwise abides in his sin, refuses to be disposed of by the providence of God, chooses a high estate, though not attained in God's way. When God's will is that he should descend into a low one, yea, he desperately says in his heart and actions, 'I will be my own chooser, and that in my own way, whatever happens or follows thereupon.'

280. Proverbs 16:33.
281. Jeremiah 15:10–11; Proverbs 16:7.

ATTEN: You have said well, in my mind. But suppose now, that Mr Badman were here. Could he not object as to what you have said, saying, 'Go and teach your brethren who are professors this lesson, for they, as I am, are guilty of breaking. Yea, I am apt to think of that which you call my knavish way of breaking, to wit, of breaking before they have need to break. But if not so, yet they are guilty of neglect in their calling,[282] of living higher, both in fare and apparel, than their trade or income will maintain. Besides, who they do break, all the world very well knows, and who they have the art to plead for a composition is very well known to men. And that it is usual with them, to hide their linen, their plate, their jewels and, 'tis to be thought, sometimes money and goods besides, is as common as four eggs a penny. And thus they beguile men, debauch their consciences, sin against their profession, and make – 'tis to be feared, their lusts in all this, and the fulfilling of them – their end.' I say, if Mr Badman were here to object thus unto you, what would be your reply?

WISE: What! Why I would say, 'I hope no good man, no man of good conscience, no man who either fears God, regards the credit of religion, the peace of God's people or the salvation of his own soul, will do thus.'

Professors: such perhaps there may be, and who, upon earth can help it? Jades there are of all colours.[283] If men will profess and make their profession a stalking horse to beguile their neighbours of their estates, as Mr Badman himself did, when he beguiled her who now is with sorrow his wife, who can help it? The churches of old were pestered with such, and therefore no marvel if these perilous difficult times be so. But mark how the apostle words it: 'Nay, ye do wrong, and defraud, and that your brethren. Know ye not that the unrighteous shall not inherit the kingdom of God? Be not deceived: neither fornicators, nor idolaters, nor adulterers, nor effeminate, nor abusers of themselves with mankind, nor thieves, nor covetous, nor drunkards, nor revilers, nor extortioners, shall inherit the kingdom of God.'[284]

282. A heavy blot upon religion.
283. If knaves will make profession their cloak to be vile, who can help it?
284. 1 Corinthians 6:8–10; 2 Timothy 3:1–5.

None of these shall be saved in this state, nor shall profession deliver them from the censure of the godly, when they shall be manifest such to be. But their profession we cannot help. How can we help it, if men should ascribe to themselves the title of holy ones, godly ones, zealous ones, self-denying ones or any other such glorious title? And while they thus call themselves, they should be the veriest rogues for all evil, sin and villainy imaginable, who could help it? True, they are a scandal to religion, a grief to the honest hearted, an offence to the world and a stumbling stone to the weak, and these offences have come, do come and will come, do what all the world can. But woe be to them through whom they come.[285] Let such professors therefore be disowned by all true Christians, and let them be reckoned among those base men of the world whom, by such actions, they most resemble. They are Mr Badman's kindred.

For[286] they are a shame to religion, I say, these sleathy,[viii] rob-shop, pickpocket men. They are a shame to religion, and religious men should be ashamed of them. God puts such a one among the fools of the world, therefore let not Christians put them among those who are wise for heaven. 'As the partridge sitteth on eggs, and hatcheth them not; so he that getteth riches, and not by right, shall leave them in the midst of his days, and at his end shall be a fool.'[287] And the man under consideration is one of these, and therefore must look to fall by this judgement.

A professor! And practice such villainies as these! Such a one is not worthy to bear that name any longer. We may say to such as the Prophet spoke to their like, to wit, to the rebellious who were in the house of Israel. 'Go ye, serve ye every one his idols, and hereafter also, if ye will not hearken unto me: but pollute ye my holy name no more with your gifts, and with your idols.'[288]

Go professors, go. Leave off profession unless you will lead your lives according to your profession. Better never profess than to make profession a stalking horse to sin, deceit, to the Devil and Hell.

285. Matthew 18:6–8.
286. Let such be disowned of all good men.
287. Jeremiah 17:11.
288. Ezekiel 20:38–39.

The ground and rules of religion allow not any such thing: 'Receive us,' says the Apostle, 'we have wronged no man, we have corrupted no man, we have defrauded no man,'[289] intimating that those who are guilty of wronging, corrupting or defrauding of any should not be admitted to the fellowship of saints, no, nor into the common catalogue of brethren with them.

Nor can men with all their rhetoric and eloquent speaking prove themselves fit for the kingdom of Heaven, or men of good conscience on earth.[290] O that godly plea of Samuel: 'Behold, here I am: witness against me before the Lord, and before his anointed: whose ox have I taken? Or whose ass have I taken? Or whom have I defrauded? Whom have I oppressed,'[291] etc? This was to do like a man of good conscience indeed. And in this his appeal, he was so justified in the consciences of the whole congregation, that they could not but with one voice, as with one mouth, break out jointly and say, 'Thou hast not defrauded us, nor oppressed us.'[292]

A professor and defraud, away with him! A professor should not owe any man anything but love. A professor should provide things not of other men's, but of his own, of his own honest getting and that not only in the sight of God, but of all men, that he may adorn the doctrine of God our saviour in all things.

ATTEN: But[293] suppose God should blow upon a professor in his estate and calling, and he should be run out before he is aware. Must he be accounted to be like Mr Badman, and lie under the same reproach as he?

WISE: No,[294] if he has dutifully done what he could to avoid it. It is possible for a ship to sink at sea notwithstanding the most faithful endeavour of the most skilful pilot under Heaven. And thus, as I suppose, it was with the Prophet who left his wife in debt to the hazarding the slavery of her children by the creditors.[295] He was no

289. 2 Corinthians 7:2.
290. Mark 10:19.
291. 1 Samuel 12:3.
292. 1 Samuel 12:4.
293. A question.
294. An answer.
295. 2 Kings 4:1–2.

profuse man, nor one who was given to defraud, for the text says he feared God. Yet, as I said, he was run out more than she could pay.

If God would blow upon a man, who can help it? And he will do so sometimes,[296] because he will change dispensations with men, and because he will try their graces.[297] Yea, also because he will overthrow the wicked with his judgements, and all these things are seen in Job. But then the consideration of this should bid men have a care that they be honest, lest this comes upon them for their sin. It should also bid them beware of launching further into the world, than in an honest way by ordinary means they can godlily make their retreat, for the further in, the greater fall. It should also teach them, to beg of God his blessing upon their endeavours, their honest and lawful endeavours. And it should put them upon a diligent looking to their steps, that if in their going they should hear the ice crack, they may timely go back again.

These things considered and duly put in practice, if God will blow upon a man, then let him be content, and with Job embrace the dunghill. Let him give unto all their dues, and not fight against the providence of God, but humble himself rather under his mighty hand, which comes to strip him naked and bare. For he that does otherwise, fights against God and declares that he is a stranger to that of Paul. 'I know both how to be abased, and I know how to abound: everywhere and in all things I am instructed both to be full and to be hungry, both to abound and to suffer need.'[298]

ATTEN: But Mr Badman would not, I believe, have put this difference between things feigned and those that fall of necessity.

WISE: If he will not, God will. Conscience will. And that not your own only, but the consciences of all those who have seen the way, and who have known the truth of the condition of such a one.

ATTEN: Well, let us at this time leave this matter, and return again to Mr Badman.

WISE: With all my heart will I proceed to give you a relation of what is yet behind of his life, in order to our discourse of his death.

ATTEN: But pray do it with as much brevity as you can.

296. Haggai 1:9.
297. God does sometimes blow upon his own people. How they should do at that time.
298. Philip 4:12.

WISE: Why? Are you a-weary of my relating of things?

ATTEN: No. But it pleases me to hear a great deal in few words.

WISE: I profess not myself an artist that way, but yet as briefly as I can, I will pass through what of his life is behind. And again I shall begin with his fraudulent dealing, as before I have showed with his creditors, so now with his customers, and those that he had otherwise to deal withal.

He dealt by deceitful weights and measures.[299] He kept weights to buy by, and weights to sell by. Measures to buy by, and measures to sell by. Those he bought by were too big, those he sold by were too little.

Besides, he could use a thing called sleight of hand, if he had to do with other men's weights and measures, and by that means make them, whether he did buy or sell, yea, though his customer or chapman looked on, turn to his own advantage.

Moreover, he had the art to misreckon men in their accounts whether by weight or measure, or money, and would often do it to his worldly advantage and their loss. What say you to Mr Badman now?

And if a question was made of his faithful dealing, he had his servants ready that to his purpose he had brought up, who would avouch and swear to his book or word. This was Mr Badman's practice. What think you of Mr Badman now?

ATTEN: Think! Why I can think no other but that he was a man left to himself, a naughty man, for these, as his other, were naughty things. If the tree, as indeed it may, ought to be judged what it is by its fruits, then Mr Badman must needs be a bad tree. But pray, for my further satisfaction, show me now by the Word of God evil of this his practice, and first of his using false weights and measures.

WISE: The evil of that! Why, the evil of that appears to every eye. The heathens who live like beasts and brutes in many things do abominate and abhor such wickedness as this. Let a man but look upon these things as he goes by, and he shall see enough in them from the light of nature to make him loathe so base a practice, although Mr Badman loved it.

ATTEN: But show me something out of the Word against it, will you?

299. More of Mr Badman's fraudulent dealing. He used deceitful weights and scales.

WISE: I will willingly do it. And first we will look into the Old Testament.[300] 'Ye shall,' says God there, 'do no unrighteousness in judgement, in meteyard,[ix] in weight, or in measure. Just balances, just weights, a just ephah, and a just hin,[x] shall ye have.'[301] This is the law of God, and that which all men according to the law of the land ought to obey. So again: 'Ye shall have just balances, and a just ephah,' etc.[302]

Now having showed you the law, I will also show you how God takes swerving therefrom. A false balance is not good. 'A false balance is abomination to the Lord.'[303] Some have just weights but false balances, and by virtue of those false balances by their just weights, they deceive the country.[304] Wherefore God, first of all, commands that the balance be made just. A just balance you shall have. Else they may be, yea, are deceivers, notwithstanding their just weights.

Now, having commanded that men have a just balance, and testifying that a false one is an abomination to the Lord, he proceeds also unto weight and measure.

'Thou shalt not have in thy bag divers weights, a great and a small.' That is one to buy by, and another to sell by, as Mr Badman had. 'Thou shalt not have in thy house divers measures, a great and a small,' and these had Mr Badman also. 'But thou shalt have a perfect and a just weight; a perfect and a just measure shalt thou have, that thy days may be lengthened in the land which the Lord thy God giveth thee. For all that do such things,' that is, who use false weights and measures, 'and all that do unrighteously, are an abomination unto the Lord.'[305] See now both how plentiful and how punctual the scripture is in this matter? But perhaps it may be objected that all this is old law and therefore has nothing to do with us under the New Testament. Not that I think you, neighbour, will object thus. Well, to this foolish objection, let us make an answer.

300. Leviticus 19:35–36.
301. Of just weights and measures.
302. Ezekiel 45:10.
303. Proverbs 20:23, 11:1.
304. The evil of deceitful balances, weights and measures.
305. Deuteronomy 25:13–16.

First, he who makes this objection, if he does it to overthrow the authority of those texts,[306] discovers that himself is first cousin to Mr Badman, for a just man is willing to speak reverently of those commands. That man therefore has, I doubt, but little conscience, if any at all, that is good who thus objects against the text. But let us look into the New Testament, and there we shall see how Christ confirms the same. Where he commands that men make to others good measure, including also that they make good weight, telling such that do thus, or those who do it not, that they may be encouraged to do it. 'Good measure, pressed down, and shaken together, and running over, shall men give into your bosom. For with the same measure that ye mete withal it shall be measured to you again,'[307] to wit, both from God and man.

For as God will show His indignation against the false man by taking away even that he has, so he will deliver up the false man to the oppressor, and the extortioner shall catch from him as well as he has caught from his neighbour. Therefore another scripture says, 'when thou shalt make an end to deal treacherously, they shall deal treacherously with thee.'[308] That the New Testament also has an inspection into men's trading, yea, even with their weights and measures, is evident from these general exhortations. Defraud not. Lie not one to another. Let no man go beyond his brother in any matter, for God is the avenger of all such. Whatsoever ye do, do it heartily, as unto the Lord, doing all in His name, to His glory, and the like.[309] All these injunctions and commandments do respect our life and conversation among men with reference to our dealing, trading, and so consequently they forbid false, deceitful, yea, all doings that are corrupt.

Having thus in a word or two showed you that these things are bad, I will next, for the conviction of those who use them, show you where God says they are to be found.[310]

306. The old and new law commands all men to be honest and upright in their weights and measures.

307. Luke 6:38.

308. Isaiah 33:1.

309. Pat scriptures for our purpose: Mark 10:19; Colossians 3:9; 1 Thessalonians 4:6; Colossians 3:23.

310. Where false weights and measures are to be found.

One – they are not to be found in the house of the good and godly man, for He, as his God, abhors them. But they are to be found in the house of evil doers,[311] such as Mr Badman's is. 'Are there, says the prophet, 'yet the treasures of wickedness in the house of the wicked, and the scant measure that is abominable?'[312] Are they there yet, notwithstanding God's forbidding, notwithstanding God's tokens of anger against those that do such things? Oh, how loath is a wicked man to let go a sweet, a gainful sin, when he hath hold of it! They hold fast deceit, they refuse to let it go.

Two – these deceitful weights and measures are not to be found in the house of the merciful but in the house of the cruel, in the house of them who love to oppress.[313] 'The balances of deceit are in his hand: he loveth to oppress.'[314] He is given to oppression and cruelty, therefore he uses such wicked things in his calling. Yea, he is a very cheat, and as was hinted before concerning Mr Badman's breaking, so I say now concerning his using these deceitful weights and measures, it is as bad, as base, as to take a purse, or pick a pocket, for it is a plain robbery. It takes away from a man that which is his own, even the price of his money.

Three – the deceitful weights and measures are not to be found in the house of such as relieve the belly, and that cover the loins of the poor, but of such as indeed would swallow them up.[315] 'Hear this, oh ye that swallow up the needy, even to make the poor of the land to fail, saying, When will the new moon be gone, that we may sell corn? And the sabbath, that we may set forth wheat, making the ephah small, and the shekel great, and falsifying the balances by deceit?' making the measure small, and the price great, 'that we may buy the poor for silver, and the needy for a pair of shoes; yea, and sell the refuse of the wheat? The Lord hath sworn by the excellency of Jacob, Surely I will never forget any of their works.'[316] So detestable and vile a thing is this in the sight of God.

311. 1. With evil doers.
312. Micah 6:10.
313. 2. With the merciless and oppressors.
314. Hosea 12:7.
315. 3. With such as would swallow up the poor.
316. Amos 8:4–7.

Four – God abominates the thoughts of calling of those who use false weights and measures by any other term than that they be impure ones[317] or the like. 'Shall I count them pure,' says He, 'with the bag of deceitful weights?'[318] No, by no means. They are impure ones. Their hands are defiled. Deceitful gain is in their houses. They have gotten what they have by coveting an evil covetousness, and therefore must and shall be counted among the impure, among the wicked of the world.

Thus you see how full and plain the Word of God is, against this sin, and them who use it. And therefore Mr Badman, for that he used by these things thus to rook and cheat his neighbours, is rightly rejected from having his name in and among the catalogue of the godly.

ATTEN: But I am persuaded that the using of these things, and the doing by them thus deceitfully, is not counted so great an evil by some.

WISE: Whether it is counted an evil or a virtue by men, it matters not. You see by the scriptures, the judgement of God upon it. It was not counted an evil by Mr Badman, nor is it by any who still are treading in his steps. But I say, 'tis no matter how men esteem of things. Let us adhere to the judgement of God. And the rather, because when we ourselves have done weighing and measuring to others, then God will weigh and measure both us and our actions. And when he does so, as he will do shortly, then woe be to him to whom and of whose actions it shall be thus said by him: 'Tekel; thou art weighed in the balances, and art found wanting.'[319] God will then recompense their evil of deceiving upon their own head, when he shall shut them out of his presence, favour and kingdom forever and ever.

ATTEN: But 'tis a wonder that since Mr Badman's common practice was to do thus, that someone or more did not find him out and blame him for this his wickedness.

WISE: For the generality of people, he went away clever with his knavery. For what with his balance, his false balance and good weight, and what with his sleight of hand to boot, he beguiled, sometimes a little and

317. 4. With impure ones.
318. Micah 6:11.
319. Daniel 5:27.

sometimes more, most that he had to deal with. Besides, those who use this naughty trade are either such as blind men with a show of religion, or by hectoring the buyer out by words. I must confess Mr Badman was not so arch at the first,[320] that is, to do it by show of religion. For now he began to grow threadbare, though some of his brethren are arch enough this way, yea, and of his sisters too, for I told you at first that there was a great many of them and of them good, but for hectoring, for swearing, for lying: if these things would make weight and measure, they should not be wanting to Mr Badman's customers.

ATTEN: Then it seem he kept good weights and a bad balance. Well that was better than that both should be bad.

WISE: Not at all. There lay the depth of his deceit.[321] For if any at any time found fault that he used them hardly, and that they wanted their weight of things, he would reply, 'Why did you not see them weighed? Will you not believe your own eyes? If you question my weights, pray carry them where you will. I will maintain them to be good and just.' The same he would say of his scales. So he blinded all by his balance.

ATTEN: This is cunning indeed. But as you say, there must be also something done or said, to blind therewith, and this I perceive Mr Badman had.

WISE: Yes. He had many ways to blind, but he was never clever at it by making a show of religion, though he cheated his wife therewith, for he was, especially by those that dwelt near him, too well known to do that, though he would bungle at it as well as he could. But there are some who are arch villains this way. They shall, to view, live a whole life religiously, and yet shall be guilty of these most horrible sins. And yet religion in itself is never the worse, nor yet the true professors of it. But as Luther says, in the name of God begins all mischief, for hypocrites have no other way to bring their evils to maturity, but by using and mixing the name of God and religion therewith.[322] Thus they become whited walls,[323] for by this white,

320 How Mr Badman did cheat, and hide his cheating.
321 Good weights and a bad balance a deep piece of knavery.
322. A cloak of religion to blind Mr Cheat's knavery.
323. Matthew 23.

the white of religion, the dirt of their actions is hidden. Thus also they become graves that appear not, and they that go over them, that have to do with them, are not aware of them, but suffer themselves to be deluded by them. Yea, if there shall, as there will sometimes, rise a doubt in the heart of the buyer about the weight and measure he should have, why, he suffers his very senses to be also deluded, by recalling of his chapman's religion to mind, and thinks verily that not his good chapman but himself is out, for he dreams not that his chapman can deceive. But if the buyer shall find it out, and shall make it apparent, that he is beguiled, then shall he be healed by having amends made, and perhaps fault shall be laid upon servants, etc. And so Master Cheat shall stand for a right honest man in the eye of his customer, though the next time he shall pick his pocket again.

Some[324] plead custom for their cheat, as if that could acquit them before the tribunal of God. And others say it came to them for so much, and therefore another must take it for so much, though there is wanting both as to weight and measure. But in all these things there are juggles. Or if not, such must know, 'That which is altogether just shalt thou follow.'[325] Suppose that I am cheated myself with a brass half-crown, must I therefore cheat another therewith? If this is bad in the whole, it is also bad in the parts. Therefore, however you are dealt withal in your buying, yet you must deal justly in selling, or you sin against your soul, and have become as Mr Badman. And know, that a pretence to custom is nothing worth. 'Tis not custom but good conscience that will help at God's tribunal.

ATTEN: But I am persuaded that that which is gotten by men this way does them but little good.

WISE: I am of your mind for that, but this is not considered by those thus minded. For if they can get it, though they get, as we say, the Devil and all, by their getting, yet they are content, and count that their getting is much.

Little good! Why do you think they consider that? No, no more than they consider what they shall do in the judgement, at the day of

324. Some plead custom to cheat.
325. Deuteronomy 16:20.

God Almighty, for their wrong getting of what they get, and that is just nothing at all.[326]

But to give you a more direct answer: this kind of getting is so far off from doing them little good, that it does them no good at all, because thereby they lose their own souls. What shall it profit a man if he shall gain the whole world, and lose his own soul?[327] He loses then, he loses greatly who gets after this fashion. This is the man who is penny-wise and pound-foolish. This is he who loses his good sheep for a halfpenny-worth of tar, who loses a soul for a little of the world. And then what does he get thereby, but loss and damage?[328] Thus he gets, or rather loses about the world to come. But what does he get in this world, more than travel and sorrow, vexation of spirit, and disappointment? Men aim at blessedness in getting, I mean, at temporal blessedness. But the man who thus gets shall not have that, for though an inheritance after this manner may be hastily gotten at the beginning, yet the end thereof shall not be blessed. They gather it indeed, and think to keep it too, but what says Solomon? God casts it away. The Lord will not suffer the soul of the righteous to famish, but he casts away the substance of the wicked.

The time, as I said, that they do enjoy it, it shall do them no good at all, but long to be sure they must not have it. For God will either take it away in their lifetime, or else in the generation following, according to that of Job: 'He,' the wicked, 'may prepare it, but the just shall put it on, and the innocent shall divide the silver.'[329]

Consider that also that is written in the Proverbs: 'A good man leaveth an inheritance to his children's children: and the wealth of the sinner is laid up for the just.'[330] What then does he get thereby, that gets by dishonest means? Why, he gets sin and wrath, Hell and damnation. And now tell me how much he does get. This, I say, is his getting. So that as David says, we may be bold to say, too, I beheld the wicked in great prosperity, and presently I cursed his habitation, for it cannot prosper with him. Fluster and huff, and make a-do for

326. They get nothing who cozen and cheat.
327. Mark 9.
328. Proverbs 10:3; Jeremiah 15:13, 17:3.
329. Job 27:17.
330. Proverbs 13:22.

a while he may, but God has determined that both he and it shall melt like grease, and any observing man may see it so. Behold, the unrighteous man in a way of injustice gets much, and loads himself with thick clay, but anon it withers, it decays, and even he, or the generation following, decline and return to beggary.

And this Mr Badman, notwithstanding his cunning and crafty tricks to get money, did die, nobody can tell whether worth a farthing or no.

ATTEN: He had all the bad tricks, I think, that it was possible for a man to have to get money. One would think that he should have been rich.

WISE: You reckon too fast, if you count these all his bad tricks to get money, for he had more besides.[331]

If his customers were in his books – as it should go hard but he would have them there, at least, if he thought he could make any advantage of them – then, then would he be sure to impose upon them his worst, even very bad commodity, yet set down for it the price that the best was sold at. Like those who sold the refuse wheat, or the worst of the wheat, making the shekel great,[332] yet hoisting up the price. This was Mr Badman's way. He[333] would sell goods that cost him not the best price by far for as much as he sold the best of all for. He had also a trick to mingle his commodity that that which was bad might go off with the less mistrust.

Besides, if his customers at any time paid him money, let them look to themselves and to their acquaintances, for he would usually attempt to call for that payment again, especially if he thought that there were hopes of making a prize thereby, and then to be sure if they could not produce good and sufficient ground of the payment, a hundred to one but they paid it again. Sometimes the honest chapman would appeal to his servants for proof of the payment of money, but they were trained up by him to say after his mind, right or wrong, so that, relief that way, he could get none.

ATTEN: It is a bad, yea, an abominable thing for a man to have such servants. For by such means a poor customer may be undone and not

331. More of Mr Badman's bad tricks.
332. Amos 8.
333. Another art to cheat withal.

know how to help himself. Alas! If the master be so unconscionable, as I perceive Mr Badman was, to call for his money twice, and if his servant will swear that it is a due debt, where is any help for such a man? He must sink. There is no remedy.

WISE: This is very bad, but this has been a practice, and that hundreds of years ago. But what says the Word of God? 'I punish all those that leap on the threshold, which fill their masters' houses with violence and deceit.'[334, 335]

Mr Badman also had this art. Could he get a man at advantage, that is, if his chapman dared not go from him, or if the commodity he wanted could not for the present be conveniently had elsewhere. Then let him look to himself, he would surely make his purse strings crack. He would exact upon him without any pity or conscience.

ATTEN: That was extortion, was it not? I pray let me hear your judgement of extortion, what it is, and when committed?

WISE: Extortion[336] is a screwing from men more than by the law of God or men is right, and it is committed sometimes by them in office about fees, rewards and the like. But 'tis most commonly committed by men of trade who, without all conscience, when they have the advantage, will make a prey of their neighbour. And thus was Mr Badman an extortioner. For although he did not exact, and force away, as bailiffs and clerks have used to do, yet he had his opportunities, and such cruelty to make use of them that he would often, in his way, be extorting and forcing of money out of his neighbour's pocket. For every man who makes a prey of his advantage upon his neighbour's necessities, to force from him more than in reason and conscience, according to the present prizes of things such commodity is worth, may very well be called an extortioner, and judged for one who has no inheritance in the kingdom of God.[337]

ATTEN: Well, this Badman was a sad wretch.

WISE: Thus you have often said before. But now we are in discourse of this, give me leave a little to go on. We have a great many people

334. Zephaniah 1:9.
335. Servants observe these words.
336. Of Extortion.
337. 1 Corinthians 6:9–10.

in the country too who live all their days in the practice and so under the guilt of extortion. People, alas, who think scorn to be so accounted.

As for example,[338] there is a poor body who dwells, we will suppose, so many miles from the market. And this man wants a bushel of grist, a pound of butter or a cheese for himself, his wife and poor children. But dwelling so far from the market, if he goes there, he shall lose his day's work, which will be eight pence or ten pence damage to him, and that is something to a poor man. So he goes to one of his masters or dames for what he wants, and asks them to help him with such a thing. 'Yes,' say they, 'you may have it.' But withal they will give him a gripe, perhaps make him pay as much or more for it at home, as they can get when they have carried it five miles to a market, yea, and that too for the refuse of their commodity. But in this the women are especially faulty, in the sale of their butter and cheese, etc. Now this is a kind of extortion. It is a-making a prey of the necessity of the poor. It is a grinding of their faces, a buying and selling of them.

But above all, your[339] hucksters who buy up the poor man's victuals by wholesale and sell it to him again for unreasonable gains by retail, and as we call it, by piecemeal. They are got into a way, after a stingeing rate, to play their game upon such by extortion. I mean such who buy up butter, cheese, eggs, bacon, etc. by wholesale, and sell it again, as they call it, by penny worths, two penny worths, a half-penny worth, or the like, to the poor, all the week after the market is past. These, though I will not condemn them all, do, many of them, bite and pinch the poor by this kind of evil dealing. These destroy the poor because he is poor, and that is a grievous sin. 'He that oppresseth the poor to increase his riches, and he that giveth to the rich, shall surely come to want.' Therefore he says again, 'Rob not the poor, because he is poor: neither oppress the afflicted in the gate. For the Lord will plead their cause, and spoil the soul of those that spoiled them.'[340] Oh, that he that grips and grinds the face of the

338. Who are extortioners.
339. Hucksters.
340. Proverbs 22:16, 22–23.

poor, would take notice of these two scriptures! Here is threatened the destruction of the estate, yea, and of the soul too, of them who oppress the poor. Their soul we shall better see where, and in what condition that is in, when the day of doom has come. But for the estates of such, they usually quickly moulter, and that sometimes all men, and sometimes no man knows how.

Besides, these are usurers. Yea, they take usury for victuals, which thing the Lord has forbidden.[341] And because they cannot so well do it on the market day, therefore they do it, as I said, when the market is over, for then the poor falls into their mouths, and are necessitated to have, as they can, for their need, and they are resolved they shall pay soundly for it. Perhaps some will find fault for my meddling thus with other folks' matters, and for my thus prying into the secrets of their iniquity. But to such I would say, since such actions are evil, 'tis time they were hissed out of the world. For all who do such things offend against God, wrong their neighbour and, like Mr Badman, do provoke God to judgement. God knows, there is abundance of deceit in the world!

WISE: Deceit! Aye, but I have not told you the thousandth part of it, nor is it my business now to rake to the bottom of that dunghill. What would you say, if I should anatomise some of those vile wretches called pawn brokers who lend money and goods to poor people who are by necessity forced to such an inconvenience, and will make, by one trick or other, the interest of what they so lend amount to thirty, forty, yea, sometimes fifty pound by the year. Notwithstanding the principle is secured by a sufficient pawn, which they will keep too at last, if they can find any shift to cheat the wretched borrower.

ATTEN: Say! Why such miscreants are the pest and vermin of the commonwealth, not fit for the society of men. But methinks by some of those things you discoursed before, you seem to import that it is not lawful for a man to make the best of his own.

WISE: If by making the best, you mean, to sell for as much as by hook or crook he can get for his commodity, then I say, it is not lawful. And if I should say the contrary, I should justify Mr Badman and all the rest of that gang. But that I never shall do, for the Word of God condemns

341. Deuteronomy 23:19.

them. But that it is not lawful for a man at all times to sell his commodity for as much as he can, I prove by these reasons.[342]

First, if it be lawful for me always to sell my commodity as dear, or for as much as I can, then 'tis lawful for me to lay aside in my dealing with others, good conscience, to them, and to God. But it is not lawful for me, in my dealing with others, to lay aside good conscience, etc. Therefore it is not lawful for me always to sell my commodity as dear, or for as much as I can.

That[343] it is not lawful to lay aside good conscience in our dealings has already been proved in the former part of our discourse. But that a man must lay it aside who will sell his commodity always as dear or for as much as he can, is plainly manifest thus.

One – he who will, as is mentioned afore, sell his commodity as dear as he can, must sometimes make a prey of the ignorance of his chapman.[344] But that he cannot do with a good conscience, for that is to overreach, and to go beyond my chapman, and is forbidden, 1 Thessalonians 4:6. Therefore he who will sell his commodity, as afore, as dear or for as much as he can, must of necessity lay aside good conscience.

Two – he who will sell his commodity always as dear as he can, must needs sometimes make a prey of his neighbour's necessity.[345] But that he cannot do with a good conscience, for that is to go beyond and defraud his neighbour, contrary to 1 Thessalonians 4:6. Therefore he who will sell his commodity, as afore, as dear or for as much as he can, must needs cast off and lay aside a good conscience.

Three – he who will, as afore, sell his commodity as dear or for as much as he can, must, if need be, make a prey of his neighbour's fondness. But that a man cannot do with a good conscience,[346] for that is still a-going beyond him, contrary to 1 Thessalonians 4:6. Therefore, he who will sell his commodity as dear or for as much as he can, must needs cast off, and lay aside good conscience.

342. Whether it be lawful for a man to make the best of his own. Proved in negative by eight reasons.
343. Good conscience must be used in selling.
344. We must not make a prey of our neighbour's ignorance.
345. Nor of his neighbour's necessity.
346. Nor of his fondness of our commodity.

The same also may be said for buying. No man may always buy as cheap as he can, but must also use good conscience in buying.[347] The which he can by no means use and keep, if he buys always as cheap as he can, and that for the reasons urged before. For such will make a prey of the ignorance, necessity and fondness of their chapman, the which they cannot do with a good conscience.

When Abraham would buy a burying place of the Sons of Heth, thus he said unto them. 'Entreat for me to Ephron the son of Zohar, that he may give me the cave of Machpelah, which he hath, which is in the end of his field; for as much money as it is worth he shall give it me.'[348] He would not have it under foot – he scorned it, he abhorred it. It stood not with his religion, credit, nor conscience. So also when David would buy a field of Ornon the Jebusite, thus he said unto him: 'Grant me the place of this threshing floor, that I may build an altar therein unto the Lord: thou shalt grant it me for the full price.'[349] He also, as Abraham, made conscience of this kind of dealing. He would not lie at catch to go beyond, no, not the Jebusite, but will give him his full price for his field. For he knew that there was wickedness, as in selling too dear so in buying too cheap, therefore he would not do it.

There ought therefore to be good conscience used, as in selling, so in buying. For 'tis also unlawful for a man to go beyond or to defraud his neighbour in buying. Yea 'tis unlawful to do it in any matter, and God will plentifully avenge that wrong. As I also before have fore-warned and testified. See also the text in the margin.[350]

But secondly, if it be lawful for me always to sell my commodity as dear or for as much as I can, then it is lawful for me to deal with my neighbour without the use of[351] charity. But it is not lawful for me to lay aside, or to deal with my neighbour without the use of charity, therefore it is not lawful for me always to sell my commodity to my neighbour for as much as I can. A man in dealing should as really design his neighbour's good, profit and advantage, as his own, for this is to exercise charity in his dealing.

347. We must use good conscience in buying.
348. Genesis 23:8–9.
349. 1 Chronicles 21; 22:24.
350. Leviticus 25:14.
351. Charity must be used in our dealings.

That I should thus use or exercise charity towards my neighbour in my buying and selling, etc., with him, is evident from the general command, 'Let all your things be done in charity.'[352] But that a man cannot live in the exercise of charity who sells, as afore, as dear, or who buys as cheap as he can, is evident by these reasons.

One – he who sells his commodity as dear or for as much money always as he can seeks himself, and himself only. But charity seeks not her own, nor her own only.[353] So then, he who seeks himself, and himself only, as he who sells, as afore, as dear as he can, does, makes not use of, nor does he exercise charity, in his so dealing.

Two – he who sells his commodity always for as much as he can get, hardens his heart against all reasonable entreaties of the buyer. But he who does so cannot exercise charity in his dealing. Therefore it is not lawful for a man to sell his commodity, as afore, as dear as he can.

Thirdly, if it be lawful for me to sell my commodity, as afore, as dear as I can, then there can be no sin in my trading, how unreasonably soever I manage my calling, whether by lying, swearing, cursing, cheating, for all this is but to sell my commodity as dear as I can. But that there is sin in these is evident, therefore I may not sell my commodity always as dear as I can.[354, 355]

Fourthly, he who sells, as afore, as dear as he can, offers violence to the law of nature,[356] for that says, 'Do unto all men even as ye would that they should do unto you.'[357] Now, were the seller a buyer, he would not that he of whom he buys, should sell him always as dear as he can. Therefore he should not sell so himself, when it is his lot to sell and others to buy of him.

Fifthly, he who sells, as afore, as dear as he can makes use of that instruction, that God has not given to others but sealed up in his hand[358] to abuse his law, and to wrong his neighbour withal, which

352. 1 Corinthians 16:14.

353. 1 Corinthians 13.

354. Ephesians 4:25.

355. There may be and is sin in trading.

356. A man in trading must not offer violence to the law of nature.

357. Matthew 7:12.

358. Job 37:7.

indeed is contrary to God.[359] God has given you more skill, more knowledge and understanding in your commodity than he has given to him who would buy of you. But what, can you think that God has given you this that you might thereby make a prey of your neighbour? That you might thereby go beyond and beguile your neighbour? No, verily, but he has given you it for his help, that you might in this, be eyes to the blind and save your neighbour from that damage that his ignorance, or necessity, or fondness would betray him into the hands of.

Sixthly, in all that a man does, he should have an eye to the glory of God,[360] but that he cannot have that sells his commodity always for as much as he can, for the reasons urged before.

Seventhly, all that a man does, he should do in the name of the Lord Jesus Christ,[361] that is, as being commanded and authorised to do it by Him. But who sells always as dear as he can, cannot so much as pretend to this without horrid blaspheming of that name, because commanded by Him to do otherwise.

Eighthly, and lastly, in all that a man does, he should have an eye to the day of Judgement, and to the consideration of how his actions will be esteemed of in that day.[362] Therefore there is not any man can or ought to sell always as dear as he can, unless he will, yea, he must say in so doing, 'I will run the hazard of the trial of that day. "If thou sell ought unto thy neighbour, or buyest ought of thy neighbour's hand, ye shall not oppress one another."'[363]

ATTEN: But why do you put in those cautionary words? They must not sell always as dear, nor buy always as cheap as they can: do you not thereby intimate that a man may sometimes do so?

WISE: I do indeed intimate that sometimes the seller may sell as dear, and the buyer buy as cheap as he can. But this is allowable only in these cases: when he who sells is a knave and lays aside all good conscience in selling, or when the buyer is a knave and lays aside all good conscience in buying. If the buyer therefore lights of a knave,

359. We must not abuse the gift we have in the knowledge of earthly things.
360. An eye to the glory of God in all we should have.
361. Colossians 3:17.
362. Acts 24:15–16.
363. Leviticus 25:14.

or if the seller lights of a knave, then let them look to themselves. But yet so, as not to lay aside conscience, because he whom you dealest with does so. But how vile or base soever the chapman is, do you keep your commodity at a reasonable price, or if you buy, offer reasonable gain for the thing you would have. And if this will not do with the buyer or seller, then seek you a more honest chapman. If you object, 'But I have not skill to know when a pennyworth is before me,' get some who have more skill than yourself in that affair, and let them in that matter dispose of your money. But if there were no knaves in the world, these objections need not be made.

And thus, my very good neighbour, have I given you a few of my reasons, why a man who has it should not always sell too dear, nor buy as cheap as he can, but should use good conscience to God, and charity to his neighbour in both.

ATTEN: But were some men here to hear you, I believe they would laugh you to scorn.

WISE: I question not that at all, for so[364] Mr Badman used to do when any man told him of his faults. He used to think himself wiser than any and would count, as I have hinted before, that he was not arrived to a manly spirit who did stick or boggle at any wickedness. But let Mr Badman and his fellows laugh. I will bear it and still give them good counsel. But I will remember also, for my further relief and comfort, that thus they that were covetous of old, served the Son of God himself. It is their time to laugh now that they may mourn in time to come.[365] And, I say again, when they have laughed out their laugh, he who uses not good conscience to God, and charity to his neighbour in buying and selling, dwells next door to an infidel, and is near of kin to Mr Badman.

ATTEN: Well, but what will you say to this question?[366] You know that there is no settled price set by God upon any commodity that is bought or sold under the sun, but all things that we buy and sell do ebb and flow, as to price, like the tide. How then shall a man of a tender conscience do, neither to wrong the seller, buyer, nor himself, in buying and selling of commodities?

364. Badman used to laugh at them who told him of his faults.

365. Luke 16:13–15; 6:25.

366. A question.

WISE: This question is thought to be frivolous by all that are of Mr Badman's way. 'Tis also difficult in itself. Yet I will endeavour to shape you an answer,[367] and that first to the matter of the question, to wit, how a tradesman should in trading keep a good conscience, a buyer or seller either. Secondly, how he should prepare himself to this work, and live in the practice of it.

For the first, he[368] must observe what has been said before, to wit, he must have conscience to God, charity to his neighbour and, I will add, much moderation in dealing. Let him therefore keep within the bounds of the affirmative of those eight reasons that before were urged to prove, that men ought not in their dealing, but to do justly and mercifully 'tween man and man. And then there will be no great fear of wronging the seller, buyer or himself.

But particularly to prepare, or instruct a man to this work:

One – let the tradesman or others consider that there is not that in great gettings, and in abundance, which the most of men do suppose, for all that a man has over and above what serves for his present necessity and supply, serves only to feed the lusts of the eye. For what good is there to the owners' thereof, save the beholding of them with their eyes?[369] Men also, many times in getting of riches, get therewith a snare to their soul.[370] But few get good by getting of them. But this consideration, Mr Badman could not abide.

Two – consider that the getting of wealth dishonestly – as he does, that gets it without good conscience and charity to his neighbour – is a great offender against God. Hence he says, 'I have smitten my hands at your dishonest gain, which you have made.'[371] It is a manner of speech that shows anger in the very making of mention of the crime. Therefore,

Three – consider that a little honestly gotten, though it may yield you but a dinner of herbs at a time, will yield more peace therewith, than will a stalled ox, ill-gotten. Better is a little with righteousness than great revenues without right.[372]

367. An answer.
368. Preparations to be a good dealer.
369. Ecclesiastes 5:10–11.
370. 1 Timothy 6:7–9.
371. Ezekiel 22:13.
372. Proverbs 15:17, 16:8, 5:21; 1 Samuel 2:5.

Four – be you confident that God's eyes are upon all your ways, and that He ponders all your goings, and also that He marks them, writes them down, and seals them up in a bag, against the time to come.[373]

Five – be you sure that you remember that you know not the day of your death. Remember also that when death comes, God will give your substance, for the which you have laboured, and for the which perhaps you have hazarded your soul, to one, you know not who, nor whether he shall be a wise man or a fool. And then, what profit has he who labours for the wind?[374]

Besides, you shall have nothing that you may so much as carry away in your hand. Guilt shall go with you if you have got it dishonestly, and they also to whom you shall leave it, shall receive it to their hurt.

These things duly considered, and made use of by you to the preparing of your heart to your calling of buying or selling, I come in the next place to show you how you should live in the practical part of this art. Are you to buy or sell?

One – if you sell, do not commend. If you buy, do not dispraise. Any otherwise, but to give the thing that you have to do with, its just value and worth, for you cannot do otherwise knowingly but of a covetous and wicked mind. Wherefore else are commodities overvalued by the seller, and also undervalued by the buyer. 'It is naught, it is naught,' says the buyer, but when he has got his bargain, he boasts thereof.[375] What has this man done now but lied in the dispraising of his bargain? And why did he dispraise it, but of a covetous mind, to wrong and beguile the seller?

Two – are you a seller, and do things grow dear? Set not your hand to help, or hold them up higher. This cannot be done without wickedness neither, for this is a making of the shekel great.[376] Are you a buyer, and do things grow dear? Use no cunning or deceitful language to pull them down, for that cannot be done but wickedly, too. 'What then shall we do?' will you say.

373. Job 14:17.
374. Ecclesiastes 5:13–15.
375. Proverbs 20:14.
376. Amos 8:5.

Why, I answer, leave things to the providence of God, and do you with moderation submit to his hand. But since, when they are growing dear, the hand that upholds the price is, for the time, more strong than that which would pull it down, that being the hand of the seller, who loves to have it dear, especially if it shall rise in his hand. Therefore I say, do you take heed, and have not a hand in it. The which you may have to your own and your neighbour's hurt, these three ways:

One – by crying out scarcity, scarcity, beyond the truth and state of things, especially take heed of doing of this by way of a prognostic for time to come. 'Twas for[377] this for which he was trodden to death in the gate of Samaria, that you read of in the book of Kings. This sin has a double evil in it. One – it belies the present blessing of God amongst us, and two – it undervalues the riches of his goodness, which can make all good things to abound towards us.

Two – this wicked thing may be done by hoarding up, when the hunger and necessity of the poor calls for it. Now that God may show his dislike against this, he does, as it were, license the people to curse such a hoarder up. 'He that withholdeth corn, the people shall curse him: but blessing shall be upon the head of him that selleth it.'[378]

Three – but if things will rise, do you be grieved. Be also moderate in all your sellings, and be sure let the poor have a pennyworth, and sell your corn to those in necessity,[379] which then you will do, when you show mercy to the poor in your selling to him, and when you for his sake, because he is poor, undersell the market. This is to buy and sell with good conscience. Your buyer you wrong not, your conscience you wrong not, yourself you wrong not, for God will surely recompense you. I have spoken concerning corn, but your duty is to 'let your moderation be known unto all men. The Lord is at hand.'[380]

ATTEN: Well, sir. Now I have heard enough of Mr Badman's naughtiness. Pray now proceed to his death.

WISE: Why, sir, the sun is not so low. We have yet three hours to night.

377. A judgement of God. 2 Kings 7.
378. Proverbs 11:26.
379. Isaiah 58:6–8.
380. Philippians 4:5.

ATTEN: Nay, I am not in any great haste, but I thought you had even now done with his life.

WISE: Done! No, I have yet much more to say.

ATTEN: Then he has much more wickedness than I thought he had.

WISE: That may be. But let us proceed. This Mr Badman, added to all his wickedness this, he was a very proud man. A very proud man.[381] He was exceeding proud and haughty in mind. He looked that what he said ought not, must not, be contradicted or opposed. He counted himself as wise as the wisest in the country, as good as the best, and as beautiful as he who had most of it. He took great delight in praising of himself, and as much in the praises that others gave him. He could not abide that any should think themselves above him, or that their wit or personage should by others be set before his.[382] He had scarce a fellowly carriage for his equals. But for those who were of an inferior rank, he would look over them in great contempt. And if at any time he had any remote occasion of having to do with them, he would show great height and a very domineering spirit. So that in this it may be said that Solomon gave a characteristical note of him, when he said, 'Proud and haughty scorner is his name, who dealeth in proud wrath.'[383] He never thought his diet well enough dressed, his clothes fine enough made or his praise enough refined.

ATTEN: This pride is a sin that sticks as close to nature I think as most sins. There is uncleanness and pride – I know not of any two gross sins that stick closer to men than they. They have, as I may call it, an interest in nature. It likes them because they most suit its lusts and fancies, and therefore no marvel though Mr Badman was tainted with pride, since he had so wickedly given up himself to work all iniquity with greediness.

WISE: You say right. Pride is a sin that sticks close to nature,[384] and is one of the first follies wherein it shows itself to be polluted. For even in childhood, even in little children, pride will first of all show itself. It is a hasty, an early appearance of the sin of the soul. It, as I may say,

381. Mr Badman a very proud man.
382. Of pride in general.
383. Proverbs 21:24.
384. Pride sticks close to nature.

is that corruption that strives for predominancy in the heart, and therefore usually comes out first. But though children are so incident to it, yet methinks those of more years should be ashamed thereof. I might at the first have begun with Mr Badman's pride, only I think it is not the pride in infancy that begins to make a difference between one and another as did and do those wherewith I began my relation of his life. Therefore I passed it over. But now, since he had no more consideration of himself, and of his vile and sinful state, but to be proud when come to years, I have taken the occasion in this place to make mention of his pride.

ATTEN: But pray, if you can remember them, tell me of some places of scripture that speak against pride. I the rather desire this, because that pride is now a reigning sin, and I happen sometimes to fall into the company of them that in my conscience are proud very much, and I have a mind also to tell them of their sin. Now when I tell them of it, unless I bring God's word too, I doubt they will laugh me to scorn.

WISE: Laugh you to scorn! The Proud man will laugh you to scorn, bring to him what text you can, except God shall smite him in his conscience by the Word. Mr Badman did use to serve them so that did use to tell him of his. And besides, when you have said what you can, they will tell you they are not proud, and that you are rather the proud man, else you would not judge nor so malapertly meddle with other men's matters as you do. Nevertheless, since you desire it, I will mention two or three texts. They are these. 'Pride and arrogancy do I hate.' 'A man's pride shall bring him low.' 'And he shall bring down their pride.' 'And all the proud, yea, and all that do wickedly, shall be stubble: and the day that cometh shall burn them up.'[385] This last is a dreadful text. It is enough to make a proud man shake. God, says he, will make the proud ones as stubble, that is, as fuel for the fire, and the day that comes shall be like a burning oven, and that day shall burn them up, says the Lord. But Mr Badman could never abide to hear pride spoken against, nor that any should say of him. He is a proud man.

ATTEN: What should be the reason of that?

WISE: He did not tell me the reason, but I suppose it to be that which is common to all vile persons. They love this vice, but care not to bear

385. Proverbs 8:13, 29:23; Isaiah 25:11; Malachi 4:1.

its name.[386] The drunkard loves the sin, but loves not to be called a drunkard. The thief loves to steal, but cannot abide to be called a thief, the whore loves to commit uncleanness, but loves not to be called a whore. And so Mr Badman loved to be proud, but could not abide to be called a proud man. The sweet of sin, is desirable to polluted and corrupted man, but the name thereof, is a blot in his scutcheon.

ATTEN: 'Tis true that you have said: but pray how many sorts of pride are there?

WISE: There are two sorts of pride:[387] pride of spirit, and pride of body. The first of these is thus made mention of in the scriptures. 'Every one who is proud in heart is abomination to the Lord.' 'A high look, and a proud heart, and the plowing of the wicked is sin.' 'The patient in spirit is better than the proud in spirit.'[388] Bodily pride these scriptures mention. 'In that day the Lord will take away the bravery of their tinkling ornaments about their feet, and their cauls, and their round tires like the moon, the chains, and the bracelets, and the mufflers, the bonnets, and the ornaments of the legs, and the headbands, and the tablets, and the earrings, the rings, and nose jewels, the changeable suits of apparel, and the mantles, and the wimples, and the crisping pins, the glasses, and the fine linen, and the hoods, and the veils.'[389] By these expressions it is evident that there is pride of body, as well as pride of spirit, and that both are sin, and so abominable to the Lord. But these texts Mr Badman could never abide to read, they were to him as Micaiah was to Ahab – they never spoke good of him, but evil.[xi]

ATTEN: I suppose that it was not Mr Badman's case alone even to malign those texts that speak against their vices, for I believe that most ungodly men, where the scriptures are, have a secret antipathy against those words of God that do most plainly and fully rebuke them for their sins.[390]

WISE: That is out of doubt, and by that antipathy, they show that sin and Satan are more welcome to them than are the wholesome instructions of life and godliness.

386. Proud men do not love to be called proud.
387. Two sorts of pride.
388. Proverbs 16:5, 21:4; Ecclesiastes 7:8.
389. Isaiah 3:17– 22.
390. Wicked men do hate that word that reproves their vice.

ATTEN: Well, but not to go off from our discourse of Mr Badman. You say he was proud, but will you show me now some symptoms of one that is proud?

WISE: Yes, that I will. And first I will show you some symptoms of pride of heart.[391] Pride of heart is seen by outward things, as pride of body in general, is a sign of pride of heart, for all proud gestures of the body flow from pride of heart. Therefore Solomon says, 'There is a generation, O how lofty are their eyes! And their eyelids are lifted up.'[392] And again, 'There is that exalteth their gate, their going.'[393] Now these lofty eyes and this exalting of the gate are a sign of a proud heart, for both these actions come from the heart. For out of the heart comes pride in all the visible appearances of it.[394] But more particularly:

One – heart pride is discovered[395] by a stretched-out neck and by mincing as they go. For the wicked, the proud have a proud neck, a proud foot, a proud tongue, by which this their going is exalted. This is that which makes them look scornfully, speak ruggedly and carry it huffingly among their neighbours.

Two – a proud heart, is a persecuting one. The wicked through his pride does persecute the poor.[396]

Three – a prayerless man is a proud man.[397]

Four – a contentious man is a proud man.[398]

Five – the disdainful man is a proud man.[399]

Six – the man who oppresses his neighbour is a proud man.[400]

Seven – he who hearkens not to God's Word with reverence and fear is a proud man.[401]

Eight – and he who calls the proud happy is, be sure, a proud man. All these are proud in heart, and this their pride of heart does thus discover itself.[402, 403]

As to bodily[404] pride, it is discovered, that is, something of it by all the particulars mentioned before, for though they are said to be

391. Signs of a proud man in general.
392. Proverbs 30:13.
393. Proverbs 17:19.
394. Mark 7.
395. In particular.
396. Psalm 10:2.
397. Psalm 10:4.
398. Proverbs 13:10.
399. Psalm 119:51.
400. Psalm 119:122.
401. Jeremiah 13:17.
402. Jeremiah 43:2.
403. Mal. 3:15.
404. Of outward pride.

symptoms of pride of heart, yet they are symptoms of that pride by their showing of themselves in the body. You know diseases that are within, are seen ofttimes by outward and visible signs, yet by them very signs even the outside is defiled also. So all those visible signs of heart pride are signs of bodily pride also. But to come to more outward signs: the putting on of gold, and pearls, and costly array, the plaiting of the hair, the following of fashions, the seeking by gestures to imitate the proud, either by speech, looks, dresses, goings or other fools' baubles, of which at this time the world is full – all these and many more, are signs as of a proud heart, so of bodily pride also.[405, 406]

But Mr Badman would not allow, by any means, that this should be called pride,[407] but rather neatness, handsomeness, comeliness, cleanliness, etc. Neither would he allow that following of fashions was anything else but because he would not be proud, singular and esteemed fantastical by his neighbours.

ATTEN: But I have been told that when some have been rebuked for their pride, they have turned it again upon the brotherhood of those by whom they have been rebuked, saying, 'Physician, heal your friends, look at home, among your brotherhood, even among the wisest of you, and see if you yourselves be clear, even you professors: for who is prouder than you professors?' Scarcely the Devil himself.

WISE: My heart aches at this answer because there is too much cause for it.[408] This very answer would Mr Badman give his wife, when she, as she would sometimes, reproved him for his pride. 'We shall have,' says he, 'great amendments in living now, for the Devil is turned a corrector of vice, for no sin reigns more in the world,' quoth he, 'than pride among professors.' And who can contradict him? Let us give the Devil his due. The thing is too apparent for any man to deny.

And I doubt not but the same answer is ready in the mouths of Mr Badman's friends, for they may and do see pride display itself in the apparel and carriages of professors. One may say, almost as much, as

405. 1 Peter 3:3–5.
406. 1 Timothy 2:2.
407. Mr Badman was not for having pride called pride.
408. Professors guilty of the sin of pride.

among any people in the land, the more is the pity. Aye, and I fear that even their extravagancies in this has hardened the heart of many a one, as I perceive it did somewhat the heart of Mr Badman himself.

For my own part, I have seen many myself, and those church members too, so decked and bedaubed with their fangles and toys, and that when they have been at the solemn appointments of God, in the way of his worship, that I have wondered with what face such painted persons could sit in the place where they were without swounding.[xii] But certainly the holiness of God, and also the pollution of themselves by sin, must needs be very far out of the minds of such people, what profession soever they make.

I have read of a whore's forehead,[409] and I have read of christian-shamefacedness. I have read of costly array, and of that which becomes women professing godliness, with good works.[410, 411] But if I might speak, I know what I know and could say, and yet do no wrong, that which would make some professors stink in their places.[412] But now I forbear.

ATTEN: Sir, you seem to be greatly concerned at this, but what I shall say more? It is whispered that some good ministers have countenanced their people in their light and wanton apparel, yea, have pleaded for their gold, and pearls, and costly array, etc.

WISE: I know not what they have pleaded for, but 'tis easily seen that they tolerate, or at least wise, wink and connive at such things, both in their wives and children. And so from the prophets of Jerusalem is profaneness gone forth into all the land.[413] And when the hand of the rulers is chief in a trespass, who can keep their people from being drowned in that trespass?

ATTEN: This is a lamentation, and must stand for a lamentation.

WISE: So it is, and so it must. And I will add it is a shame, it is a reproach, it is a stumbling-block to the blind,[414] for though men be as blind as Mr Badman himself, yet they can see the foolish lightness

409. Jeremiah 3:3.
410. 1 Timothy 2:9.
411. 1 Peter 3:1–3.
412. Jeremiah 23:15.
413. Ezra 9:2.
414. Pride in professors a shame and stumbling-block to the world.

that must needs be the bottom of all these apish and wanton extra-vagancies. But many have their excuses ready, to wit, their parents, their husbands and their breeding calls for it, and the like. Yea, the examples of good people prompt them to it. But all these will be but the spider's web when the thunder of the Word of the great God shall rattle from Heaven against them, as it will at death or judgement, but I wish it might do it before. But alas! These excuses are but bare pretences, these proud ones love to have it so. I once talked with a maid, by way of reproof, for her fond and gaudy garment. But she told me, ☞ 'The tailor would make it so,' when alas, poor proud girl, she gave order to the tailor so to make it. Many make parents, and husbands, and tailors, etc., the blind to others, but their naughty hearts, and their giving of way thereto: that is the original cause of all these evils.

ATTEN: Now you are speaking of the cause of pride. Pray show me yet further why pride is now so much in request?[415]

WISE: I will show you what I think are the reasons of it.

One – the first is[416] because such persons are led by their own hearts, rather than by the Word of God. I told you before that the original fountain of pride is the heart, for out of the heart comes pride. It is therefore because they are led by their hearts, which naturally tends to lift them up in pride. This pride of heart tempts them, and by its deceits overcomes them.[417] Yea, it does put a be-witching virtue into their peacock's feathers, and then they are swallowed up with the vanity of them.

Two – another reason why professors are so proud, for those we are talking of now, is because they are more apt to take example of those who are of the world than they are to take example of those who are saints indeed. Pride is of the world. For all that is of the world, the lusts of the flesh, the lust of the eyes and the pride of life, are not of the Father but of the world.[418] Of the world therefore professors learn to be proud. But they should not take them for example. It will be objected, no, nor your saints neither, for you are

415. Why pride is in such request.
416. First reason: Mark 7:22–23.
417. Obad. 3.
418. 1 John 2:16.

as proud as others. Well, let them take shame who are guilty. But when I say, professors should take example for their life by those who are saints indeed, I mean as Peter says, they should take example of those who were in old time, the saints, for saints of old time were the best. Therefore to these he directs us for our pattern. Let the wives' conversation be chaste and also coupled with fear, 'whose adorning,' saith Peter, 'let it not be that outward adorning of plaiting the hair, and of wearing of gold, or of putting on of apparel; but let it be the hidden man of the heart, in that which is not corruptible, even the ornament of a meek and quiet spirit, which is in the sight of God of great price. For after this manner in the old time the holy women also, who trusted in God, adorned themselves, being in subjection unto their own husbands.' [419]

Three – another reason is[420] because they have forgotten the pollution of their nature. For the remembrance of that must needs keep us humble, and being kept humble, we shall be at a distance from pride. The proud and the humble are set in opposition. God resists the proud, but gives grace to the humble. And can it be imagined that a sensible Christian should be a proud one? Sense of baseness tends to lay us low, not to lift us up with pride. Not with pride of heart, nor pride of life. But when a man begins to forget what he is, then he, if ever, begins to be proud.

Methinks it is one of the most senseless and ridiculous things in the world that a man should be proud of that which is given him on purpose to cover the shame of his nakedness with.

Four – persons who are proud have gotten God and his holiness out of their sight.[421] If God were before them, as He is behind their back, and if they saw Him in His holiness, as He sees them in their sins and shame, they would take but little pleasure in their apish knacks. The holiness of God makes the angels cover their faces, crumbles Christians when they behold it, into dust and ashes,[422] and as His Majesty is, such is his Word. Therefore they abuse it who bring it to countenance pride.

419. 1 Peter 3:1– 5.
420. Third reason.
421. Fourth reason.
422. Isaiah 6.

Lastly,[423] but what can be the end of those who are proud, in the decking of themselves after their antic manner? Why are they for going with their bulls' foretops, with their naked shoulders and paps hanging out like a cow's bag? Why are they for painting their faces, for stretching out their necks and for putting of themselves into all the formalities that proud fancy leads them to? Is it because they would honour God? Because they would adorn the Gospel? Because they would beautify religion, and make sinners to fall in love with their own salvation? No, no. It is rather to please their lusts, to satisfy their wild and extravagant fancies. And I wish none does it to stir up lust in others, to the end they may commit uncleanness with them. I believe, whatever is their end, this is one of the great designs of the Devil. And I believe also that Satan has drawn more into the sin of uncleanness by the spangling show of fine clothes than he could possibly have drawn unto it, without them. I wonder what it was, that of old was called the attire of a harlot. Certainly it could not be more bewitching and tempting than are the garments of many professors this day.

ATTEN: I like what you say very well, and I wish that all the proud dames in England who profess were within the reach and sound of your words.

WISE: What I have said I believe is true, but as for the proud dames in England who profess, they have Moses and the prophets, and if they will not hear them, how then can we hope that they should receive good by such a dull sounding ramshorn as I am? However, I have said my mind, and now if you will, we will proceed to some other of Mr Badman's doings.

ATTEN: No. Pray before you show me anything else of Mr Badman, show me yet more particularly the evil effects of this sin of pride.

WISE: With all my heart, I will answer your request.[424]

One – Then[425] 'tis pride that makes poor man so like the Devil in Hell that he cannot in it be known to be the image and similitude of God. The Angels when they became Devils, 'twas through their

423. Fifth reason.
424. The evil effects of the sin of pride.
425. First evil effect. 1 Timothy 3:6.

being lifted or puffed up with pride. 'Tis pride also that lifts or puffs up the heart of the sinner, and so makes him to bear the very image of the Devil.

Two – pride[426] makes a man so odious in the sight of God that he shall not, must not come nigh His Majesty. Though the Lord be high, yet has He respect to the lowly, but the proud He knows afar off. Pride sets God and the soul at a distance. Pride will not let a man come nigh God, nor God will not let a proud man come nigh unto Him. Now this is a dreadful thing.

Three – as[427] pride sets, so it keeps God and the soul at a distance. God resists the proud. Resists, that is, He opposes him. He thrusts him from Him. He condemns his person and all his performances. Come in to God's ordinances, the proud man may, but come into His presence, have communion with Him or blessing from Him, he shall not. For the high God does resist him.[428]

Four – the Word[429] says that the Lord will destroy the house of the proud. He will destroy his house. It may be understood, he will destroy him and his. So he destroyed proud Pharaoh, so he destroyed proud Corah,[xiii] and many others.

Five – pride,[430] where it comes and is entertained, is a certain forerunner of some judgement that is not far behind. When pride goes before, shame and destruction will follow after. When pride comes, then comes shame. Pride goes before destruction, and a haughty spirit before a fall.

Six – persisting[431] in pride makes the condition of a poor man as remediless as is that of the devils themselves.

And this I fear was Mr Badman's condition, and that was the reason that he died so as he did, as I shall show you anon.

But what need I thus talk of the particular actions, or rather prodigious sins of Mr Badman, when his whole life and all his actions, went as it were to the making up one massive body of

426. Second evil effect. Psalm 138:9.
427. Third evil effect.
428. James 4:6.
429. Fourth evil effect. Proverbs 16:25.
430. Fifth evil effect. Proverbs 11:2, 16:8.
431. Sixth evil effect. 1 Timothy 3:6.

sin?[432] Instead of believing that there was a God, his mouth, his life and actions declared that he believed no such thing. His transgression 'saith within my heart, that there is no fear of God before his eyes'.[433, 434] Instead of honouring of God, and of giving glory to Him for any of His mercies, or under any of His good providences towards him – for God is good to all, and lets His sun shine, and His rain fall upon the unthankful and unholy – he would ascribe the glory to other causes. If they were mercies, he would ascribe them, if the open face of the providence did not give him the lie, to his own wit, labour, care, industry, cunning or the like. If they were crosses, he would ascribe them, or count them the offspring of fortune, ill luck, chance, the ill management of matters, the ill will of neighbours, or to his wife's being religious and spending, as he called it, too much time in reading, praying or the like. It was not in his way to acknowledge God, that is, graciously, or His hand in things. But, as the prophet says, 'Let favour be showed to the wicked, yet will he not learn righteousness.'[435] And again, 'The people turneth not unto him that smiteth them, neither do they seek the Lord of hosts.'[436] This was Mr Badman's temper, neither mercies nor judgement would make him seek the Lord. Nay, as another scripture says, he would not see the works of God, nor regard the operations of his hands either in mercies or in judgements.[437]

But further, when by providence he has been cast under the best means for his soul – for, as was showed before, he having had a good master and before him a good father, and after all a good wife, and being sometimes upon a journey, and cast under the hearing of a good sermon, as he would sometimes for novelty's sake go to hear a good preacher – he was always without heart to make use thereof. In this land of righteousness he would deal unjustly, and would not behold the majesty of the Lord.

432. A general character of Mr Badman.
433. Psalm 36:1.
434. A brief relation of Mr Badman's ways.
435. Isaiah 26:10.
436. Isaiah 9:13.
437. Isaiah 26:11.

Instead of reverencing the Word,[438] when he heard it preached, read or discoursed of, he would sleep, talk of other business or else object against the authority, harmony and wisdom of the scriptures, saying, 'How do you know them to be the Word of God? How do you know that these sayings are true? The scriptures,' he would say, 'were as a nose of wax, and a man may turn them wheresoever he lists. One scripture says one thing, and another says the quite contrary. Besides, they make mention of a thousand impossibilities. They are the cause of all dissensions and discords that are in the land. Therefore you may,' would he say, 'still think what you will, but in my mind they are best at ease who have least to do with them.'

Instead of loving and honouring of them who did bear in their foreheads the name, and in their lives the image of Christ, they should be his song,[439] the matter of his jests and the objects of his slanders. He would either make a mock at their sober deportment, their gracious language, quiet behaviour, or else desperately swear that they did all in deceit and hypocrisy. He would endeavour to render godly men as odious and contemptible as he could. Any lies that were made by any, to their disgrace, those he would avouch for truth and would not endure to be controlled. He was much like those whom the prophet speaks of, who would sit and slander his mother's son.[440] Yea, he would speak reproachfully of his wife, though his conscience told him, and many would testify, that she was a very virtuous woman. He would also raise slanders of his wife's friends himself, affirming that their doctrine tended to lasciviousness, and that in their assemblies they acted and did unbeseeming men and women, that they committed uncleanness, etc. He was much like those who affirmed the apostle should say, 'Let us do evil that good may come,'[441] or like those of whom it is thus written, 'Report, say they, and we will report it.'[442] And if he could get anything by the end that had scandal in it, if it did but touch professors, how falsely

438. Mr Badman's judgement of the scriptures.
439. Good men Mr Badman's song.
440. Psalm 50:19–20.
441. Romans 3:7–8.
442. Jeremiah 20:10.

soever reported, Oh! Then he would glory, laugh and be glad, and lay it upon the whole party, saying, 'Hang them rogues. There is not a barrel better herring of all the holy brotherhood of them. Like to like, quoth the Devil to the collier, this is your precise crew.' And then he would send all home with a curse.

ATTEN: If those who make profession of religion be wise, Mr Badman's watchings and words will make them the more wary and careful in all things.

WISE: You say true. For when we see men do watch for our halting, and rejoice to see us stumble and fall, it should make us so much abundance the more careful.[443]

I do think it was as delightful to Mr Badman to hear, raise and tell lies, and lying stories of them who fear the Lord, as it was for him to go to bed when a-weary. But we will at this time let these things pass, for as he was in these things bad enough, so he added to these many more the like.

He was an angry,[444] wrathful, envious man, a man who knew not what meekness or gentleness meant, nor did he desire to learn. His natural temper was to be surly, huffy and rugged, and worse, and he so gave way to his temper, as to this, that it brought him to be furious and outrageous in all things, especially against goodness itself, and against other things, too, when he was displeased.[445]

ATTEN: Solomon says he is a fool who rages.

WISE: He does so, and says moreover that 'anger resteth in the bosom of fools.'[446] And truly, if it be a sign of a fool to have anger rest in his bosom, then was Mr Badman, notwithstanding the conceit that he had of his own abilities, a fool of no small size.

ATTEN: Fools are mostly most wise in their own eyes.

WISE: True. But I was a-saying, that if it be a sign that a man is a fool, when anger rests in his bosom, then what is it a sign of, think you, when malice and envy rests there? For to my knowledge Mr Badman was as malicious and as envious a man as commonly you can hear of.

443. When the wicked watch, God's people should be wary.
444. Badman an angry, envious man.
445. Proverbs 14:16.
446. Ecclesiastes 7:9.

ATTEN: Certainly, malice and envy flow[447] from pride and arrogancy, and they again from ignorance, and ignorance from the Devil. And I thought, that since you spoke of the pride of Mr Badman before, we should have something of these before we had done.

WISE: Envy flows from ignorance indeed. And this Mr Badman was so envious a one, where he set against that he would swell with it as a toad, as we say, swells with poison. He whom he maligned might at any time even read envy in his face wherever he met with him, or in whatever he had to do with him.

His envy was so rank and strong that if it at any time turned its head against a man, it would hardly ever be pulled in again. He would watch over that man to do him mischief, as the cat watches over the mouse to destroy it. Yea, he would wait seven years, but he would have an opportunity to hurt him, and when he had it, he would make him feel the weight of his envy.

Envy is a devilish thing. The scripture intimates that none can stand before it. 'A stone is heavy, and the sand weighty; but a fool's wrath is heavier than them both. Wrath is cruel, and anger is outrageous; but who is able to stand before envy?'[448, 449]

This envy, for the foulness of it, is reckoned[450] among the foulest villainies that are, as adultery, murder, drunkenness, revellings, witchcrafts, heresies, seditions, etc. Yea, it is so malignant a corruption that it rots the very bones of him in whom it dwells. 'A sound heart is the life of the flesh: but envy the rottenness of the bones.'[451]

ATTEN: This envy is the very father and mother of a great many hideous and prodigious wickednesses. I say, it is the very[452] father and mother of them. It both besets them, and also nourishes them up, till they come to their cursed maturity in the bosom of him who entertains them.

WISE: You have given it a very right description in calling of it the father and mother of a great many other prodigious wickednesses, for it is so

447. Whence envy flows.
448. Proverbs 27:3–4.
449. Envy the worst of the four.
450. Gal. 5:19–20.
451. Proverbs 14:30.
452. Envy is the father and mother of a many wickednesses.

venomous and vile a thing that it puts the whole course of nature out of order, and makes it fit for nothing but confusion, and a hold for every evil thing. For where envy and strife are, there is confusion, and every evil work.[453] Wherefore, I say you have rightly called it the very father and mother of a great many other sins. And now for our further edification, I will reckon up some of the births of envy.[454]

One – envy, as I told you before, it rots the very bones of him who entertains it. And,

Two – as you have also hinted, it is heavier than a stone, than sand. Yea, and I will add, it falls like a millstone upon the head. Therefore,

Three – it kills him who throws it, and him at whom it is thrown. 'Envy slayeth the silly one.'[455] That is, him in whom it resides, and him who is its object.

Four – 'twas that also that slew Jesus Christ himself, for his adversaries persecuted him through their envy.[456, 457]

Five – envy was that by virtue of which Joseph was sold by his brethren into Egypt.[458]

Six – 'tis envy that has the hand in making of variance among God's saints.[459]

Seven – 'tis envy in the hearts of sinners that stirs them up to thrust God's ministers out of their coasts.

Eight – what shall I say? 'Tis envy that is the very nursery of whisperings, debates, backbitings, slanders, reproaches, murders, etc.

'Tis not possible to repeat all the particular fruits of this sinful root. Therefore, it is no marvel that Mr Badman was such an ill-natured man, for the great roots of all manner of wickedness were in him, unmortified, unmaimed, untouched.

ATTEN: But it is[460] a rare case, even this of Mr Badman, that he should never in all his life be touched with remorse for his ill-spent life.

WISE: Remorse, I cannot say he ever had, if by remorse you mean repentance for his evils. Yet twice I remember he was under some trouble of mind about his condition.[461] Once when he broke his leg

453. James 3:14–15.
454. Some of the births of envy.
455. Job 5:2.
456. Matthew 27:18.
457. Mark 15:10.
458. Acts 7:9.
459. Isaiah 11:13.
460. A rare thing.
461. Mr Badman under some trouble of mind.

as he came home drunk from the alehouse, and another time when he fell sick and thought he should die. Besides these two times, I do not remember any more.

ATTEN: Did he break his leg then?

WISE: Yes. Once, as he came home drunk from the alehouse.

ATTEN: Pray, how did he break it?

WISE: Why, upon a time he was at an alehouse, that wicked house, about two or three miles from home. And having there drank hard the greatest part of the day, when night had come, he would stay no longer, but called for his horse, got up and, like a madman, as drunken persons usually ride, away he goes as hard as horse could lay legs to the ground. Thus he rode till coming to a dirty place, where his horse flouncing in, fell, threw his master and with his fall broke his leg. So there he lay.[462] But you would not think how he[463] swore at first. But after a while, he coming to himself, and feeling by his pain, and the uselessness of his leg, what case he was in, and also fearing that this bout might be his death, he began to cry out after the manner of such,[464] 'Lord help me! Lord have mercy upon me! Good God deliver me!' and the like. So there he lay till some came by, who took him up, carried him home, where he lay for some time before he could go abroad again.

ATTEN: And then, you say, he called upon God.

WISE: He cried out in his pain and would say, 'O God, and O Lord, help me!' But whether it was that his sin might be pardoned, and his soul saved, or whether to be rid of his pain, I will not positively determine. Though I fear it was but for the last,[465] because, when his pain was gone, and he had got hopes of mending, even before he could go abroad, he cast off prayer and began his old game, to wit, to be as bad as he was before. He then would send for his old companions, his sluts also would come to his house to see him, and with them he would be, as well as he could for his lame leg, as vicious as they could be for their hearts.

ATTEN: 'Twas a wonder he did not break his neck.

462. Mr Badman broke his leg.
463. He swears.
464. He prays.
465. It has no good effect upon him.

WISE: His neck had gone instead of his leg, but that God was long-suffering towards him, he had deserved it ten thousand times over. There have been many, as I have heard, and as I have hinted to you before, who have taken their horses when drunk, as he. But they have gone from the pot to the grave, for they have broken their necks 'tween the alehouse and home. One heard by us ☞ also drunk himself dead. He drank and died in his drink.

ATTEN: 'Tis a sad thing to die drunk.

WISE: So it is. But yet I wonder that no more do so. For considering the heinousness of that sin, and with how many other sins it is accompanied,[466] as with oaths, blasphemies, lies, revellings, whorings, brawlings, etc., it is a wonder to me that any who live in that sin should escape such a blow from Heaven that should tumble them into their graves. Besides, when I consider also how, when they are as drunk as beasts, they, without all fear of danger, will ride like Bedlams and madmen, even as if they did dare God to meddle with them if He dared for their being drunk. I say, I wonder that He does not withdraw his protecting providences from them and leave them to those dangers and destructions that by their sin they have deserved, and that by their Bedlam madness they would rush themselves into. Only I consider again that He has appointed a day wherein He will reckon with them,[467] and does also commonly make examples of some to show that He takes notice of their sin, abhors their way and will count with them for it at the set time.

ATTEN: It is worthy of our remark to take notice how God, to show his dislike of the sins of men, strikes some of them down with a blow, as the breaking of Mr Badman's leg, for doubtless that was a stroke from Heaven.

WISE: It is worth our remark indeed. It was an open stroke. It fell upon him while he was in the height of his sin. And it looks much like to that in Job, 'Therefore he knoweth their works, and he overturneth them in the night, so that they are destroyed. He striketh them as wicked men in the open sight of others.'[468] Or as the margent reads

466. How many sins do accompany drunkenness.
467. Acts 17:30–32.
468. Job 34:24–26.

it, in the place of beholders. He lays them with his stroke in the place of beholders. There was[469] Mr Badman laid, his stroke was taken notice of by every one. His broken leg was at this time the town talk. 'Mr Badman has broken his leg,' says one. 'How did he break it?' says another. 'As he came home drunk from such an alehouse,' said a third. 'A judgement of God upon him,' said a fourth. This his sin, his shame, and punishment, are all made conspicuous to all who are about him. I will here tell you another story or two.

I have read in *Mr Clark's Looking-glass for Sinners*[470] that upon a time, a certain drunken fellow boasted in his cups that there was neither Heaven nor Hell. Also he said, he believed, that man had no soul, and that for his own part, he would sell his soul to any who would buy it. Then did one of his companions buy it of him for a cup of wine, and presently the Devil in man's shape bought it of that man again at the same price. And so in the presence of them all laid hold on this soul-seller, and carried him away through the air, so that he was never more heard of.

In page 148, he tells us also that there was one at Salisbury, in the midst of his health drinking and carousing in a tavern. And he drank a health to the Devil, saying that if the Devil would not come and pledge him, he would not believe that there was either God or Devil, whereupon his companions, stricken with fear, hastened out of the room. And presently after, hearing a hideous noise, and smelling a stinking savour, the vintner ran up into the chamber. And coming in, he missed his guest, and found the window broken, the iron bar in it bowed and all bloody. But the man was never heard of afterwards.

Again, in page 149, he tells us of a bailiff of Hedley, who upon a Lord's Day, being drunk at Melford, got upon his horse to ride through the streets, saying that his horse would carry him to the Devil. And presently his horse threw him and broke his neck. These things are worse than the breaking of Mr Badman's leg, and should be a caution to all of his friends who are living, lest they also fall by their sin into these sad judgements of God.

469. An open stroke.
470. pag. 41.

But, as I said, Mr Badman quickly forgot all. His conscience was choked before his leg was healed. And therefore, before he was well of the fruit of one sin, he tempts God to send another judgement to seize upon him, and so He did quickly after. For not many months after his leg was well, he had a very dangerous fit of sickness, insomuch that now he began to think he must die in very deed.[471]

ATTEN: Well, and what did he think and do then?

WISE: He thought he must go to Hell. This I know, for he could not forbear but say so.[472] To my best remembrance, he lay crying out all one night for fear, and at times he would so tremble that he would make the very bed shake under him.[473] But, Oh! How the thoughts of death, of hellfire and of eternal judgement did then wrack his conscience. Fear might be seen in his face, and in his tossings to and fro. It might also be heard in his words, and be understood by his heavy groans. He would often cry, 'I am undone, I am undone! My vile life has undone me!'

ATTEN: Then his former atheistical thoughts and principles were too weak now to support him from the fears of eternal damnation.

WISE: Aye! They were too weak indeed! They may serve to stifle conscience when a man is in the midst of his prosperity, and to harden the heart against all good counsel when a man is left of God, and given up to his reprobate mind.[474] But alas, atheistical thoughts, notions and opinions must shrink and melt away when God sends, yea, comes with sickness to visit the soul of such a sinner for his sin. There was a man dwelt about twelve miles off from us who had so trained up himself in his atheistical notions that at last he attempted to write a book against Jesus Christ, and against the divine authority of the scriptures. But I think it was not printed. Well, after many days God struck him with sickness, whereof he died. So, being sick, and musing upon his former doings, the book that he had written came into his mind, and with it such a sense of his evil in writing of it, that it tore his conscience as a lion would tear a kid. He lay therefore

471. Mr Badman fallen sick.
472. His conscience is wounded.
473. He cries out in his sickness.
474. His atheism will not help him now.

upon his deathbed in sad case,[475] and much affliction of conscience. Some of my friends also went to see him, and as they were in his chamber one day, he hastily called for pen, ink and paper, which when it was given him, he took it and wrote to this purpose. 'I, ☞ such a one, in such a Town, must go to hellfire for writing a book against Jesus Christ and against the holy scriptures,' and would also have leapt out of the window of his house to have killed himself, but was by them prevented of that. So he died in his bed, such a death as it was. 'Twill be well if others take warning by him.

ATTEN: This is a remarkable story.

WISE: 'Tis as true as remarkable. I had it from them whom I dare believe, who also themselves were eye- and earwitnesses, and also who caught him in their arms and saved him when he would have leapt out of his chamber window to have destroyed himself.

ATTEN: Well, you have told me what were Mr Badman's thoughts, now being sick, of his condition. Pray tell me also what he then did when he was sick.

WISE: Did! He did many things, which I am sure he never thought to have done and which, to be sure, was not looked for of his wife and children.

In this fit of sickness, his thoughts were quite altered about his wife. I say his thoughts, so far as could be judged by his words and carriages to her.[476] For now she was his good wife, his godly wife, his honest wife, his duck, and dear and all. Now he told her that she had the best of it, she having a good life to stand by her, while his debaucheries and ungodly life did always stare him in the face. Now he told her the counsel that she often gave him was good, though he was so bad as not to take it.

Now he would hear her talk to him, and he would lie sighing by her while she so did. Now he would bid her pray for him that he might be delivered from Hell.[477]

He would also now consent that some of her good ministers might come to him to comfort him, and he would seem to show them

475. A dreadful example of God's anger.
476. What Mr Badman did more when he was sick.
477. Great alteration made in Mr Badman.

kindness when they came, for he would treat them kindly with words, and hearken diligently to what they said, only he did not care that they should talk much of his ill-spent life, because his conscience was clogged with that already. He cared not now to see his old companions. The thoughts of them were a torment to him. And now he would speak kindly to that child of his that took after its mother's steps, though he could not at all abide it before.

He also desired the prayers of good people, that God of his mercy would spare him a little longer, promising that if God would but let him recover this once, what a new, what a penitent man he would be toward God, and what a loving husband he would be to his wife, what liberty he would give her, yea, how he would go with her himself to hear her ministers, and how they should go hand-in-hand in the way to Heaven together.

ATTEN: Here was a fine show of things. I'll warrant you his wife was glad for this.

WISE: His wife! Aye, and a many good people besides. It was noised all over the town,[478] what a great change there was wrought upon Mr Badman: how sorry he was for his sins, how he began to love his wife, how he desired good men should pray to God to spare him, and what promises he now made to God in his sickness, that if ever he should raise him from his sickbed to health again, what a new penitent man he would be towards God, and what a loving husband to his good wife.

Well, ministers prayed, and good people rejoiced, thinking verily that they now had gotten a man from the Devil. Nay, some of the weaker sort did not stick to say that God had began a work of grace in his heart. And his wife, poor woman,[479] you cannot think how apt she was to believe it so. She rejoiced, and she hoped as she would have it. But, alas! Alas! In little time things all proved otherwise.

After he had kept his bed a while, his distemper began to abate, and he to feel himself better. So he in little time was so finely mended that he could walk about the house, and also obtained a very fine

478. The town-talk of Mr Badman's change.
479. His wife is comforted.

stomach to his food.[480] And now did his wife and her good friends stand gaping to see Mr Badman fulfil his promise of becoming new towards God and loving to his wife, but the contrary only showed itself. For so soon as ever he had hopes of mending, and found that his strength began to renew, his troubles began to go off his heart, and he grew as great a stranger to his frights and fears as if he had never had them.

But verily, I am apt to think, that one reason of his no more regarding or remembering of his sickbed fears, and of being no better for them, was some words that the doctor who supplied him with physic said to him when he was mending. For as soon as Mr Badman began to mend, the doctor came and sat him down by him in his house, and there fell into discourse with him about the nature of his disease. And among other things, they talked of Badman's trouble, and how he would cry out, tremble and express his fears of going to Hell when his sickness lay pretty hard upon him, to which the doctor replied[481] that those fears and outcries did arise from the height of his distemper, for that disease was often attended with lightness of the head, by reason the sick party could not sleep and for that the vapours disturbed the brain. 'But you see, sir,' quoth he, 'that so soon as you got sleep and betook yourself to rest, you quickly mended, and your head settled, and so those frenzies left you.'

'And was it so indeed,' thought Mr Badman. 'Were my troubles only the effects of my distemper, and because ill vapours got up into my brain? Then surely, since my physician was my saviour, my lust again shall be my God.' So he never minded religion more, but betook him again to the world, his lusts and wicked companions. And there was an end of Mr Badman's conversion.

ATTEN: I thought, as you told me of him, that this would be the result of the whole, for I discerned by your relating of things that the true symptoms of conversion were wanting in him, and that those that appeared to be anything like them were only such as the reprobates may have.

480. Mr Badman recovers and returns to his old course.
481. Ignorant physicians kill souls while they cure bodies.

WISE: You say right, for there wanted in him, when he was most sensible, a sense of the pollution of his nature. He only had guilt for his sinful actions, the which Cain, and Pharaoh, and Saul, and Judas, those reprobates, have had before him.[482]

Besides, the great things that he desired were to be delivered from going to Hell – and who would willingly? – and that his life might be lengthened in this world. We find not by all that he said or did that Jesus Christ the Saviour was desired by him from a sense of his need of his righteousness to clothe him and of his Spirit to sanctify him.[483]

His own strength was whole in him. He saw nothing of the treachery of his own heart, for had he, he would never have been so free to make promises to God of amendment. He would rather have been afraid that if he had mended, he should have turned with the dog to his vomit, and have begged prayers of saints and assistance from Heaven upon that account that he might have been kept from doing so.

'Tis true he did beg prayers of good people, and so did Pharaoh of Moses and Aaron, and Simon Magus of Simon Peter.[484]

His mind also seemed to be turned to his wife and child. But alas! 'Twas rather from conviction that God had given him concerning their happy estate over his than for that he had any true love to the work of God that was in them. True, some shows of kindness he seemed to have for them, and so had rich Dives, when in Hell, to his five brethren who were yet in the world. Yea, he had such love as to wish them in Heaven, that they might not come there to be tormented.[485]

ATTEN: Sickbed repentance is seldom good for anything.

WISE: You[486] say true. It is very rarely good for anything indeed. Death is unwelcome to nature, and usually when sickness and death visit the sinner, the first taking of him by the shoulder and the second standing at the bedchamber door to receive him, then the sinner begins to look about him and to bethink with himself, 'These will have me away before God, and I know that my life has not been as it should. How

482. Genesis 4:13–14; Exodus 9:27; 1 Samuel 15:24; Matthew 27:3–5.

483. The true symptoms of conversion wanting in all Mr Badman's sense of sin and desires of mercy.

484. Exodus 19:28; Acts 8:24.

485. Luke 16:27–28.

486. Of sickbed repentance, and that it is to be suspected.

147

shall I do to appear before God?' Or if it be more the sense of the punishment, and the place of the punishment of sinners, that also is starting to a defiled conscience, now roused by death's lumbering at the door.

And hence usually is sickbed repentance and the matter of it, to wit, to be saved from Hell and from death, and that God will restore again to health till they mend, concluding that it is in their power to mend as is evident by their large and lavishing promises to do it.

I have known many who, when they have been sick, have had large measures of this kind of repentance, and while it has lasted, the noise and sound thereof has made the town to ring again. But alas! How long has it lasted? Ofttimes scarce so long as until the party now sick has been well. It has passed away like a mist or a vapour. It has been a thing of no continuance. But this kind of repentance is by God compared to the howling of a dog, 'And they have not cried unto me with their heart, when they howled upon their beds.'[487]

ATTEN: Yet one may see by this the desperateness of man's heart,[488] for what is it but desperate wickedness to make promise to God of amendment if he will but spare them, and yet so soon as they are recovered or quickly after, fall to sin as they did before and never to regard their promise more.

WISE: It is a sign of desperateness, indeed, yea, of desperate madness. For surely they must needs think that God took notice of their promise that he heard the words that they spoke,[489] and that he has laid them up against the time to come, and will then bring out and testify to their faces that they flattered him with their mouth, and lied unto him with their tongue[490] when they lay sick, to their thinking upon their deathbed, and promised him that if He would recover them they would repent and amend their ways. But thus, as I have told you, Mr Badman did. He made great promises that he would be a new man, that he would leave his sins and become a convert, that he would love, etc., his godly wife, etc. Yea, many fine words had Mr Badman in his sickness, but no good actions when he was well.

487. Hos. 7:14.
488. A sign of the desperateness of man's heart.
489. Deuteronomy 1:34–35.
490. Psalm 78:34–37.

ATTEN: And how did his good wife take it when she saw that he had no amendment, but that he returned with the dog to his vomit, to his old courses again?

WISE: Why, it[491] broke her heart. It was a worse disappointment to her than the cheat that he gave her in marriage. At least she laid it more to heart, and could not so well grapple with it. You must think that she had put up many a prayer to God for him before, even all the time that he had carried it so badly to her. And now, when he was so affrighted in his sickness, and so desired that he might live and mend, poor woman, she thought that the time had come for God to answer her prayers. Nay, she did not let with gladness to whisper it out amongst her friends that 'twas so. But when she saw herself disappointed by her husband's turning rebel again, she could not stand up under it, but fell into a languishing distemper, and in a few weeks gave up the ghost.

ATTEN: Pray, how did she die?

WISE: Die! She died bravely, full of comfort of the faith of her interest in Christ, and by Him, of the world to come. She had many brave expressions in her sickness, and gave to those who came to visit her many signs of her salvation. The thoughts of the grave, but especially of her rising again, were sweet thoughts to her. She would long for death because she knew it would be her friend. She behaved herself like to some who were making of them ready to go meet their bridegroom.[492] 'Now,' said she, 'I am going to rest from my sorrows, my sighs, my tears, my mournings and complaints. I have heretofore longed to be among the saints, but might by no means be suffered to go. But now I am going, and no man can stop me, to the great meeting, "to the general assembly and church of the firstborn, which are written in heaven".[493] There I shall have my heart's desire. There I shall worship without temptation or other impediment. There I shall see the face of my Jesus, whom I have loved, whom I have served, and who now, I know, will save my soul.[494] I have prayed often for my husband, that he might be converted, but there has been no answer

491. Mr Badman's wife's heart is broken.
492. Her Christian speech.
493. Hebrews 12:22–24.
494. Her talk to her friends.

of God in that matter. Are my prayers lost? Are they forgotten? Are they thrown over the bar? No. They are hanged upon the horns of the golden altar, and I must have the benefit of them myself that moment that I shall enter into the gates, in at which the righteous nation that keeps truth shall enter. I say, I shall have the benefit of them. I can say as holy David. I say, I can say of my husband, as he could of his enemies. "As for me, when they were sick, my clothing was sackcloth: I humbled my soul with fasting; and my prayer returned into mine own bosom."[495] My prayers are not lost, my tears are yet in God's bottle. I would have had a crown and glory for my husband, and for those of my children who follow his steps. But so far as I can see yet, I must rest in the hope of having all myself.'

ATTEN: Did she talk thus openly?

WISE: No, this she spoke but to one or two of her most intimate acquaintances, who were permitted to come and see her when she lay languishing upon her deathbed.

ATTEN: Well, but pray go on in your relation. This is good. I am glad to hear it. This is as a cordial to my heart while we sit thus talking under this tree.

WISE: When she drew near her end, she called for her husband, and when he had come to her, she told him[496] that now he and she must part. And said she, 'God knows, and you shall know, that I have been a loving, faithful wife unto you. My prayers have been many for you, and as for all the abuses that I have received at your hand, those I freely and heartily forgive, and still shall pray for your conversion, even as long as I breathe in this world. But husband, I am going there where no bad man shall come, and if you do not convert, you will never see me more with comfort. Let not my plain words offend you. I am your dying wife, and of my faithfulness to you, would leave this exhortation with you. Break off your sins, fly to God for mercy while mercy's gate stands open. Remember that the day is coming when you, though now lusty and well, must lie at the gates of death as I do. And what will you then do, if you shall be found with a naked soul to meet with the cherubims with their flaming swords? Yea, what will

495. Psalm 35:13.
496. Her talk to her husband.

you then do, if death and Hell shall come to visit you, and you in your sins, and under the curse of the law?'

ATTEN: This was honest and plain. But what said Mr Badman to her?

WISE: He did what he could to divert her talk[497] by throwing in other things. He also showed some kind of pity to her now and would ask her what she would have, and with various kind of words put her out of her talk. For when she saw that she was not regarded, she fetched a deep sigh and lay still. So he went down, and then she called for her children and began to talk to them. And first she spoke to those who were rude,[498] and told them the danger of dying before they had grace in their hearts. She told them also that death might be nearer them than they were aware of, and bade them look, when they went through the churchyard again, if there were not little graves there. And, 'ah, children,' said she, 'will it not be dreadful to you, if we only shall meet at the day of Judgement, and then part again, and never see each other more?' And with that she wept. The children also wept, so she held on her discourse. 'Children,' said she, 'I am going from you. I am going to Jesus Christ, and with Him there is neither sorrow, nor sighing, nor pain, nor tears, nor death.[499] There would I have you go also, but I can neither carry you nor fetch you there. But if you shall turn from your sins to God, and shall beg mercy at His hands by Jesus Christ, you shall follow me, and shall, when you die, come to the place where I am going, that blessed place of rest. And then we shall be forever together, beholding the face of our redeemer, to our mutual and eternal joy.' So she bade them remember the words of a dying mother when she was cold in her grave, and themselves were hot in their sins, if perhaps her words might put check to their vice, and that they might remember and turn to God.

Then they all went down but her[500] darling, to wit, the child that she had most love for, because it followed her ways. So she addressed herself to that. 'Come to me,' said she, 'my sweet child, you are the child of my joy. I have lived to see you a servant of God. You

497. He diverts her discourse.
498. Her speech to her children who were rude.
499. Revelation 7:16, 21:3–4.
500. Her speech to her darling.

shall have eternal life. I, my sweetheart, shall go before, and you shall follow after. If you shall hold the beginning of your confidence steadfast to the end.[501] When I am gone, do you still remember my words: love your Bible, follow my ministers, deny ungodliness still. And if troublous times shall come, set a higher price upon Christ, his Word and ways, and the testimony of a good conscience, than upon all the world besides. Carry it kindly and dutifully to your father, but choose none of his ways. If you may, go to service. Choose that rather than to stay at home, but then be sure to choose a service where you may be helped forwards in the way to Heaven. And that you may have such a service, speak to my minister. He will help you, if possible, to such a one. I would have you also, my dear child, to love your brothers and sisters, but learn none of their naughty tricks. Have no fellowship with the unfruitful works of darkness, but rather reprove them.[502] You have grace, they have none. Do you therefore beautify the way of salvation before their eyes by a godly life, and conformable conversation to the revealed will of God, that your brothers and sisters may see and be the more pleased with the good ways of the Lord. If you shall live to marry, take heed of being served as I was, that is, of being beguiled with fair words, and the flatteries of a lying tongue. But first be sure of godliness, yea, as sure as it is possible for one to be in this world. Trust not your own eyes, nor your own judgement, I mean, as to that person's godliness that you are invited to marry. Ask counsel of good men, and do nothing therein if he lives without my minister's advice. I have also myself desired him to look after you.' Thus she talked to her children and gave them counsel, and after she had talked to this a little longer, she kissed it, and bade it go down.

Well, in short, her time drew on and the day that she must die. So she[503] died with a soul full of grace, a heart full of comfort and by her death ended a life full of trouble. Her husband made a funeral for her, perhaps because he was glad he was rid of her, but we will leave that to be manifest at judgement.

501. Hebrews 3:14.
502. Ephesians 5:11.
503. Her death.

ATTEN: This woman died well. And now we are talking of the dying of Christians, I will tell you a story of one who died some time since in our town. The man was a godly old Puritan, for so the godly were called in time past. This man after a long and godly life, fell sick of the sickness whereof he died. And as he lay drawing on, the woman who looked to him thought she heard music, and that the sweetest that ever she heard in her life, which also continued until he gave up the ghost. ☞ Now when his soul departed from him, the music seemed to withdraw and to go further and further off from the house, and so it went until the sound was quite gone out of hearing.

WISE: What do you think that might be?

ATTEN: For ought I know, the melodious notes of angels who were sent of God to fetch him to Heaven.

WISE: I cannot say but that God goes out of his ordinary road with us poor mortals sometimes. I cannot say this of this woman, but yet she had better music in her heart than sounded in this woman's ears.

ATTEN: I believe so. But pray tell me, did any of her other children hearken to her words so as to be bettered in their souls thereby?

WISE: One of them did,[504] and became a very hopeful young man. But for the rest, I can say nothing.

ATTEN: And what did Badman do after his wife was dead?

WISE: Why even as he did before. He scarce mourned a fortnight for her, and his mourning then was, I doubt, more in fashion than in heart.

ATTEN: Would he not sometimes talk of his wife when she was dead?

WISE: Yes, when the fit took him and could commend her too extremely, saying she was a good, godly, virtuous woman. But this is not a thing to be wondered at. It is common with wicked men to hate God's servants while alive, and to commend them when they are dead. So served the pharisees the prophets. Those of the prophets who were dead, they commended, and those of them who were alive they condemned.[505]

ATTEN: But did not Mr Badman marry again quickly?

504. One of her children converted by her dying words.
505. Matthew 23.

WISE: No, not a good while after. And when he was asked the reason, he would make this slighty answer, 'Who would keep a cow of their own, who can have a quart of milk for a penny?'[506] Meaning who would be at the charge to have a wife, who can have a whore when he lists? So villainous, so abominable did he continue after the death of his wife. Yet at last there was one was too hard for him. For, getting of him to her upon a time, and making of him sufficiently drunk, she was so cunning as to get a promise of marriage of him, and so held him to it, and forced him to marry her.[507] And she, as the saying is, was as good as he[508] at all his vile and ranting tricks. She had her companions as well as he had his, and she would meet them too at the tavern and alehouse more commonly than he was aware of. To be plain, she was a very whore, and had as great resort came to her where time and place was appointed, as any of them all. Aye, and he smelt it too, but could not tell how to help it. For if he began to talk, she could lay in his dish the whores that she knew he haunted, and she could fit him also with cursing and swearing, for she would give him oath for oath, and curse for curse.

ATTEN: What kind of oaths would she have?

WISE: Why damn her, and sink her, and the like.

ATTEN: These are provoking things.

WISE: So they are. But God does not altogether let such things go unpunished in this life. Something of this I have showed you already, and will here give you one or two instances more.

There lived, says one,[509] in the year 1551, in a city of Savoy, a man who was a monstrous curser and swearer, and though he was often admonished and blamed for it, yet would he by no means mend his manners. At length a great plague happening in the city, he withdrew himself into a garden, where being again admonished to give over his wickedness, he hardened his heart more, swearing, blaspheming God and giving himself to the Devil. And immediately the Devil snatched him up suddenly, his wife and kinswoman looking on, and carried him quite away. The magistrates advertised hereof, went to the place and examined the woman, who justified the truth of it.

506. Mr Badman's base language.
507. He marries again, and how he got this last wife.
508. What she was, and how they lived.
509. *Clark's Looking-glass*.

Also at Oster in the duchy of Magalapole, saith Mr Clark, a wicked woman used in her cursing to give herself body and soul to the Devil, and being reproved for it, still continued the same, till being at a wedding feast, the Devil came in person and carried her up into the air with most horrible outcries and roarings. And in that sort carried her round about the town that the inhabitants were ready to die for fear. And by and by he tore her in four pieces, leaving her four quarters in four several highways, and then brought her bowels to the marriage feast, and threw them upon the table before the mayor of the town, saying, 'Behold, these dishes of meat belong to you, whom the like destruction waits for, if you do not amend your wicked life.'

ATTEN: Though God forbears to deal thus with all men who thus rend and tear His name, and that immediate judgements do not overtake them, yet he makes their lives by other judgements bitter to them, does he not?

WISE: Yes, yes. And for proof, I need go no further than to this Badman and his wife, for their railing, and cursing, and swearing ended not in words. They would fight and fly at each other, and that like cats and dogs. But it must be looked upon as the hand and judgement of God upon him for his villainy. He had an honest woman before, but she would not serve his turn, and therefore God took her away, and gave him one as bad as himself. Thus that measure that he meted to his first wife, this last did mete to him again. And this is a punishment wherewith sometimes God will punish wicked men. So said Amos to Amaziah, 'thy wife shall be an harlot in the city'.[510] With this last wife Mr Badman lived a pretty while, but, as I told you before, in a most sad and hellish manner. And now he would bewail his first wife's death – not of love that he had to her godliness, for that he could never abide, but for that she used always to keep home, whereas this would go abroad. His first wife was also honest and true to that relation, but this last was a whore of her body. The first woman loved to keep things together, but this last would whirl them about as well as he. The first would be silent when he chid, and would take it patiently when he abused her, but this would give him word for word,

510. Amos 7:16–17.

blow for blow, curse for curse, so that now Mr Badman had met with his match.[511] God had a mind to make him see the baseness of his own life in the wickedness of his wives.[512] But all would not do with Mr Badman. He would be Mr Badman still. This judgement did not work any reformation upon him, no, not to God nor man.

ATTEN: I warrant you that Mr Badman thought when his wife was dead that next time he would match far better.

WISE: What he thought I cannot tell, but he could not hope for it in this match. For here he knew himself to be caught. He knew that he was by this woman entangled, and would therefore have gone back again, but could not. He knew her, I say, to be a whore before, and therefore could not promise himself a happy life with her. For he or she that will not be true to their own soul will neither be true to husband nor wife. And he knew that she was not true to her own soul, and therefore could not expect she should be true to him, but Solomon says, 'a whore is a deep pit',[513] and Mr Badman found it true. For when she had caught him in her pit, she would never leave him till she had got him to promise her marriage. And when she had taken him so far, she forced him to marry indeed. And after that, they lived that life that I have told you.

ATTEN: But did not the neighbours take notice of this alteration that Mr Badman had made?

WISE: Yes, and many of his neighbours, yea, many of those who were carnal said[514] 'tis a righteous judgement of God upon him, for his abusive carriage and language to his other wife. For they were all convinced that she was a virtuous woman, and he, vile wretch, had killed her, I will not say, with, but with the want of kindness.

ATTEN: And how long I pray did they live thus together?

WISE: Some fourteen or sixteen years, even until, though she also brought something with her, they had sinned all away and parted as poor as howlets.[515, xiv] And, in reason, how could it be otherwise? He would have his way, and she would have hers, he among his

---

511. He is punished in his last wife for his bad carriages towards his first.

512. He is not at all the better.

513. Proverbs 23:27.

514. None did pity him for his sorrow, but looked upon it as a just reward.

515. Badman and this last wife part as poor as howlets.

companions, and she among hers, he with his whores, and she with her rogues. And so they brought their noble to nine pence.

ATTEN: Pray, of what disease did Mr Badman die, for now I perceive we are come up to his death?

WISE: I cannot so properly say that he died of one disease,[516] for there were many who had consented and laid their heads together to bring him to his end. He was dropsical, he was consumptive, he was surfeited, was gouty and, as some say, he had a tang of the pox in his bowels. Yet the captain of all these men of death who came against him to take him away was the consumption, for 'twas that that brought him down to the grave.

ATTEN: Although I will not say, but the best men may die of a consumption, a dropsy or a surfeit, yea, that these may meet upon a man to end him. Yet I will say again that many times these diseases come through man's inordinate use of things. Much drinking brings dropsies, consumptions, surfeits and many other diseases. And I doubt that Mr Badman's death did come by his abuse of himself in the use of lawful and unlawful things. I ground this my sentence upon that report of his life that you at large have given me.

WISE: I think verily that you need not call back your sentence, for 'tis thought by many that by his cups and his queens he brought himself to this his destruction. He was not an old man when he died, nor was he naturally very feeble, but strong and of a healthy complexion. Yet, as I said, he mouldered away, and went, when he set a-going, rotten to his grave. And that which made him stink when he was dead, I mean, that made him stink in his name and fame was that he died with a spice of the foul disease upon him. A man whose life was full of sin, and whose death was without repentance.

ATTEN: These were blemishes sufficient to make him stink indeed.

WISE: They were so, and they did do it. No man could speak well of him when he was gone.[517] His name rotted above ground, as his carcass rotted under. And this is according to the saying of the wise man, 'The memory of the just is blessed: but the name of the wicked shall rot.'[518]

516. Mr Badman's sickness and diseases of which he died.
517. Badman's name stinks when he is dead.
518. Proverbs 10:7.

This text, in both the parts of it, was fulfilled upon him and the woman that he married first, for her name still did flourish, though she had been dead almost seventeen years, but his began to stink and rot before he had been buried seventeen days.

ATTEN: That man who dies with a life full of sin, and with a heart void of repentance, although he should die of the most golden disease, if there were any that might be so called, I will warrant him his name shall stink, and that in heaven and earth.

WISE: You say true, and therefore does the name of Cain, Pharaoh, Saul, Judas and the Pharisees, though dead thousands of years ago, stink as fresh in the nostrils of the world as if they were but newly dead.

ATTEN: I do fully acquiesce with you in this. But, sir, since you have charged him with dying impenitent, pray let me see how you will prove it. Not that I altogether doubt it, because you have affirmed it, but yet I love to have proof for what men say in such weighty matters.

WISE: When I said he died without repentance, I meant so far as those who knew him could judge, when they compared his life, the word and his death together.

ATTEN: Well said. They went the right way to find out whether he had, that is, did manifest that he had repentance or no. Now then show me how they did prove he had none?

WISE: So I will.[519] And first,[520] this was urged to prove it. He had not, in all the time of his sickness, a sight and sense of his sins, but was as secure, and as much at quiet, as if he had never sinned in all his life.

ATTEN: I must needs confess that this is a sign he had none. For how can a man repent of that of which he has neither sight nor sense? But 'tis strange that he had neither sight nor sense of sin now, when he had such a sight and sense of his evil before, I mean when he was sick before.

WISE: He was, as I said, as secure now as if he had been as sinless as an angel, though all men knew what a sinner he was, for he carried his sins in his forehead. His debauched life was read and known of all men, but his reputation was read and known of no man, for, as I said,

519. That Mr Badman dies impenitent is proved.
520. First proof that he died impenitent.

he had none. And for ought I know, the reason he had no sense of his sins now was because he profited not by that sense that he had of them before. He liked not to retain that knowledge of God then that caused his sins to come to remembrance. Therefore God gave him up now to a reprobate mind, to hardness and stupidity of spirit. And so was that scripture fulfilled upon him, 'He hath blinded their eyes.'[521] And that, 'Let their eyes be darkened that they may not see.'[522] Oh! For a man to live in sin, and to go out of the world without repentance for it is the saddest judgement that can overtake a man.

ATTEN: But, sir, although both you and I have consented that[523] without a sight and sense of sin there can be no repentance, yet that is but our bare say-so. Let us therefore now see if by the scripture we can make it good.

WISE: That is easily done. The three thousand that were converted, Acts the second, repented not till they had sight and sense of their sins.[524] Paul repented not till he had sight and sense of his sins. The gaoler repented not till he had sight and sense of his sins, nor could they. For of what should a man repent? The answer is, of sin. What is it to repent of sin? The answer is, to be sorry for it, to turn from it.[525] But how can a man be sorry for it who has neither sight nor sense of it? David did not only commit sins, but abode impenitent for them, until Nathan the Prophet was sent from God to give him a sight and sense of them.[526] And then, but not till then, he indeed repented of them. Job, in order to his repentance, cries unto God, 'Show me wherefore thou contendest with me.' And again, 'That which I see not teach thou me: if I have done iniquity, I will do no more.'[527] That is not in what I know, for I will repent of it, nor yet in what I know not, when you shall show me it. Also Ephraim's repentance was after he was turned to the sight and sense of his sins, and after he was instructed about the evil of them.[528]

ATTEN: These are good testimonies of this truth, and do – if matter of fact with which Mr Badman is charged, be true – prove indeed that

521. John 12:40.

522. Romans 11:10.

523. No sense of sin, no repentance proved.

524. Acts 2:9–16.

525. Psalm 38:18.

526. 2 Samuel 12.

527. Job 10:2, 34:32.

528. Jeremiah 31:18–20.

he did not repent, but as he lived, so he died in his sin. For without repentance a man is sure to die in his sin, for they will lie down in the dust with him,[529] rise at the Judgement with him, hang about his neck like cords and chains when he stands at the bar of God's tribunal, and go with him too when he goes away from the judgement seat, with a 'Depart from me ye cursed into everlasting fire, prepared for the Devil and his angels,' and there shall fret and gnaw his conscience, because they will be to him a never-dying worm.[530]

WISE: You say well, and I will add a word or two more to what I have said. Repentance, as it is not produced without a sight and sense of sin, so every sight and sense of sin cannot produce it. I mean, every sight and sense of sin cannot[531] produce that repentance, that is, repentance unto salvation, repentance never to be repented of. For it is yet fresh before us that Mr Badman had a sight and sense of sin, in that fit of sickness that he had before, but it died without procuring any such godly fruit, as was manifest by his so soon returning with the dog to his vomit. Many people think also that repentance stands in confession of sin only, but they are very much mistaken, for repentance, as was said before, is a being sorry for and a turning from transgression to God by Jesus Christ. Now, if this be true, that every sight and sense of sin will not produce repentance, then repentance cannot be produced there where there is no sight and sense of sin. That every sight and sense of sin will not produce repentance, to wit, the godly repentance that we are speaking of, is manifest in Cain, Pharaoh, Saul and Judas, who all of them had sense, great sense of sin, but none of them repentance unto life.

Now I conclude, that Mr Badman did die impenitent, and so a death most miserable.

ATTEN: But pray now, before we conclude our discourse of Mr Badman, give me another proof of his dying in his sins.

WISE: Another proof is this.[532] He did not desire a sight and sense of sins that he might have repentance for them. Did I say he did not desire it, I will add, he greatly desired to remain in his security, and

529. Job 20:11; Proverbs 5:22.
530. Matthew 25; Isaiah 66:24; Mark 9:44.
531. Every sight and sense of sin cannot produce repentance.
532. Second proof that he died impenitent.

that I shall prove by that which follows. First, he could not endure that any man now should talk to him of his sinful life, and yet that was the way to beget a sight and sense of sin, and so of repentance from it in his soul. But, I say, he could not endure such discourse. Those men who did offer to talk unto him of his ill-spent life, they were as little welcome to him in the time of his last sickness as was Elijah when he went to meet with Ahab, as he went down to take possession of Naboth's vineyard. 'Hast thou found me,' said Ahab, 'O mine enemy?'[533] So would Mr Badman say in his heart to and of those that thus did come to him, though indeed they came even of love, to convince him of his evil life, that he might have repented thereof and have obtained mercy.

ATTEN: Did good men then go to see him in his last sickness?

WISE: Yes. Those who were his first wife's acquaintance, they went to see him and to talk with and to him, if perhaps he might now, at last, bethink himself and cry to God for mercy.

ATTEN: They did well to try now at last if they could save his soul from hell. But pray how can you tell that he did not care for the company of such?

WISE: Because of the differing carriage that he had for them from what he had when his old carnal companions came to see him. When his old companions came to see him, he would stir up himself as much as he could both by words and looks, to signify they were welcome to him. He would also talk with them freely, and look pleasantly upon them, though the talk of such could be none other but such as David said, carnal men would offer to him when they came to visit him in his sickness, 'If he comes to see me,' says he, 'he speaketh vanity, his heart gathereth iniquity to itself.'[534] But these kind of talks, I say, Mr Badman better brooked than he did the company of better men.

But I will more particularly give you a character[535] of his carriage to good men and good talk when they came to see him.

One – when they were come, he would seem to fail in his spirits at the sight of them.

533. 1 Kings 21:17–21.
534. Psalm 41:6.
535. How Badman carried it to good men when they came to visit him in his last sickness.

Two – he would not care to answer them to any of those questions that they would at times put to him, to feel what sense he had of sin, death, Hell, and judgement: But would either say nothing, or answer them by way of evasion, or else by telling of them he was so weak and spent that he could not speak much.

Three – he would never show forwardness to speak to or talk with them, but was glad when they held their tongues. He would ask them no question about his state and another world, or how he should escape that damnation that he had deserved.

Four – he had got a haunt at last to bid his wife and keeper, when these good people attempted to come to see him, to tell them that he was asleep or inclining to sleep, or so weak for want thereof, that he could not abide any noise. And so they would serve them time after time, till at last they were discouraged from coming to see him any more.

Five – he was so hardened now, in this time of his sickness, that he would talk, when his companions came unto him, to the disparagement of those good men – and of their good doctrine, too – that of love did come to see him, and that did labour to convert him.

Six – when these good men went away from him, he would never say, 'Pray, when will you be pleased to come again, for I have a desire to more of your company, and to hear more of your good instruction?' No, not a word of that, but when they were going would scarce bid them drink, or say, 'Thank you for your good company and good instruction.'

Seven – his talk in his sickness with his companions would be of the world, as trades, houses, lands, great men, great titles, great places, outward prosperity, or outward adversity, or some such carnal thing.

By all which I conclude that he did not desire a sense and sight of his sin that he might repent and be saved.

ATTEN: It must needs be so as you say, if these things be true that you have asserted of him. And I do the rather believe them, because I think you dare not tell a lie of the dead.

WISE: I was one of them who went to him, and who beheld his carriage and manner of way, and this is a true relation of it that I have given you.

ATTEN: I am satisfied. But pray if you can, show me now by the Word, what sentence of God does pass upon such men?

WISE: Why, the man that is thus averse to repentance, that desires not to hear of his sins, that he might repent and be saved, is said to be a man who says unto God, 'Depart from me, for I desire not the knowledge of thy ways.'[536] He is a man who says in his heart and with his actions, 'I have loved strangers, [sins] and after them I will go.'[537] He is a man who shuts his eyes, stops his ears, and who turns his spirit against God. Yea he is the man who is at enmity with God, and who abhors Him with his soul.[538]

ATTEN: What other sign can you give me that Mr Badman died without repentance?

WISE: Why, he did never heartily cry to God for mercy all the time of his affliction.[539] True, when sinking fits, stitches or pains took hold upon him, then he would say as other carnal men use to do, 'Lord help me,' 'Lord strengthen me,' 'Lord deliver me,' and the like. But to cry to God for mercy, that he did not, but lay, as I hinted before, as if he never had sinned.

ATTEN: That is another bad sign indeed, for crying to God for mercy is one of the first signs of repentance. When Paul lay repenting of his sin, upon his bed, the Holy Ghost said of him, 'Behold, he prayeth.'[540] But he who has not the first signs of repentance, 'tis a sign he has none of the other, and so indeed none at all. I do not say, but there may be crying, where there may be no sign of repentance. 'They cried,' says David, 'unto the Lord, but he answered them not,'[541] but that He would have done, if their cry had been the fruit of repentance. But, I say, if men may cry and yet have no repentance, be sure, they have none that cry not at all. It is said in Job, 'They cry not when he bindeth them.'[542] That is because they have no repentance. No repentance, no cries. False repentance, false cries. True repentance, true cries.

536. Job 21:14.
537. Jeremiah 2:25.
538. Zechariah 7:11–12; Acts 28:26–27.
539. Third proof that he died impenitent.
540. Acts 9:11.
541. Psalm 18:41.
542. Job 36:13.

WISE: I know that it is as possible for a man to forbear crying who has repentance, as it is for a man to forbear groaning who feels deadly pain. He who looks into the Book of Psalms, where repentance is most lively set forth even in its true and proper effects, shall there find that crying, strong crying, hearty crying, great crying, and incessant crying have been the fruits of repentance. But none of this had this Mr Badman, therefore he died in his sins.

That crying is an inseparable effect of repentance is seen in these scriptures. Have mercy upon me, O God, according to the multitude of your tender mercies, blot out my transgressions. 'Have mercy upon me, O Lord; for I am weak: O Lord, heal me; for my bones are vexed. My soul is also sore vexed: but thou, O Lord, how long? Return, O Lord, deliver my soul: oh save me for thy mercies' sake.' 'O Lord, rebuke me not in thy wrath: neither chasten me in thy hot displeasure. For thine arrows stick fast in me, and thy hand presseth me sore. There is no soundness in my flesh because of thine anger; neither is there any rest in my bones because of my sin. For mine iniquities are gone over mine head: as a heavy burden they are too heavy for me. My wounds stink and are corrupt because of my foolishness. I am troubled; I am bowed down greatly; I go mourning all the day long. For my loins are filled with a loathsome disease: and there is no soundness in my flesh. I am feeble and sore broken: I have roared by reason of the disquietness of my heart.'[543]

I might give you a great number more of the holy sayings of good men whereby they express how they were, what they felt and whether they cried or no when repentance was wrought in them. Alas, alas, it is as possible for a man, when the pangs of guilt are upon him to forbear praying, as it is for a woman when pangs of travel are upon her to forbear crying. If all the world should tell me that such a man has repentance, yet if he is not a praying man, I should not be persuaded to believe it.

ATTEN: I know no reason why you should, for there is nothing can demonstrate that such a man has it. But pray, sir, what other sign have you by which you can prove that Mr Badman died in his sins, and so in a state of damnation?

543. Psalm 51:1, 6:1–4, 38:1–8.

WISE: I have this to prove it.[544] Those who were his old sinful companions in the time of his health were those whose company and carnal talk he most delighted in in the time of his sickness. I did occasionally hint this before, but now I make it an argument of his want of grace, for where there is indeed a work of grace in the heart, that work does not only change the heart, thoughts and desires, but the conversation also, yea, conversation and company, too. When Paul had a work of grace in his soul, he assayed to join himself to the disciples. He was for his old companions in their abominations no longer. He was now a disciple, and was for the company of disciples. And he was with them coming in and going out in Jerusalem.[545]

ATTEN: I thought something when I heard you make mention of it before. Thought I, this is a shrewd sign that he had not grace in his heart. Birds of a feather, thought I, will flock together. If this man was one of God's children, he would herd with God's children, his delight would be with and in the company of God's children. As David said, 'I am a companion of all them that fear thee, and of them that keep thy precepts.'[546]

WISE: You say well, for what fellowship has he who believes with an infidel? And although it be true, that all that join to the godly are not godly, yet they who shall inwardly choose the company of the ungodly and open profane rather than the company of the godly, as Mr Badman did, surely are not godly men, but profane. He was, as I told you, out of his element when good men did come to visit him, but then he was where he would be when he had his vain companions about him. Alas! Grace, as I said, alters all – heart, life, company, and all – for by it the heart and man is made new. And a new heart, a new man, must have objects of delight that are new, and like himself. Old things are passed away. Why? For 'all things are become new'.[547] Now if all things have become new, to wit, heart, mind, thoughts, desires and delights, it follows by consequence that the company must be answerable. Hence it is said that they who believed were together, that they went to their own company, that they were added

544. Fourth proof that he died impenitent.
545. Acts 9:26–28.
546. Psalm 119:63.
547. 2 Corinthians 5:17.

to the Church, that they were of one heart and of one soul,[548] and the like. Now if it is objected that Mr Badman was sick, and so could not go to the godly, yet he had a tongue in his head and could, had he had a heart, have spoken to some to call or send for the godly to come to him. Yea, he would have done so, yea, the company of all others, especially his fellow sinners, would, even in every appearance of them before him, have been a burden and a grief unto him. His heart and affection standing bent to good, good companions would have suited him best. But his companions were his old associates. His delight was in them, therefore his heart and soul were yet ungodly.

ATTEN: Pray, how was he when he drew near his end, for I perceive that what you say of him now has reference to him and to his actions at the beginning of his sickness? Then he could endure company and much talk. Besides, perhaps then he thought he should recover and not die, as afterwards he had cause to think, when he was quite wasted with pining sickness, when he was at the grave's mouth. But how was he, I say, when he was as we say at the grave's mouth, within a step of death, when he saw and knew, and could not but know, that shortly he must die and appear before the judgement of God?

WISE: Why,[549] there was not any other alteration in him than what was made by his disease upon his body. Sickness, you know, will alter the body. Also pains and stitches will make men groan, but for his mind he had no alteration there. His mind was the same, his heart was the same. He was the self-same Mr Badman still. Not only in name but conditions, and that to the very day of his death, yea, so far as could be gathered to the very moment in which he died.

ATTEN: Pray, how was he in his death? Was death strong upon him? Or did he die with ease, quietly?

WISE: As quietly as a[550] lamb. There seemed not to be in it, to standers-by, so much as a strong struggle of nature. And as for his mind, it seemed to be wholly at quiet. But pray, why do you ask me this question?

548. Acts 4:32–33, 2:44–47.
549. How Mr Badman was when near his end.
550. He died like a lamb.

ATTEN: Not for my own sake, but for others. For there is such[551] an opinion as this among the ignorant that if a man dies, as they call it, like a lamb, that is quietly, and without that consternation of mind that others show in their death, they conclude, and that beyond all doubt, that such a one has gone to Heaven, and has certainly escaped the wrath to come.

WISE: There is no judgement to be made by a quiet death of the eternal state of him who so dies. Suppose one man should die quietly, another should die suddenly and a third should die under great consternation of spirit. No man can judge of their eternal condition by the manner of any of these kinds of deaths. He who dies quietly, suddenly or under consternation of spirit may go to Heaven, or may go to Hell. No man can tell where a man goes by any such manner of death. The[552] judgement therefore that we make of the eternal condition of a man must be gathered from another consideration, to wit, did the man die in his sins? Did he die in unbelief? Did he die before he was born again? Then he is gone to the Devil and Hell, though he died never so quietly. Again, was the man a good man? Had he faith and holiness? Was he a lover and a worshipper of God by Christ, according to His Word? Then he is gone to God and Heaven, how suddenly, or in what consternation of mind soever he died. But Mr Badman was naught. His life was evil, his ways were evil – evil to his end. He therefore went to Hell and to the Devil, how quietly soever he died.

Indeed there is, in some cases, a judgement to be made of a man's eternal condition by the manner of the death he dies.[553] As suppose now a man should murder himself, or live a wicked life, and after that die in utter despair – these men without doubt do both of them go to Hell. And here I will take an occasion to speak of two of Mr Badman's brethren, for you know I told you before that he had brethren, and of the manner of their death. One of them killed himself, and the other after a wicked life died in utter despair. Now I should not be afraid to conclude of both these, that they went by, and through their death to Hell.

551. The opinion of the ignorant about his manner of dying.
552. How we must judge whether men die well or no.
553. When we may judge of a man's eternal state by the manner of his death.

ATTEN: Pray tell me concerning the first, how he made away himself?

WISE: Why, he took a knife and cut his own throat, and immediately gave up the ghost and died. Now what can we judge of such a man's condition, since the scripture says no murderer has eternal life, etc., but that it must be concluded that such a one has gone to Hell. He was a murderer, a self-murderer, and he is the worst murderer – one who slays his own body and soul. Nor do we find mention made of any but cursed ones who do such kind of deeds. I say, no mention made in holy writ of any others but such who murder themselves.

And this is the sore judgement of God upon men, when God shall, for the sins of such, give them up to be their own executioners, or rather to execute his judgement and anger upon themselves. And let me earnestly give this caution to sinners. Take heed, sirs: break off your sins lest God serves you as he served Mr Badman's brother, that is, lest he gives you up to be your own murderers.

ATTEN: Now you talk of this, I did once know a man, ☞ a barber, who took his own razor and cut his own throat, and then put his head out of his chamber window to show the neighbours what he had done, and after a little while died.

WISE: I can tell you ☞ a more dreadful thing than this, I mean, as to the manner of doing the fact.[554] There was about twelve years since, a man who lived at Brafield by Northampton named John Cox who murdered himself. The manner of his doing of it was thus. He was a poor man, and had for some time been sick, and the time of his sickness was about the beginning of hay time, and taking too many thoughts how he should live afterwards, if he lost his present season of work, he fell into deep despair about the world, and cried out to his wife the morning before he killed himself, saying, 'We are undone.' But quickly after, he desired his wife to depart the room, 'Because,' said he, 'I will see if I can get any rest.' So she went out. But he, instead of sleeping, quickly took his razor, and therewith cut up a great hole in his side, out of which he pulled and cut off some of his guts, and threw them, with the blood up and down the chamber. But this not speeding of him so soon as he desired, he took the same razor and therewith cut his own throat. His wife, then hearing of him

554. The story of John Cox.

sigh and fetch his wind short, came again into the room to him, and seeing what he had done, she ran out and called in some neighbours, who came to him where he lay in a bloody manner, frightful to behold. Then said one of them to him, 'Ah! John, what have you done? Are you not sorry for what you have done?' He answered roughly, ''Tis too late to be sorry.' Then said the same person to him again, 'Ah! John, pray to God to forgive you this bloody act of yours.' At the hearing of which exhortation, he seemed much offended, and in angry manner said, 'Pray!' And with that flung himself away to the wall and, so after a few gasps, died desperately. When he had turned him of his back, to the wall, the blood ran out of his belly as out of a bowl, and soaked quite through the bed to the boards, and through the chinks of the boards, it ran pouring down to the ground. Some said that when the neighbours came to see him, he lay groping with his hand in his bowels, reaching upward, as was thought, that he might have pulled or cut out his heart. 'Twas said also that some of his liver had been by him torn out and cast upon the boards, and that many of his guts hung out of the bed on the side thereof. But I cannot confirm all particulars. But the general of the story, with these circumstances above mentioned, is true. I had it from a sober and credible person who himself was one who saw him in this bloody state, and who talked with him, as was hinted before.

Many other such dreadful things might be told you, but these are enough, and too many, too, if God in his wisdom had thought necessary to prevent them.

ATTEN: This is a dreadful story, and I would to God that it might be a warning to others to instruct them to fear before God, and pray, lest he gives them up to do as John Cox has done. For surely self-murderers cannot go to Heaven. And therefore, as you have said, he who dies by his own hands has certainly gone to Hell. But speak a word or two of the other man you mentioned.

WISE: What, of a wicked man dying in despair?

ATTEN: Yes, of a wicked man dying in despair.

WISE: Well, then.[555] This Mr Badman's other brother was a very wicked man, both in heart and life. I say in heart, because he was so

555. Of dying in despair.

in life, nor could anything reclaim him – neither good men, good books, good examples, nor God's judgements. Well, after he had lived a great while in his sins, God smote with a sickness of which he died. Now in his sickness, his conscience began to be awakened, and he began to roar out of his ill-spent life insomuch that the town began to ring of him. Now when it was noised about, many of the neighbours came to see him, and to read by him, as is the common way with some. But all that they could do ☞ could not abate his terror, but he would lie in his bed gnashing of his teeth, and wringing of his wrists, concluding upon the damnation of his soul. And in that horror and despair he died, not calling upon God, but distrusting in his mercy, and blaspheming of his name.

ATTEN: This brings to my mind a man that a friend of mine told me of. ☞ He had been a wicked liver. So when he came to die, he fell into despair, and having concluded that God had no mercy for him, he addressed himself to the Devil for favour, saying, 'Good Devil, be good unto me.'

WISE: This is almost like Saul, who being forsaken of God, went to the Witch of Endor, and so to the Devil for help.[556] But alas, should I set myself to collect these dreadful stories, it would be easy in little time to present you with hundreds of them. But I will conclude as I began. They who are their own murderers, or who die in despair after they have lived a life of wickedness, do surely go to Hell.

And here I would put in a caution: Every one who dies under consternation of spirit, that is, under amazement and great fear, do not therefore die in despair. For a good man may have this for his bands in his death,[557] and yet go to Heaven and glory. For, as I said before, he who is a good man, a man who has faith and holiness, a lover and worshipper of God by Christ, according to his Word, may die in consternation of spirit. For Satan will not be wanting to assault good men upon their deathbed, but they are secured by the Word and power of God, yea, and are also helped, though with much agony of spirit, to exercise themselves in faith and prayer, the which he who dies in despair can by no means do.

556. 1 Samuel 28.
557. Psalm 73:4.

But let us return to Mr Badman, and enter further discourse of the manner of his death.

ATTEN: I think you and I are both of a mind, for just now I was thinking to call you back to him also. And pray now, since it is your own motion to return again to him, let us discourse a little more of his quiet and still death.

WISE: With all my heart. You know we were speaking before of the manner of Mr Badman's death.[558] How that he died very stilly and quietly, upon which you made observation, that the common people conclude, that if a man dies quietly, and as they call it, like a lamb, he has certainly gone to Heaven. When alas, if a wicked man dies quietly, if a man who has all his days lived in notorious sin, dies quietly, his quiet dying is so far off from being a sign of his being saved, that it is an uncontrollable proof of his damnation. This was Mr Badman's case. He lived wickedly even to the last, and then went quietly out of the world. Therefore Mr Badman has gone to Hell.

ATTEN: Well, but since you are upon it, and also so confident in it, to wit, that a man who lives a wicked life till he dies, and then dies quietly, has gone to Hell, let me see what show of proof you have for this your opinion.

WISE: My first argument is drawn from the necessity of repentance. No man can be saved except he who repents, nor can he repent who sees not, who knows not that he is a sinner, and he who knows himself to be a sinner, will, I will warrant him, be molested for the time by that knowledge.[559] This, as it is testified by all the scriptures, so it is testified by Christian experience. He who knows of himself to be a sinner is molested, especially if that knowledge comes not to him until he is cast upon his deathbed. Molested, I say, before he can die quietly. Yea, he is molested, dejected and cast down. He is also made to cry out, to hunger and thirst after mercy by Christ, and if at all he shall indeed come to die quietly, I mean with that quietness that is begotten by faith and hope in God's mercy, to the which Mr Badman and his brethren were utter strangers, his quietness is distinguished

558. Further discourse of Mr Badman's death.
559. He that after a sinful life dies quietly, that is, without repentance, goes to Hell:
first proof.

by all judicious observers by what went before it, by what it flows from and also by what is the fruit thereof.

I must confess I am no admirer of sickbed repentance, for I think verily it is seldom[560] good for anything. But I say, he who has lived in sin and profaneness all his days, as Mr Badman did, and yet shall die quietly, that is, without repentance steps in 'tween his life and death, he has assuredly gone to Hell, and is damned.

ATTEN: This does look like an argument indeed, for repentance must come, or else we must go to hellfire. And if a lewd liver shall, I mean, who so continues till the day of his death, yet go out of the world quietly, 'tis a sign that he died without repentance, and so a sign that he is damned.

WISE: I am satisfied in it, for my part, and that from the necessity and nature of repentance. It is necessary because God calls for it, and will not pardon sin without it. Except you repent, you shall all likewise perish. This is that which God has said, and he will prove but a foolhardy man who shall yet think to go to Heaven and glory without it. Repent, for the axe is laid to the root of the tree, every tree therefore that brings not forth good fruit – but no good fruit can be where there is not sound repentance – shall be hewn down and cast into the fire.[561] This was Mr Badman's case. He had attending of him a sinful life, and that to the very last, and yet died quietly, that is, without repentance. He is gone to Hell and is damned. For the nature of repentance, I have touched upon that already, and showed that it never was where a quiet death is the immediate companion of a sinful life, and therefore Mr Badman has gone to Hell.

Secondly,[562] my second argument is drawn from that blessed Word of Christ, While the strong man armed keeps the house, his goods are in peace, till a stronger than he comes,[563] but the strong man armed kept Mr Badman's house, that is, his heart, and soul, and body, for he went from a sinful life quietly out of this world. The stronger did not disturb by intercepting with sound repentance, between his sinful life and his quiet death. Therefore Mr Badman has gone to Hell.

560. Sickbed repentance seldom good for anything.
561. Luke 13:1–7.
562. Second proof.
563. Luke 11:21–22.

The strong man armed is the Devil, and quietness is his security. The Devil never fears losing of the sinner, if he can but keep him quiet. Can he but keep him quiet in a sinful life, and quiet in his death, he is his own. Therefore he says, his goods are in peace, that is, out of danger. There is no fear of the Devil's losing such a soul, say, because Christ, who is the best judge in this matter, says, his goods are in peace, in quiet, and out of danger.

ATTEN: This is a good one, too,[564] for doubtless peace and quiet with sin is one of the greatest signs of a damnable state.

WISE: So it is. Therefore, when God would show the greatness of his anger against sin and sinners in one word, He says they are joined to idols, let them alone.[565] Let them alone, that is, disturb them not. Let them go on without control. Let the Devil enjoy them peaceably. Let him carry them out of the world unconverted quietly. This is one of the sorest of judgements, and bespeaks the burning anger of God against sinful men. See also when you come home, the fourteenth verse of the chapter last mentioned in the margin: 'I will not punish your daughters when they commit whoredom. I will let them alone.'[566] They shall live and die in their sins. But,

Thirdly, my third argument[567] is drawn from that saying of Christ, 'He hath blinded their eyes, and hardened their heart; that they should not see with their eyes, nor understand with their heart, and be converted, and I should heal them.'[568]

There are three things that I will take notice of from these words.

One – the first is that there can be no conversion to God where the eye is darkened, and the heart hardened. The eye must first be made to see, and the heart to break and relent under and for sin, or else there can be no conversion. He has blinded their eyes, and hardened their hearts, lest they should see, and understand and so be converted. And this was clearly Mr Badman's case. He lived a wicked life, and also died with his eyes shut and heart hardened, as is manifest in that a sinful life was joined with a quiet death, and

564. Peace in a sinful state is a sign of damnation.
565. Hosea 4:17.
566. Hosea 4:14.
567. Third proof.
568. John 12:40.

all for that he should not be converted, but partake of the fruit of his sinful life in hellfire.

Two – the second thing that I take notice of from these words is that this is a dispensation and manifestation of God's anger against a man for his sin. When God is angry with men, I mean, when he is so angry with them, this among many is one of the judgements that He gives them up unto, to wit, to blindness of mind, and hardness of heart, which He also suffers to accompany them till they enter in at the gates of death. And then and there, and not short of then and there, their eyes come to be opened. Hence it is said of the rich man mentioned in Luke, 'He died, and in Hell he lift up his eyes,'[569] implying that he did not lift them up before. He neither saw what he had done, nor where he was going till he came to the place of execution, even into Hell. He died asleep in his soul. He died bespotted, stupefied, and so consequently for quietness, like a child or lamb, even as Mr Badman did. This was a sign of God's anger. He had a mind to damn him for his sins, and therefore would not let him see nor have a heart to repent for them, lest he should convert, and his damnation, which God had appointed, should be frustrated, 'Lest they should be converted, and I should heal them.'[570]

Three – the third thing that I take notice of from hence is that a sinful life and a quiet death annexed to it is the ready, the open, the beaten, the common highway to Hell. There is no surer sign of damnation than for a man to die quietly after a sinful life. I do not say that all wicked men who are molested at their death with a sense of sin and fears of Hell do therefore go to Heaven, for some are also made to see, and are left to despair, not converted by seeing, that they might go roaring out of this world to their place. But I say, there is no surer sign of a man's damnation, than to die quietly after a sinful life, than to sin and die with his eyes shut, than to sin and die with a heart that cannot repent. He has blinded their eyes and hardened their heart that they should not see with their eyes, nor understand with their heart – no, not so long as they are in

569. Luke 16:22.
570. Mark 4:12.

this world – lest they should see with their eyes, and understand with their heart, and should be converted, and I should heal them.[571]

God has a judgement for wicked men. God will be even with wicked men. God knows how to reserve the ungodly to the day of Judgement to be punished.[572] And this is one of His ways by which He does it. Thus it was with Mr Badman.

Four – fourthly,[573] it is said in the Book of Psalms, concerning the wicked, there is no bands in their death, but their strength is firm. By no bands, he means no troubles, no gracious chastisements, no such corrections for sin as fall to be the lot of God's people for theirs, yea, that many times falls to be theirs at the time of their death. Therefore he adds concerning the wicked, 'They are not in trouble as other men; neither are they plagued like other men,' but go as securely out of the world as if they had never sinned against God, and put their own souls into danger of damnation. There is no band in their death. They seem to go unbound and set at liberty out of this world, though they have lived notoriously wicked all their days in it. The prisoner who is to die at the gallows for his wickedness must first have his irons knocked off his legs, so he seems to go most at liberty, when indeed he is going to be executed for his transgressions. Wicked men also have no bands in their death. They seem to be more at liberty when they are even at the wind-up of their sinful life than at anytime besides.

Hence you shall have them boast of their faith and hope in God's mercy, when they lie upon their deathbed. Yea, you shall have them speak as confidently of their salvation, as if they had served God all their days, when the truth is the bottom of this their boasting is because they have no bands in their death.

Their sin and base life comes not into their mind to correct them and bring them to repentance, but presumptuous thoughts, and a hope and faith of the spider's – the Devil's – making, possesses their soul to their own eternal undoing.[574]

Hence wicked men's hope is said to die not before but with them.

571. Romans 2:1–5; Acts 28:26–27.
572. 2 Peter 2.
573. Fourth proof. Psalm 73:4–6.
574. Job 8:13–14.

They give up the ghost together. And thus did Mr Badman. His sins and his hope went with him to the gate, but there his hope left him, because it died there, but his sins went in with him to be a worm to gnaw him in his conscience forever and ever.

The opinion therefore of the common people concerning this kind of dying is[575] frivolous and vain, for Mr Badman died like a lamb, or as they call it, like a chrism child, quietly and without fear. I speak not this with reference to the struggling of nature with death, but as to the struggling of the conscience with the judgement of God. I know that nature will struggle with death. I have seen a dog and sheep die hardly. And thus may a wicked man do because there is an antipathy between nature and death. But even while, even then, when death and nature are struggling for mastery, the soul, the conscience, may be as besotted, as benumbed, as senseless and ignorant of its miserable state, as the block or bed on which the sick lies. And thus they may die like a chrism child in show, but indeed like one who by the judgement of God is bound over to eternal damnation. And that also by the same judgement is kept from seeing what they are, and where they are going till they plunge down among the flames.

And as it is a very great judgement of God on wicked men who so die, for it cuts them off from all possibility of repentance, and so of salvation,[576] so it is as great a judgement upon those who are their companions who survive them. For by the manner of their death, they dying so quietly, so like unto chrism children as they call it, they are hardened and take courage to go on in their course.

For comparing their life with their death, their sinful cursed lives with their childlike, lamb-like death, they think that all is well, that no damnation is happened to them. Though they lived like devils incarnate, yet they died like harmless ones. There was no whirlwind, no tempest, no band, nor plague in their death. They died as quietly as the most godly of them all, and had as great faith and hope of salvation, and would talk as boldly of salvation as if they had assurance of it. But as was their hope in life, so was their death. Their hope was

575. A frivolous opinion.

576. When a wicked man dies in his sins quietly, it is a judgement of God upon his wicked beholder.

without trial because it was none of God's working, and their death was without molestation because so was the judgement of God concerning them.

But I say, at this their survivors take heart to tread their steps, and to continue to live in the breach of the law of God, yea, they carry it stately in their villainies, for so it follows in the Psalm. There is no bands in their death, but their strength is firm, etc. 'Therefore pride compasseth them [the survivors] about as a chain; violence covereth them as a garment.'[577] Therefore they take courage to do evil, therefore they pride themselves in their iniquity. Therefore, wherefore? Why, because their fellows died after they had lived long in a most profane and wicked life, as quietly and as like to lambs as if they had been innocent.

Yea, they are bold by seeing this to conclude that God either does not or will not take notice of their sins. They speak wickedly, they speak loftily. They speak wickedly of sin, for that they make it better than by the Word it is pronounced to be. They speak wickedly concerning oppression that they commend and count it a prudent act. They also speak loftily. They set their mouth against the heavens, etc. And they say, 'How does God know, and is there knowledge in the most High?' And all this, so far as I can see, arises in their hearts from the beholding of the quiet and lamb-like death of their companions.[578]

'Behold, these are the ungodly, who prosper in the world,' that is, by wicked ways, 'they increase in riches.'[579]

This therefore is a great judgement of God both upon that man who dies in his sins, and also upon his companion who beholds him so to die. He sins, he dies in his sins, and yet dies quietly. What shall his companion say to this? What judgement shall he make how God will deal with him by beholding the lamb-like death of his companion? Be sure he cannot as from such a sight say, 'Woe be to me,' for judgement is before him. He cannot gather that sin is a dreadful and a bitter thing by the childlike death of Mr Badman, but must

577. Psalm 73:6.
578. Psalm 73:8–11.
579. Psalm 73:12.

rather, if he judges according to what he sees, or according to his corrupted reason, conclude with the wicked ones of old, 'Every one that doeth evil is good in the sight of the Lord, and he delighteth in them; or, Where is the God of judgement?'[580]

Yea, this is enough to puzzle the wisest man. David himself was put to a stand by beholding the quiet death of ungodly men. 'Verily,' says he, 'I have cleansed my heart in vain, and have washed my hands in innocency.'[581] They to appearance fare better by far than I. Their eyes stand out with fatness, they have more that heart can wish. 'But all the day long have I been plagued, and chastened every morning.' This, I say, made David wonder, yea, and Job and Jeremiah, too. But he goes into the sanctuary, and then he understands their end, nor could he understand it before. 'I went into the Sanctuary of God.' What place was that? Why, there where he might enquire of God, and by him be resolved of this matter. 'Then,' says he, 'understood I their end. Then I saw that thou hast set them in slippery places, and that thou castest them down to destruction.' Castest them down, that is, suddenly, or as the next words say, 'as in a moment! they are utterly consumed with terrors,' which terrors did not cease them on their sickbed, for they had no bands in their death. The terrors therefore ceased them there, where also they are held in them forever. This he found out, I say, but not without great painfulness, grief and pricking in his reins. So deep, so hard and so difficult did he find it rightly to come to a determination in this matter.

And indeed, this is a deep judgement of God towards ungodly sinners. It is enough to stagger a whole world. Only the godly who are in the world have a sanctuary to go to, where the oracle and Word of God is, by which his judgements, and a reason of many of them are made known to, and understood by them.

ATTEN: Indeed this is a staggering dispensation. It is full of the wisdom and anger of God. And I believe, as you have said, that it is full of judgement to the world. Who would have imagined who had not known Mr Badman, and yet had seen him die, but that he had been a man of a holy life and conversation, since he died so stilly, so quietly,

580. Malachi 2:17.
581. Psalm 73:13.

so like a lamb or chrism child? Would they not, I say, have concluded, that he was a righteous man? Or that if they had known him and his life, yet to see him die so quietly, would they not have concluded that he had made his peace with God? Nay, further, if some had known that he had died in his sins and yet that he died so like a lamb would they not have concluded that either God does not know our sins, or that he likes them, or that he wants power, or will, or heart, or skill to punish them, since Mr Badman himself went from a sinful life so quietly, so peaceably, and so like a lamb as he did?

WISE: Without controversy, this is a heavy judgement of God upon wicked men.[582] One goes to Hell in peace, another goes to Hell in trouble. One goes to Hell being sent there by his own hands, another goes to Hell, being sent there by the hand of his companion. One goes there with his eyes shut, and another goes there with his eyes open. One goes there roaring, and another goes there boasting of Heaven and happiness all the way he goes. One goes there like Mr Badman himself, and others go there as did his brethren. But above all, Mr Badman's death, as to the manner of dying, is the fullest of snares and traps to wicked men. Therefore they who die as he are the greatest stumble to the world. They go, and go, they go on peaceably from youth to old age, and thence to the grave, and so to Hell, without noise. They go as an ox to the slaughter, and as a fool to the correction of the stocks, that is, both senselessly and securely. Oh! But having come at the gates of Hell! Oh! But when they see those gates set open for them. Oh! But when they see that that is their home, and that they must go in there, then their peace and quietness flies away forever. Then they roar like lions, yell like dragons, howl like dogs and tremble at their judgement, as do the devils themselves. Oh! When they see they must shoot the gulf and throat of Hell! When they shall see that Hell has shut her ghastly jaws upon them! When they shall open their eyes, and find themselves within the belly and bowels of Hell! Then they will mourn, and weep, and hack, and gnash their teeth for pain. But this must not be, or if it must, yet very rarely, till they are gone out of the sight and hearing of those mortals whom they do leave behind them alive in the world.

582. Job 21:23.

ATTEN: Well, my good neighbour wiseman, I perceive that the sun grows low, and that you have come to a conclusion with Mr Badman's life and death, and therefore I will take my leave of you. Only first, let me tell you, I am glad that I have met with you today, and that our hap was to fall in with Mr Badman's state. I also thank you for your freedom with me in granting of me your reply to all my questions. I would only beg your prayers that God will give me much grace, that I may neither live nor die as did Mr Badman.

WISE: My good neighbour Attentive, I wish your welfare in soul and body, and if ought that I have said of Mr Badman's life and death, may be of benefit unto you, I shall be heartily glad. Only I desire you to thank God for it, and to pray heartily for me, that I with you may be kept by the power of God through faith unto salvation.

ATTEN: Amen. Farewell.

WISE: I wish you heartily farewell.

NOTES

i. As in an engraving or illustration.

ii. Corah, Dathan and Abiram headed a rebellion against Moses, which was punished by their being swallowed up by the ground (Numbers 16).

iii. Poultry.

iv. Sly or crafty person.

v. 'Damme', a person using the oath 'damn me!'; 'blade', a dashing, pleasure-seeking fellow.

vi. His favourite.

vii. Cast down, dejected.

viii. Slovenly.

ix. A measuring rod or standard of measurement.

x. Ephah, hin: biblical measurements.

xi. Micaiah (truthfully) prophesied against Ahab, prompting the king to say of him, 'Didn't I tell you that he never prophesies anything good about me, but only bad?' (1 Kings 22:18).

xii. Fainting, swooning.

xiii. See note ii.

xiv. Owl, owlet.

Writer and preacher John Bunyan was born at Elstow, near Bedford, in 1628, the son of a brazier. In his autobiographical work *Grace Abounding to the Chief of Sinners* Bunyan describes his early years as reckless; it was his first wife who introduced him to the religious life. In 1653 he was baptised into a Non-conformist church, and in 1655 he became a deacon and began to preach.

As an itinerant tinker, Bunyan was judged by the authorities to be a subversive influence, and in 1658 he was indicted for preaching without a licence; he was imprisoned on these grounds in November 1660. He remained in prison for almost twelve years, during which time he wrote nine books, including his spiritual autobiography, *Grace Abounding to the Chief of Sinners*, and started work on *The Pilgrim's Progress*.

On his release in 1672 he was appointed pastor of the Non-conformist church in Bedford, but was imprisoned again in 1677, during which confinement he finished the first part of *The Pilgrim's Progess*, perhaps the best-known allegory ever written. The first part was published in 1678; the second part, together with the whole work, was published in 1684. Bunyan was soon released from this second imprisonment and, due to his popularity, was not arrested again.

Aside from his two best-known works, in total Bunyan wrote around sixty books and tracts, including *The Life and Death of Mr Badman*, written as a counterpart to *The Pilgrim's Progress*, and *The Holy War*. Bunyan died in 1688.

SELECTED TITLES FROM HESPERUS PRESS

Author	Title	Foreword writer
Pedro Antonio de Alarcón	The Three-Cornered Hat	
Louisa May Alcott	Behind a Mask	Doris Lessing
Edmondo de Amicis	Constantinople	Umberto Eco
Gabriele D'Annunzio	The Book of the Virgins	Tim Parks
Pietro Aretino	The School of Whoredom	Paul Bailey
Pietro Aretino	The Secret Life of Nuns	
Pietro Aretino	The Secret Life of Wives	Paul Bailey
Jane Austen	Lady Susan	
Jane Austen	Lesley Castle	Zoë Heller
Jane Austen	Love and Friendship	Fay Weldon
Honoré de Balzac	Colonel Chabert	A.N. Wilson
Charles Baudelaire	On Wine and Hashish	Margaret Drabble
Aphra Behn	The Lover's Watch	
Giovanni Boccaccio	Life of Dante	A.N. Wilson
Charlotte Brontë	The Foundling	
Charlotte Brontë	The Green Dwarf	Libby Purves
Charlotte Brontë	The Secret	Salley Vickers
Charlotte Brontë	The Spell	Nicola Barker
Emily Brontë	Poems of Solitude	Helen Dunmore
Giacomo Casanova	The Duel	Tim Parks
Miguel de Cervantes	The Dialogue of the Dogs	Ben Okri
Geoffrey Chaucer	The Parliament of Birds	
Anton Chekhov	The Story of a Nobody	Louis de Bernières
Anton Chekhov	Three Years	William Fiennes
Wilkie Collins	The Frozen Deep	
Wilkie Collins	A Rogue's Life	Peter Ackroyd
Wilkie Collins	Who Killed Zebedee?	Martin Jarvis
William Congreve	Incognita	Peter Ackroyd